Books by Corey Mesler:

Poetry

For Toby, Everything for Toby (1997) Wing & The Wheel Press
Ten Poets (1999) editor, only Wing & The Wheel Press
Piecework (2000) Wing & The Wheel Press
Chin-Chin in Eden (2003) Still Waters Press
Dark on Purpose (2004) Little Poem Press
The Hole in Sleep (2006) Wood Works Press
The Agoraphobe's Pandiculations (2006) Little Poem Press
The Lita Conversation (2006) Southern Hum
The Chloe Poems (2007) Maverick Duck Press
Some Identity Problems (2007) Foothills Publishing
Pictures from Lang and Fellini (2007) Sheltering Pines Press
Grit (2008) Amsterdam Press
The Tense Past (2010) Flutter Press
Before the Great Troubling (2011) Unbound Content
Mitmensch (2011) Folded Word Press
The Heart is Open (2011) Right Hand Pointing
To Writing You (2012) Origami Poems Project
Our Locust Years (2013) Unbound Content
My Father is Still Dying (2013) Flutter Press
Body (2013) Chapbook Journal
The Catastrophe of my Personality (2014) Blue Hour Press
The Sky Needs More Work (2014) Upper Rubber Boot Books
The Medicament Predicament (2015) Redneck Press
Stone (2015) Origami Poems (chapbook)
Opaque Melodies that Would Bug Most People (2015) After the
Pause Books
Mountain (2015) Fairfield Press
Home (2016) Fairfield Press
Among the Mensans (Iris Press) 2017
River (Fairfield Press) 2018
Madstones (BlazeVOX Books) 2018
Alphabeticon (Staring Problem Press) 2019
Dog (Fairfield Press) 2019

Prose

Talk: A Novel in Dialogue (2002) Livingston Press
We Are Billion-Year-Old Carbon (2005) Livingston Press
Short Story and Other Short Stories (2006) Parallel Press
Following Richard Brautigan (chapbook) (2006) Plan B Press
Publisher (2007) Writers Write Journal Press
Listen: 29 Short Conversations (2009) Brown Paper Press
The Ballad of the Two Tom Mores (2010) Bronx River Press
Following Richard Brautigan (full-length novel) (2010)
Livingston Press
Notes toward the Story and Other Stories (2011) Aqueous Books
Gardner Remembers (2011) Pocketful of Scoundrel
I'll Give You Something to Cry About (2011) Queen's Ferry Press
Frank Comma and the Time-Slip (2012) Wapshott Press
The Travels of Cocoa Poem Lorry (2013) Leaf Garden Press
Diddy-Wah-Diddy: A Beale Street Suite (2013) Ampersand Press
As a Child: Stories (2014) MadHat Press
Memphis Movie (2015) Soft Skull Press
Robert Walker (2016) Livingston Press
Camel's Bastard Son (2020) Cabal Books

The Adventures of Camel Jeremy Eros

Corey Mesler

Červená Barva Press
Somerville, Massachusetts

Červená Barva Press
P.O. Box 440357
W. Somerville, MA 02144-3222

www.cervenabarvapress.com

Bookstore: www.thelostbookshelf.com

Cover Art: "Mound City" by Karen Bottlecapps

Cover Design: William J. Kelle

ISBN: 978-1-950063-08-6

Library of Congress Control Number: 2020947370

ACKNOWLEDGMENTS

"Let the Light Stand" appeared originally in *Poetry*.
"California" in *Rusty Nail*.
"Camel and Richard take a vacation" and part of "More Bitter Lemon" appeared originally in *We Are Billion-Year-Old Carbon*.
"When Camel met Allen" in *Desdemona*.

Special thanks to John Beifuss, Cheryl Mesler, Chelsea Laine Wells, Deborah Martin, Susan Tepper, Robert Gordon, Greg Hunt, Heather Minette, Mike Keith, Fredric Koeppel, Susan Cushman, and especially Rebecca Tickle for her perspicacious editing.

for my Cheryl, who is my past, present and future and for Sylvi Mesler, who is the fitful gleam seen through mists of dream

I didn't know the full dimensions of forever, but I knew it was longer than waiting for Christmas to come.
—Richard Brautigan

Reality is a movie.
—Abbie Hoffman

Another cosmic custard pie please.
—Wavy Gravy

Prologue

You don't know about me without you have read a book by the name of <u>We Are Billion-Year-Old Carbon</u>, but that ain't no matter. That book was made by Mr. Creole Myers, and he told the truth, mainly. There was things he stretched, but mainly he told the truth. That is nothing.

Thus, Camel Jeremy Eros, Memphis Metrist, Bard of the Bluffs, began his autobiography. He never went further for reasons unknown. The spiral notebook with these words was found among his personal effects by movie director/screenwriter, Sandy Shoars, after Mr. Eros' death.

The tale is here told, gathered from other sources. The interpretation of incidents recollected and revived can be here judged, though it will produce nothing more solid than the interpretation of dreams, as Dr. F knows.

We go on:

Camel Jeremy Eros, Memphis poet, provocateur, heiromonk and bon vivant, who once upon a ghost-drenched highway gave a ride to Jack Kerouac (maybe); who once faced down the ghastly ghoul of the banana purveying Piggly Wiggly; who once became involved with some motion picture wizards which may have cost him his life; who once was part of a nefarious plot to explode the Doughboy Statue in Overton Park in protest against the Vietnam, you know, *War;*

who was once known as the Rector of the Boo Enema; and who once boarded a celestial microbus with compatriot Richard Brautigan, ganja-enlivened sights set upon The Garden, being, as it were, rebuilt on Farmer Yasgur's Land in Upstate New Mesopotamia.

These tales, myths, hometruths and mendacities are part of extant texts, both exoteric and inscrutable.

But we must go back and back to begin again.

The Adventures of Camel Jeremy Eros

PART ONE: THE BEGINNING OF THE ADVENTURES

The first chapter

When Camel Jeremy Eros was a teen he said: "I want to read all the books and fuck all the women." When he got a bit older he amended that to: "I want to read *and write* all the books and fuck all the women."

As a boy, growing up in one of the poorer sections of Frayser, a poorer section of Shelby County, north of perpetually poor Memphis, Camel ran with a group of toughs, whose favorite pastimes included putting firecrackers in frogs, M80s in mailboxes, and burning paper bags of excrement on front porches. This small aggregate of toughs (called hoods back in the back time) were conscienceless and nasty and they had more fun than a dozen Republicans ripping off their constituents. Though Camel was long and lithe he was good at sports, especially corkball, roundball and ferret legging. This was cachet enough for Camel's entrance into their smudgy, malicious band.

"Camel," Peck, the ostensible tummler of the boys needled, "Whatcha reading?"

This was a running joke among the 4-6 members of the clique: Camel read books that he didn't have to. He read *for pleasure.*

3

"Peck," Camel said, drawing himself up to his full, scrawny height (he was always taller than his peers), "A little volume called *The Tales and Poems of Edgar Allan Poe.*"

"Who wrote it, Shakespeare?" Peck snorted, laughing at himself for no good reason. Shakespeare is the name Peck used, sometimes, to bedevil Camel. Peck was not asking if Shakespeare wrote the works of Edgar Allan Poe.

"A drunkard and child-molester," Camel said, with an 11-year old's irony.

The irony sat on the air for a moment, like a butterfly. The other boys looked at their shoes or drew dirty pictures in the Frayser dust. They weren't following the conversation, except they were hoping it might end in fisticuffs. If it didn't, they could care less about palaver regarding books.

Peck, however, was intrigued.

"Sounds good," he said, at last. "Maybe you'll loan it to me when you're done."

He clapped a hand on Camel's shoulder, almost on tiptoe to reach it, and nodded toward the road ahead of them. Adventure waited.

Camel's boats

Sometimes, when it rained heavily in this forsake corner of Shelby County, the storm drains would back up and water would flow down the curbs of St. Elmo Avenue in a slender torrent. Camel was sure that the small freshet was his alone and that it went directly to the Mississippi River (which Camel had only seen once, briefly, when his father took him to the downtown Christmas parade to see, not Santa, but Sivad, Your Monster of Ceremonies) and from the Mississippi on to the Seven Oceans of the world, ending, for whatever reason, at Africa, where Tarzan lived, with his foundling son, his gorgeous wife, and an antic simian named, for whatever reason, Cheetah.

And Camel fashioned his particular boats out of the pages of poetry books and he let them go, three, four, five, six a day, saying, "Go little boats. Take these poems to Africa or beyond. Take them to where people need poems to get by."

And he believed in them. They were like prayers. And, like the best prayers, they were the highest work of man and womankind, versifiers like Poe and Yeats and Dickinson and Whitman and Blake and Robert Service. He imagined that "Sailing to Byzantium" would go straight *there*.

The adventure of the dead boar

This rowdy troupe of boys was free to wander the marshy woodlands around their homes. Suburban neighborhoods in the early 1950s were more open, at least in these backwater spots in the Southern United States of, you know, America. Every kid was Tom Sawyer or Huck Finn. The woods were lovely, dark and deep.

They built forts there. They built pits with sharpened bamboo in the bottom and covered them with frondescent branches. They hiked far and wide, regardless of weather, or time of day. They were as free as the neighborhood dogs, who at that time had a more powerful union than the dogs of today. Few houses had added chain-link fences. Everyone knew the dogs and the dogs tolerated the boys, often following them on their excursions. Patches was a long-eared Irish Setter, a particular favorite of Peck and his gang. Patches had been hit by cars a half-dozen times, sometimes in the boys' presence, and she lived on, stumbling, loyal and as lasting as the vestal fire. Her beautiful red noggin must have been Portland Cement.

Once, following some half-assed trail deeper into a particularly marshy area, the boys stopped and, simultaneously, raised their dirty sleeves to their collective nostrils.

"Whoo, what a stink," Izzy, one of the smaller boys said.

"Smells like an old asshole," Peck said.

They pushed on. And there, half-in, half-out of a poor man's stream, was the body of a large wild pig. It was decidedly deceased and larger than frozen chaos. It was also putrefying, turning slowly from wild pig to sempiternal pap.

"I never seen a pig that big," another boy said.

"It's feral," Camel said.

"What's feral, Shakespeare?"

"Wild. This pig didn't come from anyone's farm. It has lived in these woods for centuries. It was a pig here before the first red man built a wall at Chucalissa."

A reverent hush fell around them like a dome of stars.

Camel broke the silence. "It's the Lord of the Flies," he said, in a near whisper.

"What are you on about?" Peck said. Perhaps he felt the mantle of leadership slipping from his young, semi-squared shoulders.

"It's in a novel I read. These boys trapped on an island stick a pig's head on a pike and call it the Lord of the Flies. A false god. They'd created their own false god."

Peck looked around the faces of the minions.

"Get busy," he said, handing his Bowie knife to Izzy.

"What the hell?" Izzy said, with some heat.

"Cut its head off. Camel, find us a whatever you said. A pike."

"Bloody hell," Izzy said.

Peck gave him the Fiery Angel look. Izzy bent reluctantly to his work.

Once a slit was accomplished in the rough hide various humors exited and the stink increased by about 38%. Izzy looked up at Peck and found a stone face. He looked to Camel for his release. Before Camel could speak Izzy turned his head and upchucked onto the boar's ugly face.

"Jaysus," Peck said. He thought about it for a moment. "I guess that fucks up that god," he said, a royal pronouncement.

So they did not make a god. They went home instead.

Later, Camel dreamed about the bristly monster. In his dream Camel's head was on the pike and the boar, who walked on his hind legs dressed as a cavalier, kept saying to Camel, "You don't look like Shakespeare now. You don't look like Shakespeare *now*."

Camel's begetters

Camel's father, Axel Eros, was a jazz musician. He used to play in Harlem with some of the greats. Cosy Cole taught him how to play drums. Sweetie Sykes, who played with Lady Day's band, taught Axel how to play the licorice stick. This became his preferred instrument.

Camel's mother, Maya nee Revel, was once a singer, and was once seamstress for the band (some say the *zuit suit* came from her experiments working with Memphis tailor, Louis Lettes), and later a hydrocrystalophone adept . The couple met at a party at Cecil Taylor's house and, after making love in one of the spare bedrooms, came downstairs naked, save for bright red lipstick circles around their navels, announcing to the room that they had just consummated their evening-long flirtation and now would like to be considered a married couple.

Dizzy Gillespie puffed out his cheeks and exhaled a long, verdant sigh.

"Let it be so," Earl Hines said.

"Where's the head?" said Cow Cow Davenport.

It took a boo-smoked half minute for the assembled to understand he meant the little jazzman's room and not their fearless leader.

So, the Eroses always said that they were married by Earl Hines, which is why, in some circles, he is now called Fatha. His piano piece, "Axel Maya All Night," was later included on his seminal LP, *Once Upon a Time.*

Camel was born in St. Elizabeth's hospital on Christmas Day, 1941. Axel named him Camel after Camel Ibn Kufte, an obscure 15th century, Persian poet, thus marking Camel's future with a red felt pen (he couldn't have possibly known?), and Maya added Jeremy after Jeremy Bentham, because she felt it might ground him in utilitarianism, though, truthfully, truth, to Maya, was a shape-shifter and utilitarianism a trash heap philosophy.

"Still, Bentham argued for separation of church and state and development of the welfare state," she told her husband as he was cleaning an old clarinet he had gotten second hand.

"Good enough for the Eroses," Axel said, looking up into his wife's watery, green eyes.

"He jumped," she said.

"He better jump," Axel said fiddling with a stuck key. "He's gonna be a colorful baby."

When the jazzy couple moved to Memphis in the 1940s, so that Axel could work at the Grace Chemical Plant on Fite Road, they became a staple act at Club BingoBango on Beale. While entertaining there they composed a number of what have become jazz standards, "America the Mulligrubs," which was covered by Winston Marsalis, and "Wobble Over Me for A While," which was a hit for Diana Krall and covered by artists as diverse as Van Morrison, Jan Hammer and Vicki Lawrence. It is also told among the cognoscenti that the upbeat, swinging "Zeus Couldn't Keep it in His Pants," featured lyrics by a very young Camel Jeremy

Eros. The song showed up on a KayTell compilation but, today, is as hard to find as a mind that's chaste.

The adventure of Camel in high school

Camel and Peck both attended Trezevant High School, though 'attended' was not quite in Peck's vocabulary. His name is in the records. His grades are not. He was a ghost student and, as such, he began to fade out of Camel's life like the dye of his pegleg pants.

Camel was early on recognized for his writing skills and, some teachers, who saw the writing on the wall as well as in his notebooks, pushed Camel to develop his gift. Some teachers will do that. Imagine. The world would be a better place, a richer place, if more teachers celebrated the gifts of their talented students. Of course it would be.

The adventure of Tamerlane and the Paphian

And, at this unenlightened time in human history, Trezevant High School was without a literary magazine, like many high schools, not just in the backwater South, but in the gray etch-a-sketch of 1950s Amerika. And, lo, it came to pass that Camel came up with the idea that there should be one and that he, Camel Jeremy Eros, sophomore forward for the

Trezevant Mighty Bears, would be its progenitor. And he would call this rag, *Tamerlane*.

He took the idea to his English teacher, Mrs. Goff. Mrs. Goff looked like Catherine Deneuve and she was almost as tall as Camel. So Camel was speaking straight into her lovely mug, haloed by her caramel hair. Sometimes in her class Camel (as well as the other horny pubescent males in the room) could not concentrate on Julius Caesar for staring at the teacher's legs sheathed in dark hose. Sometimes you could catch a glimpse of a part of the hose, higher on the thigh, which was darker, the way that the grave is darker than the surrounding God's little acre.

"A literary magazine, Camel Dear?" Mrs. Goff said. There may have been a lilt on the *dear*.

Camel was nonplussed. A literary magazine? Who cares about literary magazines when women who smell like honeysuckle, with lips like strawberry wine, are within reach? Which was quite a thought for a young fellow whose sexual experience consisted of Playboy magazine blanket drill and one quick handjob from one of the cheerleaders the night he scored 41 points.

"Camel?"

"A literary magazine?" Camel said. "Yes, ma'am, that sounds like a good idea."

"It's yours."

"Oh, yes ma'am."

"So. Tell me more. Who, besides you, writes? Do you have friends who are literary also?" She smiled encouragement.

"In Frayser?" Camel asked.

This wasn't going well and Mrs. Goff was now nonplussed.

"Perhaps you haven't thought this through," Mrs. Goff said, and she placed a soft, fawn hand on Camel's bicep. Camel looked at the hand. Its nails were five small, red mirrors. In them he saw his blood workup.

Simultaneously, Camel was awakened to the Carnal (again, but more *profoundly*), and awakened to the Mantle of Literature. For the rest of his life sex and literature were intertwined in his popgun head. Getting an acceptance in the mail from a poetry magazine was akin to getting a postcard from a beautiful woman far away who, up until that point, Camel had no idea was interested in him as a sexual being. By the same subway token, getting a love letter from a woman gave Camel the same kind of frisson he received from seeing his name in print.

But now: If there was to be an appreciation for fine writing in Frayser, it would have to begin with him.

"Wait," Camel said. He shook his head and his head rattled like a gourd. "We can make it together."

Mrs. Goff looked at him. Were her cheeks reddening?

"Camel? I. I am not sure."

"Mrs. Goff. We can make literature happen. Here. Now."

"Oh, oh yes," and she laughed a little silver laugh. "I thought—ha, ha—never mind. Yes." She brushed her fawn hand through her caramel hair.

"Oh, you thought I meant make it together. Heh, heh, now I see. We're talking at cross purposes."

"Yes," Mrs. Goff said. "That must have been it. We can do this magazine thing. Yes. I'll bring it up at the next staff meeting. Whew."

"Ha ha. Ridiculous. Crossed wires. Ha."

"Yes. Whew."

"Whew."

Outside the last ice cream truck of the season went by playing a carnival tune. It might have been "Let's Make Whoopee."

Camel looked into Mrs. Goff's pale green eyes. She was a cat.

"Is there a Mr. Goff?" Camel said.

"There was," Mrs. Goff said. She hesitated on the threshold of eternity. "He's passed on."

"But you're so young," Camel said.

"I'm still here. He's dead. He was much older. We thought he was hale and strong. He had arms like a lumberjack's. And his body was strong, muscular, rippling. He died on top of me."

She was obviously babbling. She took a deep breath. She licked her lips.

"Camel, I don't know why I'm rattling on. You're standing so close to me. Camel, I can feel the heat of your body."

"Does that door lock?" Camel asked.

Mrs. Goff's expression jactitated like a swerving automobile, before settling into a one-quarter smile. She turned slowly and walked to her classroom door. She locked it with calm, deliberate motion. There was a small window in the door at face level. She walked just as deliberately to her desk and picked up the first page of someone's essay. The paper said, "Was Charles Dickens a Pirate?" by College Herpes. She reached into the drawer of her desk and took out a roll of masking tape. She tore strips of tape off with her small, sharp teeth and covered the small window with the sheet. All this time she had not looked at Camel. Now she turned toward him.

She shook her hair because she had seen women shake their hair in movies. She was hypnotized. She was about to cross a dead black line but the ethics required to halt what had been set in motion were trapped in the ether. Etherized ethics. She undid the top two buttons of her dress. Her skin was lightly freckled over the tops of her two medium-size breasts.

There were only four more words spoken in that room for the next half hour. Mrs. Goff, at one point said this, "Camel! You're not circumcised."

And this is how Camel Jeremy Eros lost his virginity, to his sophomore English teacher, in a locked classroom, on top of his peers' reports, on top of a proctor-sized wooden desk, in the dim regions of Weir, North of Memphis, Tennessee, on the same day the Trezevant literary magazine, *Tamerlane*, was born, with the music of summer fading away into the distance, toward the river, toward parts of the United States where summer was already extinct, already deaf to music.

The adventures of Camel as a new man

Once shown the gift of estrus it is only human nature to spread it around. Having seen Paris Camel did not linger on the farm. Working on *Tamerlane* became, for Camel, an erotogenic activity. It stirred him in many ways.

He found writers in odd places. Joey White, the basketball team's black point guard, admitted to Camel that he had written a science fiction short story called, "Frank Comma on the Planet Sniff." Camel took it home with him and laughed at its wild rimshots and cockeyed humor. He accepted it for Issue One.

Jimpy Hoar, who was shunned by much of the student population due to his bad clothes and perfervid body odor, came to Camel and handed him a small group of smudgy notecards.

"You probably don't want these," he said.

Each card held a little poem, rounded off like a perfect egg. Camel accepted two of them.

One of the cheerleaders, a small, bronzed beauty with legs like an ocelot, found Camel working alone in Mrs. Goff's room. Camel was editing an essay which one of the parking lot hoods wrote, called "I'm Gonna Kick Some Coon Ass." Camel was trying, in his egalitarian way, to rescue a glint of gem from this pile of manure.

"Camel," came a soft feminine voice from the doorway.

Camel looked up. He knew her name. She was a senior, co-captain of the cheerleaders, and she was called Eedy Durrette. She was the cheerleader who could do back flips from one corner of the basketball court to the other. She was not the cheerleader who gave Camel the handjob. Her name was Lips Leeds and she had abruptly left Trezevant mid-year. Eedy had strong, dark thighs the size of hams.

"Hi, Eedy," he said.

"I heard you're starting a literary magazine," she purred and stepped into the room.

"I am. I have."

"That's so wild," Eedy said.

"Thank you."

"I wrote something."

"Don't be shy. Lemme see it."

She crossed the room. Her gavotte set loose all the hamsters in Camel's heart's cage.

"It's called, 'My Vagina'."

"Provocative title."

"Yes. Should I change it? Cuz I will. I will do anything you say to get published. I'd much rather be a poet than a cheerleader. If the poem is no good I want you to tell me. I want you to be honest because I want to learn. You can teach me, right, Camel?"

Eedy sat on the edge of the desk next to Camel's. Her cheerleader's uniform could not hide her animal sexuality. It was quite a speech from someone Camel had never spoken to before.

"Lemme read it and see."

Eedy handed him the poem, written in curly longhand on a yellow sheet of line paper. The word vagina was used 4 times in the first 3 lines. All her I's dotted with hearts.

"It's—it's provocative," Camel repeated. It was also terrible.

"It's just so—well, when I write, I feel so—sexy. I just—pffftt—let it all go!"

"I get that," Camel said. He smiled. Eedy smiled back.

"I bet editing a literary magazine is really sexy," Eedy said. She was savoring saying the word, sexy.

"Eedy, let me tell you something I've learned in my short time editing *Tamerlane*."

Eedy sat forward. Her hair fell over one blue eye.

"I've learned that Mrs. Goff's door locks."

The adventure of Camel in high school, take two

Twice, Camel was suspended from Trezevant High. Both times the basketball coach held a closed door meeting with the principal, and Camel returned early. The first suspension was for wearing an American flag on the seat of his jeans. In truth, it was Mrs. Eros who sewed the fragment of flag over Camel's thinned out jeans.

"It was close at hand," she told the principal. "Camel's father had burned the rest of the flag a few years earlier in protest over the Rosenbergs' execution."

"It's ok, Mom," Camel said.

"It's not ok," the principal said.

The second suspension came in Mrs. Gaines social studies class. During a discussion of Sherman Antitrust Act Mrs. Gaines became distracted by a rhythmic tapping somewhere in the back row.

It was Camel using his pencil as a drumstick while Hoagy Carmichael's "Hong Kong Blues" ran through his benighted head.

"Camel!" Mrs. Gaines snapped suddenly.

Camel's attention was drawn back to his teacher's angry mug.

"Mrs. Gaines," Camel said, in acknowledgement. And to soften his response he offered Mrs. Gaines a pious smile.

"What is that?" Mrs. Gaines snapped again.

"Hong Kong Blues," Camel said.

"No, that, *that.*"

Camel looked at his hand. He looked back at Mrs. Gaines. He looked back at his makeshift drumstick.

"It's a number two pencil," Camel said. "It's for writing shit down."

In the annual

There is a picture in the Trezevant High School annual, 1958, of a Camel Eroes (sic), with sideburns the size of paperback books, with hair just short enough to not get expelled, with a benighted smile upon his almost handsome mug, and underneath that picture it says. "Unofficial Poet Laureate." And underneath "Unofficial Poet Laureate," there is this snippet from William Blake: "Imagination is the real and eternal world of which this vegetable universe is but a faint shadow." This last part was added by Camel himself.

By the time he graduated, with mediocre grades except in English, he had fallen in love a dozen times and out of love about half that many. He broke some hearts. Some hearts broke his. His steadiest girlfriend from this era was Myriad Bling. Perhaps she deserves her own chapter.

The chapter about Myriad Bling

Camel did not meet Myriad Bling through his editing of *Tamerlane* (whose publication continued long after Camel's stewardship, hitting its stride during the 70s when it was edited by Edmund St. Charles Burton--about *his* later years no one needs reminding). Instead he met her at a donkey basketball game in the school gym one sere autumn evening. (Or as Camel liked to say, "a Sears autumn evening.")

She and Camel had come to protest the mistreatment of the donkeys. They were a protest rally of two. Camel's sign said, "Do Not Covet Thy Neighbor's Ass or Cause him to Be Humiliated in a High School Gymnasium." Myriad's read, "Leave My Ass Alone."

Camel smiled at her and she smiled at Camel. She wore a tight skirt and an army green Army shirt with the name "E. D. Slovik" on the pocket, underneath which was one of two ample bosoms. Camel was drawn both to the sign of protest and to the ample bosoms. Myriad Bling was constructed with circular precision: she was as round as a berry so ripe it threatened to burst its burnished skin.

"Yours is better," Camel said as a shot across her lovely bough.

"Excuse me," she said with feminist wariness.

"Your sign. It's more succinct. And I call myself a poet."

Now she laughed. "Well, people generally, probably, don't go after your ass the way they do mine. So the double meaning would be lost."

"I have a pretty good ass," Camel said. The smile between his muttonchops was like a hammock slung between bending trees.

"You do," Myriad said. "Myriad." She put out her hand, thus signaling to Camel that she had just given him his name and he was to give his back.

"Camel," he said, taking her small white offering between his large, soft meathooks.

"I know," she said. "Editor of *Tamerlane*. Poet. Gangly forward with a soft hook shot. Skirt-chaser."

"I," Camel started to protest. Myriad Bling held up her hand like a traffic cop.

"It's ok," she said. "You have charm. You are charming."

"Thank you," Camel said.

"And a nice ass."

"You've been paying attention."

"I am a great reader. Not a writer myself. Sometimes I think there are too many writers and not enough readers, people who aren't ashamed to say, I can't do it myself but I love reading some really fine writing."

"Ah," Camel said, in his slow, drawling way. "And I like a good ass myself, though tire quickly of boys who know only how to complement mine by grunting or whistling."

"Thank you, Kind Lady," Camel said, and he executed a killer Sir Walter Raleigh bow.

Eros and bling

So they dated.

They dated in time-honored high school fashion, in Jeremy's dad's car, a Studebaker wagon as large as a river barge. Jeremy often clipped its corners on anything overhanging the side of the road. The car looked like it had been pummeled or stoned from all compass points.

Camel would bring it home, sheepishly slipping into the house through his bedroom window, leaving behind the evidence of his lack of depth perception. In the morning Axel would be sitting over his bowl of cornflakes, his face buried in the newspaper, spoon dangling from one hand, seemingly rapt by world events or his own swimmy thoughts. Sometimes he was humming compositions he didn't know he was writing.

Camel gently got his own bowl. Camel gently poured Sugar Smacks into his bowl. Camel gently opened the fridge and gently poured milk over the cereal. Camel sat down at the other end of the kitchen table, gently, gently.

He ate.

"Goddamn Dodgers," Axel said.

"Who—ahem—who pitched?" Camel asked, gently.

Axel looked up as if he was suddenly aware he was not alone.

"Who pitched what?" he asked in all seriousness.

"The—the ball, you know. The," Camel said.

Axel went back to his paper.

Camel bolted his meal. He rose and was putting the bowl in the sink just as his mother entered the room, her head full of bees, her lovely tresses tangled. She rubbed her eyes like a sleepy toddler.

"Morning, Eros Men," she said.

"Morning, Mom. Gotta run," Camel said, scooping his books off the dryer in the utility room.

And just as he opened the door his father spoke.

"What did you hit this time?"

"Llewellyn's mail box. Stop sign on the corner of Gillespie and Kane."

"The red paint?"

"The Marcrum's Buick."

"It's almost symmetrical, your pattern of dents," Axel said, in his dreamy voice. "It's almost car art."

Camel smiled and exited, pursued by ghosts.

One night Camel and Myriad went to the Frayser Drive-In. It was a double feature of *Attack of the Crab Monster* and *It Conquered the World*.

"Camel, these are terrible," Myriad said, one hand in a tub of popcorn and one hand on Camel's thigh.

"I know. I love them."

"Wait, that actress. We saw her last week."

"Beverly Garland. In *Swamp Women*. Isn't she gorgeous?"

"Sure, Camel."

Myriad put her head back and closed her eyes. She let the creaks and screams and bent-saw melody wash over her. Camel was quiet for a long time. He was gripped by rubber movie monsters.

"Whoa," Camel said. Myriad lifted her head.

"I didn't see that coming." He smiled at his date.

"Camel, can we get in the back yet? Do we have to watch all of both films?"

"No," Camel said. "Wait just one minute."

On screen something was happening. You could tell because the music went all wobbly.

"There," Camel said, as if he'd just put a period after a particularly graceful sentence.

"Let's go," he said.

He opened his door, smoothly lifting the speaker out of harm's way and then repositioning it on the window so he could still hear.

He joined Myriad in the rear where there was an Eros family quilt spread upon the car's hard floor. The quilt, its pattern a mandala, contained a piece of Bird's jacket, a scrap from Stan Getz's castoff pants.

"Camel," Myriad whispered. "You love me?"

"I do," Camel said.

"For more than this?"

This was a question Camel would hear for the rest of his life, oftener and oftener, but this, being the first time, drew him up short and indignant.

"Myr, you know me. Am I like that?"

"You're not. You're a beautiful cat, Camel."

"Then open your shirt," Camel said with his shiteating grin.

Myriad did. And, without further inquiry, she removed her bra.

"You have gorgeous orbs," Camel said.

"Orbs," Myriad snickered.

Just as Camel began to suckle someone passed close to the car.

"Camel," a voice in the darkness said.

Camel lifted his mouth. "Selvidge," he answered.

He re-nursed. Myriad loved to have her nipples sucked. Camel knew that once he did that everything was on. So they did everything, short of Camel coming inside his luscious, leftist girlfriend's luscious, leftist beehive. He pulled out like a gentleman, but, on this night, once he did he lost his well-wrought erection.

"Aw, Baby," Myriad said. "Let me finish you."

And just as she put Camel's considerable manhood all the way into her throat and Camel's honey rose toward her uvula a voice from beyond spoke: *We are unquestionably on the brink of a great discovery. It is not likely that that discovery will be of a pleasant nature. That is the sum of my knowledge.*

The Adventures of Camel high

When Camel was 15 he got his first doobie. His parents gave it to him.

"Camel," his mother said, softly. "This is pot. It's Earth medicine. Use it to open your chakras but don't tell anyone else about it. For some reason it's illegal."

Camel did not tell anyone except Myriad. He did not even tell his best friend, Bandy Lob, who was a musician and songwriter. Bandy was as cool as the eyes of infants but, even he had not smoked pot; at this time, in Frayser, Tennessee, it was still an exotic substance, like myrrh, or amrita.

Once upon a time, high at highschool, in Advanced Math class, Camel was nonplussed and almost subtracted when Mrs. Deer popped a pop quiz. In. Advanced. Math. Camel stared vigorously at the numbers. He read the words sine and cosine and he felt sure that if he concentrated hard enough they would give up their mysteries and tell him the Secret of the Sphinx. It took Camel half the class, thirty minutes, to read over the entire one-sheet test. Finally, his third eye opened. The next thirty minutes he bent his head and wrote. The next day, when the sheets were handed back,

Camel scored the only 100% in the class. Mrs. Deer asked to see him as the class filed out.

"Camel, Dear," Mrs. Deer said. "A remarkable accomplishment. I threw in a bonus puzzle with material we haven't even covered yet."

"Yes, ma'am," Camel said. He was high again and elderly Mrs. Deer suddenly looked like Beverly Garland to him.

"And your cartoon on the bottom of the sheet was appreciated too." Mrs. Deer actually twinkled.

Camel looked at the sheet. At the bottom he had drawn a small quincunx. Camel stared at it and his gaze penetrated the simple pencil lines. His mind smoked.

"What is it?" Mrs. Deer asked.

Camel looked up at her. She had Beverly Garland's eyes. Camel blinked his own. "I have no idea," he said.

Another time, buying beer at a convenience store (Camel was rarely carded because, with his fanciful facial hair, he looked 25), Camel was asked for his ID. High as a chaparral, he fumbled the contents of his wallet out onto the counter. And, stuck to the back of his student ID card, was a half-smoked joint. Camel looked down at it as if the clerk had conjured it.

"Sorry," Camel mumbled, and pulling the joint off the stickum, the paper split and the dope spilled onto the counter like a small overflow of cremains. Camel looked up at the clerk and grinned.

"What kinda tobacco is that?" the bespectacled fellow asked.

"Asian," Camel said.

"You been to Asia?" The old guy apparently wanted to chat.

"Burma, Myanmar, Nepal," Camel said.

"All those places in Asia?"

"To be honest I don't know."

"Right. Well, that'll be 3.63 for the beer and snacks. That's a powerful lot of puffed cheese things."

"They're good for you," Camel said. And, from an inner pocket of his vest, Camel removed a perfectly shaped doobie, rolled tightly by his meticulous father. He handed it to the clerk.

"Thank you, sir," the old fellow said. "I'll smoke this tonight with the wife."

But, the most memorable highs Camel experienced from these days were with his girlfriend, Myriad Bling.

The first time they got stoned together was at a party at Bandy's house while Bandy's parents were out of town. Bandy and his band, The Coronados, were playing some jazzy folk stuff that was quite pleasant and the gathered teens were mellow, contented as puppies whose bellies were being rubbed. A couple couples, or more, were making out in various chairs.

"I got something for you, Babe," Camel whispered in Myriad's ear.

"I know you do, Studmuffin."

"Something new," Camel whispered back.

"A second dick?" Myriad asked, making with the cow eyes.

"Yes," Camel said. "Let's go upstairs."

They found a bedroom that looked like a hotel room.

"This must be the parents' bedroom," Myriad said, as if they were disturbing the dust of long dead kings.

"I believe it is," Camel said. He took Myriad's hand and led her to the large bed, covered with a counterpane with Jesus's face on it. They sat with crossed legs facing each other.

Camel pulled out the joint and held it in front of Myriad's face. Camel's grin was eating shit to beat the band.

"You don't smoke," Myriad said. Her pretty face twisted into a childlike query.

"It's not tobacco."

Myriad thought for a moment. "Camel!" she said.

"Yeah, quiet now. Let's share this fizgig."

Camel lit it and took one good long toke, drawing it deeply into his bony chest. He passed it back to Myriad. She choked on the first draw.

"Slow, Sweetheart," Camel said.

She tried again, held it, and they passed it back and forth until it was the size of a ladybug.

"It's kinda sleepy-making, isn't it?" Myriad said.

"Yes, Baby."

Camel pulled Myriad to him and kissed her softly, holding the liplock for a long time. When he backed away Myriad's eyes were like crystal balls.

"Camel," she said, her voice girly. "Whoosh."

"Yeah?"

"Is it an aphrodisiac?" she asked.

"If it isn't it will do till they invent one," Camel said solemnly.

They undressed just as solemnly. When they had removed all their clothes they returned to the bed, facing each other again, again legs crossed in front of them, forming laps like carnal pools. Myriad's subterranean, black-haired crotch looked like the absence of space. Camel found himself (as he lost himself) staring at it. He imagined that he could crawl inside and that, once inside, he fancied that the genii of romance would illuminate their underground palaces to receive the sons of men.

"Camel, wow," Myriad said, like millions of stoners before and after her. "You're like traveling up my pussy."

"You're feeling it too?"

"And how." And here Myriad looked down at her own lap. Her pubic hair seemed beautiful to her and she made a silent prayer of thanks for a god who would add beautiful, bountiful pubic hair to his humans.

Myriad looked up slowly. She only got about waist high.

"Camel," she whispered. "Your cock is glowing."

"I know, Baby."

"It's turning colors like a Christmas tree revolvy thing."

"I know, Baby. When it gets to yellow I want you to eat it like a banana."

"I will, Camel. I'm watching close."

"What color is it now, Baby?"

"Orange. No, wait—there it is. It's yellow."

And Myriad positioned herself in fetal fashion, her head in Camel's soft lap, and she began to suck on his dick as if it were a baby bottle.

Later—it might have been days—they made love in five different positions. At one point Bandy walked in. He watched them for a while. It was better than *Gunsmoke*. They never broke their clutch and, eventually, Bandy left, closing the door quietly.

Around midnight, on Earth, Camel came inside his girlfriend. It was hot like magma and Myriad's face flushed devil-red. They held each other and, when the dawn came, they kissed, unaware that their mystic coupling had already begun a small zygote, the size of a tadpole and the color of a baked beet. A wee human girl child, in its necromantic first hour, already speaking the tongues of angels.

(This child, never mentioned again in these annals, whose father was never aware of its existence, was adopted by a couple who lived on the Isle of Guernsey. There, under the name Grace Durrell, she became a botanist of some renown. Also, in secret, she wrote poems about the natural world. These poems were beautiful and full of import but were later lost in a house fire, never making their way out into the walking-around world. She quit writing then, confiding to a friend, "I don't know what I was thinking anyway. I'm not a poet. I'm a scientist.")

PART TWO: THE ADVENTURES OF CAMEL AT BERKELEY

Hondo Minimum

Hondo Minimum, a couple groovy years ahead of Camel at UC-Berkeley, spent long hours, talking over doobies and wine, schooling the young but hip Memphis poet on the politics of the day. They talked initials: FSM, SDS, HUAC. They talked committees: Fair Play for Cuba Committee, Committee to Free Caryl Chessman, Committee for Civil Rights, Jazz in the Karmic Circle Committee, Committee to Free Theseus *and* the Minotaur. The Artist's Liberation Front.

Camel listened. He absorbed like a sponge, or like a small blotter hungry for its drop of acid. Camel was a damn good listener.

Hondo reminisced about his psychology professor, Richard Alpert, who had absconded to the green pastures of Harvard with his Felix the Cat bag of tricks and his mind working on synthetic medicaments. "Alpert rearranged my chromosomes," Hondo said. "His classes were inspiration refined. He walked the walk of a psychiatrist but you could tell his soul wanted to dance like Nick Bottom."

"Tell me more about these synthetic leechdom."

"I'm not hip to all what's going on cuz he went far away to do his best work. But I hear tell he's working on a powder that will make the Paramatman appear in your sensorium, dissolve there, and leave you with the head of a yogi. And he's growing mushrooms that allow you to travel in time."

"These are stories, just stories perhaps," Camel said.

"Stories create reality, Camel. Stories create truth."

Camel paused over this. Finally he nodded his head of curly hair.

"Thank you, Brother Minimum. Let's expand our cathedral."

Cindy Ingaq

It was underneath Sather Gate, that liminal space between campus and the wide world of color, that Camel met Cindy Ingaq. She was manning (womanning, though the woman's movement was only a gleam in Betty Friedan's eye at this time) a table with hand-printed pamphlets decrying her message, "June Cleaver isn't Clever," and "Stone Donna Stone." She wore her jet-black hair pulled away from her impressive forehead with a scrap of shoestring forming a ponytail sloppy enough to be an old nag. Her bangs were cut straight across her impressive forehead, like the female agent in *The President's Analyst,* a film unmade at this recollecting, but one that would later be part of Camel's filmic DNA. Perhaps it was the agent who looked like Cindy Ingaq, perhaps the music, or the film's unmitigated cool, but Camel, later, memorized the hipster movie the same way he memorized 'The Second Coming.' Cindy Ingaq's nose turned up slightly like a rose petal. Camel was smitten on the spot. He hiked his chest upward, expanded his already formidable height, and approached her. She wore a t-shirt which read, "Stop Looking at my Tits," which, naturally, made it impossible to *not* look at her tits. They were middling-size and round as the O in Stop.

Camel feigned interest in the literature. Cindy Ingaq stood back, arms crossed now over her medium-sized message.

"You print these yourself?" he asked, looking upward with his sweet grin shining like second sight.

Cindy looked him up and down, her detectometer set on stun.

"With shome help," she said. She lisped. Camel's heart pumped a few extra pumps.

"Nicely done," he said. "I'm thinking about starting a poetry rag, maybe just pamphlet size things at first, like City Lights." This now became exactly what he wanted to do, though he had up until that moment thought his editorship days behind him.

"You a poet?" Cindy asked.

Camel put forth his camel-colored hand. "Camel Jeremy Eros," he said.

She uncrossed her hirsute but delicate arms and took the hand. Was that a chimpish grin at the corner of her bow-shaped mouth?

"Shindy Ingaq."

Camel was pretty certain she meant Cindy but could not think of a graceful way of making sure. He picked up one of the pamphlets and began to read, searching in vain for her name on the frangible fascicle.

"I write poetry, too," Camel continued. He set the pamphlet down. "Maybe I'll write a poem for you, Cindy Ingaq."

Now Cindy recrossed her arms. The crossing guard back on duty.

"How do you spell that name?"

"I-n-g-a-q," she said, her mouth a drawn line.

"First name?"

"With a C," Cindy, with a C said.

"Ah."

Now Camel shuffled. His gangly frame shook a bit like Bojangles nervous before his duet with Shirley Temple.

"Wanna take me for coffee?" Cindy Ingaq said.

When they were seated in a coffeehouse called Sinkers and Joe, just down the hill from the campus, she spoke again for the first time. The walk there had been done in gelid silence.

"I don't know why I shed that, to be honest," she said, when the cups were set in front of them.

"What's that?"

"Wanna take me for coffee. I'm not usually—what? – bold."

"It was rather bold. I liked it."

"Ok."

"Because I was about to ask you the same question."

They sat in a companionable silence for a bit, sipping their heavily creamed coffees.

"This is a nice place," Camel said, finally.

"I come here a lot. They have a poetry night. Thurshdays."

Camel's smile curled upward. He spotted the waitress and signaled to her.

"Is the manager here?" he asked.

And this was how Camel's persona as a public poet was a-born. It was also the start of Cindy and Camel, a formidable duo on the soon-to-be fomenting Berkeley campus.

Soon Camel was hosting poetry nights and Cindy Ingaq

Love is hot, truth is molten.
—Donovan

After several weeks of Camel reading his own verse, little odes he was frantically cobbling together late nights after he'd written his papers for his classes, high on Cindy's thick black joe and Benzedrine—they were small but potent: Camel was finding his voice, the orotund voice by which he would soon be known across the hip, hairy midsection of 1960s America—Camel began booking poets he'd gotten to know at City Lights and in the basement jazz clubs of San Francisco.

For, after his first visit to City Lights Bookstore, a young poetess on his arm (pre-Ingaq), Camel began to cultivate a self that he never thought possible growing up in Frayser, Tennessee. He developed something of a Jerusalem syndrome. Because of City Lights he felt himself a poet, in *italics*. Camel was a little full of himself, a little cocky, a little giddy. He told the young poetess afterward that he wanted to take her home and lick her like a stamp.

"Oh, Camel," the young poetess said. "I'm walking on airmail."

Ahem, the Camel Series:

Gary Snyder read. Ginsberg. Gregory Corso. Ferlinghetti. Rudder Amidships. A young devotchka named Alexandra Naughton read from her first book, *I Will Always be Your Whore*, in a short, fairy skirt and legs like the answer to every question. She had a storm of red hair and her freckles were a map to Paradiso. She turned men into spados. Later, Camel, in thinking of her wrote his poem, "California," (cf.) from which one may intuit that Camel knew more about her than her sestinas and well-turned ankles.

And Camel's work was beginning to be noticed in the little ill-lit corners from whence poetry springs. His style was often compared to Frank O'Hara's, possibly because of the pop culture references and the attic wit ("Virginia Mayo was a Tomato"), but his spiritual forefather was William Carlos Williams, whose plain-speaking Camel attempted to limn. "Write a straight line," Camel told himself. "Listen to the rhythm of your inner voice."

Also, Camel grew close to Rudder Amidships, whose first collection, *I Expect my Drugs to do Nothing*, came from Big Table Books. His reading from it at Les Joulins Jazz Bistro, with Ishmael Reed, and accompanied by Pops Foster, was a wow, reviewed in the Examiner as "Incomparable Reed and Foster welcome New Raw Poet."

Rudder was a big man, built along the proportions of The Ghost of Christmas Present, with a bass voice that could shake the bats from the rafters, or from the dugout, or from your own belfry. His poetry was caustic, loud and immediate. There was blood and guts in it and Camel could only marvel.

"Your words make mine seem sickly things, poor little worms in a single spadeful of the shallow grubby earth."

"Nonsense," Rudder boomed. "You are the one catching lightning in a bottle. Your "Jenny Never Kissed Me," is worth any ten of mine."

"You're very kind, Rudder," Camel said, quietly, stroking his mustache. "I have to work harder. I'm nowhere near what you're doing. A book is a long way away."

"You're young, son, younger than yesterday. And you're poisoning your mind in the university, listening to Mario and the rabble-rousers. Politics. Spit it out of your mouth. Don't get involved, Camel. The page, the page is all that matters."

Rudder was a notorious anti-academic. Once, a professorial type, at one of Rudder's readings, asked him if he had never heard that free verse was low hanging fruit. Rudder reddened. The retort was acid on his tongue, burning him. But he only stared goggle-eyed, and there were murmurings in the audience. The rest of the reading went badly, Rudder's voice running down like an old clock. His final poem's final line was spoken in a whisper, which also died prematurely, so that his final word was only a thought.

Afterward he tried to find the Ivy-league fellow in the dark street.

"Where is he?" he asked Snyder. "I'm going to beat him like Drummer Hoff's best skin."

He did not find him and Gary Snyder procured a bottle of red wine and they went and sat on Potrero Hill and got poetically sotted.

Camel's poetry nights at Sinkers and Joe became legendary. How he balanced his hosting with his schoolwork is a mystery. Bennies, sure, but he was also running on hematic speed. His soul was on fire.

And so were his loins. Cindy Ingaq was Camel's first expert lover. In bed she was as creative as Camel was on the page, or in front of the mic.

I wanna shuck you

Cindy had her own apartment. Camel never did figure out how she afforded it. If pressed she became vague on the subject and told apocryphal stories of about where Eugene Debs lived, or how Gloria Steinem took Playboy bunny money and turned the sexual tables.

In that apartment, though sparsely furnished, there was a well-stocked bar and refrigerator (Cindy was an eager consumer of foods. She ate and never gained weight.), and a bookcase full of leftish literature.

Her bedroom was dimly lit and the walls were scrawled with slogans and hand-written sections from some of Cindy's favorite books. Camel spent the first night there walking the entire room until, his eyes straining in the murk, he had inspected everything stuck to the mucky walls. He felt he knew Cindy better after reading her room.

"Interesting," was all he could think of to say. She stood aside and watched his walk, pulling hard on a Marlboro cigarette.

"You're interesting, too," she said, with a smirk the size of a semi-colon.

"Thanks," Camel muttered.

He kissed her at the door that night. He didn't exactly skulk out but his head was full of the butterflies which normally take flight in one's GI. The kiss at the door, however, was deep and wet, and Cindy's tongue was as plump as a plum. He could have sucked on it all night. Instead he went home and wrote a poem entitled "Cindy Ingaq and the Night at the Wall."

The 2nd date, after exotic seafood in Chinatown, the two soon-to-be lovers, barely made it inside the door before their arms were flailing, casting clothing hither and yon. At dinner their hand-holding and warm conversation had made this a foregone conclusion, but they were still thrilled, as if this were something humans normally did not accomplish.

Cindy stood, clad only in bra and panties, on the toes of Camel's boots, so she could reach his lips and neck and ears with her lips and tongue. Camel's hands were trying to undo the bra clasp while not losing his concentration on that thick, vigorous tongue. It was a daunting magic trick and Camel couldn't quite complete it.

Cindy de-tongued and smiled her chimpish smile. She reached back and undid the clasp and her breasts fell forward like ripe fruit.

"I'm surprised you wear a bra," Camel said, flummoxed by the beauty of her marmoreal (snow-white with blue veins) breasts.

"Backache otherwise," Cindy said, stepping onto Camel's boots, his only clothing save for his white briefs, and re-tonguing.

They had just about exhausted the upright position, their hands exploring everything within reach, and Cindy broke the buss and put her wet lips against Camel's left ear. She circled its spiral with her tongue, licking the shell clean of its animal accrual, and then, wetly whispered, "I wanna shuck you."

Camel pulled his head back. "I'm sorry," he said.

"Camel, I wanna shuck you. I wanna shuck your dick. Ish that bad to shay?"

Camel had never seen the shy side of Cindy Ingaq, which made his heart go ka-chunk, and, finally grasping what she was desiring, he laughed his Southern drawl of a laugh, throwing his leonine head back.

"Yes!," he said. "Cindy Ingaq, most beautiful woman in California, as Molly said, yes, yes, yes."

On the futon in the bedroom Camel lay on his back, now denuded entirely, and spread his legs wide like a patient at the gynecologist. It allowed Cindy easy access and it invited her to see the whole package and play with the soft maracas underneath Camel's hard stick. Camel loved to have his balls played with while being sucked.

"Camel," Cindy said, her arms resting on his Y'd legs, her beautiful, baseball tits hanging slightly in view, her body comfortably spread out beneath her, "your dick is a thing of beauty. Itsh—itsh—like a clarinet."

"Cindy, O Cindy."

"Now for my sholo," she said.

And a so low solo, she did. That mouth that could French kiss so well, could also treat a man's most important organ like it was divinely inspired, which, of course, it was. She swirled it, twirled it, deep-throated it, tickling the base with her sharp nails. She put both hands on Camel's balls and squeezed, while placing her mouth entirely flush with his lower stomach. Camel's head was full of posies and pansies and song. Cindy made sloppy, slippery noises too. She was trying to make a good impression, to really do her best work this first time, and she was blowing Camel's mind, while blowing his Timmy.

Then she slowed her action, like a jazz musician changing the mood, pulling it in and out. Her sensitive lips could feel Camel fill and, just before it exploded, she pushed her pinky finger into Camel's anus.

His orgasm was a masterpiece, the best poem he'd ever written. It was *Guernica*. It was "Take Five." It was *Ulysses*. After he was emptied he flipped around a bit, the aftershocks electric.

"Holy cats," Camel said, once he got his breath back. Cindy's mouth was still covering him. She almost looked like she had fallen asleep.

"Cindy?" he said, softly.

She slowly removed Camel's now flaccid penis from her mouth with a gourmand's delicacy. She put her pointer and a raised pinky on the deflated snail, and smiled at Camel, now her lover, her poet-lover.

"You ok?" Camel asked. "That was—that was."

"The poet is wordlesh," she said. She was rolling something around in her mouth, making her lisp even soggier.

"I thought—I thought—"

"Wait," she said. She stuck out her tongue. There was an opalescent pool there. "I'm still shwallowing."

"Oh, my sweet," Camel said.

"You come bunches."

"I would think so. That was a—a supersonic blowjob."

"I'm good."

"You are. You put the lick in phallic."

Camel gently pulled her forward until she lay on him chest to chest.

"Give me a few minutes."

"For what, lover?"

"Say it again."

"Lover."

"A short rest and then I will return the favor."

"Yesh?" Cindy said. It was almost girlish.

Camel looked at her dark eyes and her dark hair and that forehead upon which he wanted to paint *The Book of Genesis*. "Yes," he said. "I can only hope to do half as well."

And he did even better than that. Cindy Ingaq came 3 times on Camel's tongue and, a little later, twice more, sitting astride him.

"I love you, Cindy Ingaq," Camel said.

"I know, beautiful man. I knew and I know."

She didn't say she loved Camel that night. Only later did Camel realize that she hadn't.

Mario

"But how shall we educate men to goodness, to a sense of one another, to a love of truth? And more urgently, how shall we do this in a bad time?"
—*Daniel Berrigan*

Through Cindy Camel met Mario Savio, the key figure in The Free Speech Movement. He was intense, even in personal conversation. He carried his body and mind as if a soldier. Though short he stood tall, his chest pushed outward, his handsome face as intense as a black pudding: Mario was one of the most committed men Camel had ever met.

Mario protested HUAC when many people still thought that esteemed phalanx of self-appointed nabobs had credibility. Mario protested against the UN-Berkeley's nuclear weapons lab. Mario talked about CORE and SLATE and, later, FSM, his own Free Speech Movement, which began with a campus protest about the right to protest, and spread nationally, like a fresh stream flooding the corrupted alluvial plane of the United States of America, becoming The Civil Rights Movement, the Anti-Vietnam War movement, The Struggle for Women's Rights, and, eventually, the Gay Pride Movement.

"That's a lot of movement," Camel said. "Let's hope it's all forward. Till I came out here the only movement I wholeheartedly supported was my own bowels, that and the movement of nouns and adjectives and adverbs and shy little commas around the surface of a white piece of paper, not to prejudice anyone against colored paper."

Mario smiled. His smile was cunning, like Abbie Hoffman's, like Dylan's.

"We need poets, man," Mario said.

"I don't know, man. I'm just a wee basketball player from Memphis, Tennessee."

"I've seen you play ball. You're a great poet."

Camel didn't know if this was a joke or not.

"Sometimes the juice is worth the squeeze."

"Yes," Camel said.

"One more thing, Camel," Mario said, leaning in close, "Express yourself but bring a little something for the cops."

Despite his initial belief that he had little to offer Mario and his team, Camel joined the protestors on the steps of the administration building the first afternoon the police turned the firehoses on them and dumped the gathered pre-hippies ceremoniously down the concrete steps, bump bump bump, until the ground was awash in sopping and sore student demonstrators.

Many felt the hoses were a form of baptism better than any Baptist dunker had devised.

"First bath you've had in a while," one porcine officer spoke to Camel, nose to nose.

"Sir," Camel said, standing straighter, bringing his lanky, dripping, hairy self erect, "I am cleaner than your wife's diary."

While the heated peace officer thought about that, Camel slithered through the crowd and made a slippery escape. In the melee he had lost Cindy and now, more than anything, he wanted her at his side. He suddenly felt mumpish, lonely, as if all this activity around him was for naught (though he could not know what was to come), and he was, personally, bereft of direction. It was a brown study of a blue funk, not the first in Camel's life, not the last.

Instead of returning to Cindy's and stripping off their wet clothing in front of her gas stove, Camel returned to his dorm room and wrote the desultory ode, "Mario, My Captain." It was later published in *Antigone's Jockstrap*, and Camel caught some flak from the left, reading into the poem that Camel was not committed to the Free Speech

Movement, or the Peace Movement, or the movements after them.

Melancholia

Is what Camel suffered from. He liked the word but not the bone-draining experience.

In an early poem, "Camel's Blues," (later collected in the chapbook *Ghost Milk* (Small Totem Press, 1965, OP) he wrote, "What I found beneath me, beneath us all all/along, was a chthonic library,/of black emotion."

Camel inherited it from his mother. (He has blue genes.) His mother smoked weed to take the edges off the blues. Camel could only do the same, smoke weed, take pills, drop acid. Still the blues came back like acne.

Many who knew Camel, especially in those heady days on campus, would be surprised to know he suffered from paradoxical anhedonia. The noonday demon.

"Meet my pet black dog," Camel would say. "His barque sits on the River Styx."

The Movement

"You will not be able to stay home, brother.
You will not be able to plug in, turn on and cop out.

You will not be able to lose yourself on skag and skip,
Skip out for beer during commercials,
Because the revolution will not be televised."
—Gil Scott-Heron

Camel didn't know he was in at the beginning of something grand, something that would change the world for the better, something that would effloresce and send ripples out into history. The pebble, Grasshopper, with perpetual motion ripples of eternity. He only knew that he was among right-thinking people.

Camel initially joked, when asked about his commitment, that the only movement he was wholly committed to was the one that led to sexual engagement. Now he was in planning sessions with Mario, Cindy, Ruth Rosen, Jentri Anders (Camel, even with his head on right could not help but be attracted to the beautiful females who were turning into hippie earthmothers right before his eyes), Barry Melton (sometimes), Stokely Carmichael (sometimes) and a cat named Episcopal Dan, who was tripping and high during meetings, and who sat perfectly still with a blissful grin on his face while policy was debated, and who, when push came to shove, was always on the front lines getting truncheoned.

Episcopal Dan wore a flower on top of his head, a real flower, with a hand-sized mound of planter's soil securing it to his blond scalp. He also wore a grin that cast sparks like a struck flint. Camel thought Dan was beautiful and entertained the idea that, if he were gay, Dan would be his man. (Even straight as an angel's flight Camel once necked with Episcopal Dan in the back of Abbie Hoffman's van.)

One protestor, Camel never found out his name, wore a skeleton mask and carried a sign saying, "Napalm: It isn't Just for Breakfast." Something about this figure gave Camel the fantods. The skull mask. *Memento mori.* Death from the skies. Death from within. Camel stared at the face as if it were an oracle and could teach him a dark truth, a secret to life he, Camel, did not want to know. Does anyone want the unknown known? Let the dark stay dark.

When Governor Reagan spoke out about the students on the Berkeley campus, calling them hooligans and trespassers on government land, it galvanized the movement. If Reagan was against you you must be doing something right.

At the rallies, often held off campus, Country Joe and the Fish would play. Joan Baez would play and sing and speak. Allen Ginsberg would speak. Phil Ochs would play and sing and speak. Fred Cody of Cody's Books in Berkeley would speak. His bookstore became part of the scene. He sold out of Saul Alinsky and Leon Trotsky and Pierre-Joseph Proudhon.

But Mario spoke last. "Put your bodies upon the gears," he would say, and the crowd would cheer. They knew. They understood. Power could wind up in the hands of those whose cause was just. Free speech. End the war. Subvert the corrupt power elite. True democracy was busy being born.

Day Break

The examined life, so much a writer's haven, had its pitfalls. It also had its glories. Camel tasted both.

When Camel looked back on his Berkeley years he marveled at how much he did, extra-curricularly, and still managed to make good grades, even with professors who were opposed to the student movements on campus and off. Camel wrote well. This made school easier. And, for the record, Camel graduated Summa Cum Laude in 1963, with a double degree in literature and political science (this 2nd degree due to the convictions of his paramour, by whose side he felt safe and savvy); he stayed on campus taking nothing but literature classes for another 18 months, and was invited to top graduate schools in Amerika and beyond. But, by that time, Camel's literary career had been launched and he left academia's groovy groves for the mythical highway.

The book that decided this was Camel's first full-length poetry collection, *Jokes my Kidnappers Told Me* (Lower Power Books, 1964). The day it arrived in his mailbox was a holy day, a day Camel remembered the rest of his life, for it was on this day, also, that Cindy told him she loved him. ("I love you," she said. "Look! My new book!" Camel said. More on this later.)

On one of these extra-curricular afternoons, Camel and Cindy, along with Hondo and his woman of the moment, Destiny Dingle (beautiful, half-Cherokee woman, who wore on her umber cheek a small tattooed ankh), went to lunch at John's Grill in San Francisco. John's Grill was as famous for its mention in Dashiell Hammett's *The Maltese Falcon*, as it was for its toothsome steaks. Hondo was a fan of hard-boiled mysteries. In later years he penned one himself (*The Bride with the Grenade*, The Mysterious Press, 1977), though it sold fewer copies than Camel's poetry books, and was soon remaindered and many copies pulped. By 1990 a firm first edition paperback was selling for a cool $1000. Hondo was one of the first 'staff' writers on the *Berkeley Barb* (1965-1980).

At this lunch the men dug into their steaks, while Destiny, a vegetarian picked at a house salad, and Cindy had fish. The conversation was wide-ranging, touching on politics and literature, music and television, Huey Newton and Baby Huey, James Joyce and James Cagney, Diane di Prima and

Diana Dors, *The Doors of Perception* and *No Exit*, Artaud and Art Tatum. It was a lively lunch and all four were relishing the good food and good folk. This is friendship. This lasts.

After lunch, though their moseying took them along a cable car route, they decided to walk off the meal. The two men hung back while the women, arm in arm, lead the way.

"It's a fine view," Hondo said, lighting a cigarette with a flip-top lighter. Hondo was known for his ability to roll a joint in one hand like a cow-puncher of olde.

"The cerulean sky or the behinds of the women as they lead us astray?"

"The sky is blue?" Hondo said, expelling a snort of smoke.

"Destiny is the right stuff," Camel said.

"She is fine," Hondo said, "A woman with a lot of soul."

"Tell me again where you met her."

"A party at her sister's house. I had a class with her sister. Her twin sister, I should add."

"Identical?"

"Indeed identical."

'How do you know you're with the right one today?" Camel said, smiling through his mustache.

"Does it matter?" Hondo asked in return.

"Not to me, Brother."

They were moving toward the bay. There was a cool mist in the air even this far inland. The women swayed as they walked, their heads inclined together, as they discussed politics, a sororal intimacy that men could only stand outside of and admire.

"Both sisters," Hondo said, as if finishing a thought he had not till then formulated as speech.

Camel, no Maupin, scrunched up his face and turned toward his friend. "What?"

"Oh, both sisters. I've been with both sisters," Hondo said from his personal brume.

"Oh," Camel said. "That's fine, isn't it?"

"They're beautiful."

"They are," Camel affirmed, extrapolating from the one.

"Destiny says there's a new bookstore along here," Cindy called back over her shoulder. "You wanna?"

"Absolutely," Camel said.

"At once," Hondo said, sotto voce.

"Hm?" Camel hummed.

"I had both sisters at once. Best night of my short life."

"Ah," Camel said. He put an arm around his friend's shoulders. "We're going to a bookstore."

"Oh, oh, sure," Hondo said. "Destiny told me there's a new one around here somewhere, by coincidence."

A Buyer's Market

Was the name of the bookstore.

Its white façade, like a house in Hooterville, gave no hint of the quality of its contents. San Francisco was awash in great bookstores, and this one seemed to take its place in such august company with aplomb, and a little polish. The interior was all blond wood and ceiling fans and long, long shelves, stretching from the front door into the turbid outer-regions of fairyland.

The man behind the counter, at the front, was as slim as Hoagy Carmichael. He wore his brown hair cut short but his beard was a long braid, woven with small flowers. His name tag said, "Benny Profane."

"Nice name," Camel said, sauntering over.

"I stole it from *V*," the clerk said. His voice was plummy, friendly.

"Oh, Benny, yeah. I love Benny. I meant the name of the store," Camel said pleasantly in return.

"Right, of course. You know Anthony Powell?"

"Um, no," Camel said. "Is he local?

"No, no. British writer. At work on the English

59

language *Remembrance of Things Past*. I just finished the 6ᵗʰ novel. I think that's halfway, but we'll see."

"Camel," Camel said, stretching his long, stretchy form forward and extending his long-fingered hand.

"Mark," Benny Profane said, grasping Camel's hand firmly. "Short for Remark. Remark Kramer. My parents loved palindromes."

"Ha," Camel laughed. "Mayhaps I should change my name to Sore Eros. These are my friends, Hondo, Cindy..." but as he turned they had already wandered away down the shotgun aisles of the bookstore. "Anyway. Want to look around a bit, too. Nice to meet you."

"You too," Remark Kramer said. "Oh!"

Kramer's eyes grew wide.

"You're Camel Eros!"

"Yeah, yeah, that's me."

"Listen, dammit. I wasn't paying attention. You're Camel Jeremy Eros. I love your book."

"Oh, nice, man, you know my book?"

"Know it? It's beautiful, my friend. It's written with a burning stick."

"Jesus, thanks, Mark."

Mark Kramer hustled from behind the counter and bade Camel follow. Sure enough. There in the poetry section were ten copies of *Jokes my Kidnappers Told Me*, face out, their modest flesh-colored covers wearing Camel's stoned smile.

"That's beautiful," Camel said.

"Sign them?"

"Of course, yeah." Camel pulled a ballpoint from his vest pocket.

"And inscribe one to me and my wife, please."

"Sure, Mark. What's her name?"

"Eedy," Mark Kramer said.

Camel looked up and blinked slowly a few times.

"Eedy Durrette?" Camel said.

"Nee Durrette, yes. How did you know?"

"She's from Memphis," Camel said.

"Right, right. You're from Memphis?" The coincidence seemed astounding to the bookseller.

"I am. Frayser High School. Eedy went there, too."

"Yeah, I know. Wild. Did you know her in high school? She wanted to be a poet, I think. You must have known her."

"Not well," Camel said, "Not well." He bent over the book and wrote:

"For Remark and Eedy Kramer, friends across the great wash of time. Love, Camel."

The tinkle of the front door bell acted on Kramer like Pavlov's bell. His head swiveled as two thin young men entered the bookstore.

"Excuse me" he said. "And thanks," he waved his inscribed copy at Camel.

Camel found the other three in his party lost in the shelves, each to his own passion. He sidled up to Cindy in the philosophy section. She was holding a copy of Kropotkin's *Fields, Factories and Workshops.*

"Score," she said, holding the book up for Camel to appreciate.

"It's a used copy?" Camel said.

"The store is a mix of used and new. There are some great bargains here."

Hondo was browsing through fiction. Under his arm he already had Vonnegut's *Cat's Cradle* (new) and *The Stories of Anton Chekhov* (used).

"You read this?" Hondo said, reaching into the shelf and pulling out a plum, a shiny copy of John Barth's *The End of the Road.*

"I haven't," Camel said.

"I'm buying it for you," Hondo said.

"I got pelf," Camel said, smiling.

"My gift."

"Hey!" Camel exclaimed. He reached into the shelf and his hand returned with a 2nd hand copy of Powell's *A Buyer's Market*. He tucked it under his arm.

Camel wandered over to poetry again, where Destiny was now browsing.

"Camel, do you know this guy?" Destiny was holding a small, red pamphlet-sized book called *The Galilee Hitch-hiker*, by someone named Richard Brautigan. Camel took it from her and flipped it open. His eyes widened, squinted, widened again. It could have been myopia or it could have been something had just seeped into his soul.

"I've heard his name," Camel said, almost inaudibly. White Rabbit Press, Camel read to himself, feeling as if he had just fallen down the hole. The poems inside were small othernesses, half machine, half insect. He'd never seen anything like them.

"Are you buying this?" Camel asked.

"Should I?" Destiny asked anxiously. She was slightly cowed by Camel, his height, his wit, his pen.

"Lemme buy it. If it's good I'll give it to you. If it's bad I'll keep it and you've lost nothing."

"That's groovy, Camel," Destiny said, giving Camel her best wide-mouth, toothy smile. She had one helluva good wide-mouth smile.

Camel had no intention of ever giving up the book. He had already been hooked by it. He also found a small brown cardboard box by Gregory Corso, called *Earth Egg*. Inside were some postcards, some pornography, some poetry. Camel loved it instantly.

At the checkout counter, Remark Kramer shook his head and smiled at all their choices.

"Nice, nice," he kept saying. "Nice choice."

When it was Camel's turn, he said, "Oh, lemme replace this 2nd hand *Buyer's Market* with an equally lovely copy of the first book in the series, *A Question of Upbringing*. You gotta read them in order."

"Ok, thanks, Mark," Camel said. "I'll take both though just to, you know, support you."

"Cool," Mark said. "Oh and Richard will be so pleased."

"Pardon?" Camel said.

"You're buying Richard's chapbook. I assume you know him."

"I do not," Camel said.

"I'll introduce you. You wanna come to dinner at mine and Eedy's place? I'll see if Richard and his easy rider can come."

"Yes," Camel said. "Yes, that would be lovely."

The dinner with Remark and Eedy

Remark and Eedy lived in a painted lady in Haight-Ashbury. The bright pastels of it, aside its contiguous neighbors, looked like a fairy cake in the middle of an illusory city. Richard gave Cindy a tight smile on the doorstep. Cindy looked like Alice right before she falls.

"Hashbury," Camel chuntered.

"It's gonna be nice, Camel. What are you worried about? The woman or the writer?"

"The lady or the tiger?"

"You think this Brautigan is a tiger."

"He's certainly a lion. A literary lion."

"You have the jimjams about meeting him?"

"No, I don't think so. I feel—an anticipatory vibration."

"Ok. It's precognitive, that's cool."

"Ok," Camel parroted back. "Precognitive."

"You're not thinking about the old girlfriend?"

"Richard's old girlfriend? No—sorry, my mind wandered. Eedy? No."

The door opened. Eedy stood there dressed in a thin white dress, light and diaphanous, and as short as a bird's song. Her legs were immaculate. Camel was staring at them. Cheerleader legs.

"Camel!" Eedy squeaked. Camel forgot she squeaked. "Goddamn, it's good to see you!"

Her arms went around Camel's neck and he almost tumbled backwards. She was climbing Camel as if he were a monkey puzzle tree.

"Eedy, my love," Camel said, involuntarily.

"Who would have thunk it, right? Both of us from Frayser and here we are together again in this coastal Oz."

Eedy was trying too hard. She had perhaps prepared this speech ahead of time.

"Eedy, this is my friend, Cindy. Cindy, Eedy."

They shook hands. Cindy appraised her. She couldn't help but stare at her legs, so smooth, shapely and so *there*, under that impossibly small dress. Cindy wanted Eedy suddenly. Just like that, lightning.

"Come in, come in, I'm sorry I am leaving my guests on the stoop. I guess I'm a stoop, ha ha."

Turning she bellowed as if calling for her team to play better defense: "MARK!"

The interior of the house was as shiny as a new car, lots of nice wood, warm rugs, pleasing art. Miro, Rivers, Noland: surely not originals. Parquet floors and ceilings in the clouds. There was more money here than a bookstore makes in its entire life.

"Camel, wonderful," Mark said, rushing forward. In his hand was a pastry cutter. The men managed a half-handshake/hug.

"Mark, beautiful place, man. Really beautiful."

Mark osculated Cindy's cheek.

"Family money," Mark said to the unspoken question.

"Ah, that's good money, family money," Camel said with a grin.

"Richard's late as usual. Come in and sit."

The living room was so white it was like a blizzard of light. They sat on a plush couch the size of an ocean liner. There were wines, cheese, and a bong on the coffee table.

"Mark's making a pie for dessert," Eedy said, crossing those legs, tanned and polished as a new play-pretty. "He's the cook, thank God. I think he'll join us soon. So, Camel, long time no looky, cookie. Tell me what you've been doing since Trezevant High."

"Well, the day after I graduated, I remember I had a hamburger and fries at Whataburger. That night I listened to an old recording of Lady Day my dad gave me and when I went to bed I dreamed I was a buccaneer with a limp and a pet wolf named Belmondo."

"Stop it, Camel," Cindy said. "You're full of yourself."

Only then did Eedy realize it was a joke and she laughed a horsey, cheerleader laugh.

The doorbell rang. The chimes sounded like coins dropping.

"Richard!" Remark shouted and rushed to the door, his hands white with flour.

A few moments later Mark ushered Richard Brautigan and a beautiful brunette woman into the living room. Brautigan was as tall as Camel and had the same sort of graceful slouch. His hair was ear-level, blondish red, and his mustache a shaggy, chipped thing of beauty.

"Richard," Camel said. "I've been reading you."

"Oh, mm, yes," Richard said. "This is Frankie."

The brunette made a flirty curtsey and smiled as if she knew a secret that could affect them all.

"Aw, Jesus," Mark said. "I got flour on your vest."

Richard tried to crane his head around. There were two perfect white handprints on the back of his dark vest.

"I'm sure that's alright," Richard said. His voice was not exactly soft but it was mollescent. A wee voice, almost girlish.

The dinner, held around a long glass table as long as the white couch, was a roaring success. The talk was books and politics, movies and politics, food and politics. Eedy played hostess mostly but when she spoke everyone stopped to listen as if she were an oracle. Mark smiled at her with such adoration the room seemed to expand with warmth.

"I'm working on a new short story. Short short story," Richard said.

"You're so prolific it makes me tired," Mark said. "Give us a hint."

Richard looked around the table with an imp's grin. "It's based on the ugly duckling fairy tale. That's all I want to say."

Richard's date blurted out, "Spoiler alert. The duckling is a swan."

There was a tittering. Richard's face was inscrutable. He may have been thinking about changing the ending. He may have been thinking about the lover who would follow Frankie.

After dinner they all sat in the backyard and passed the small, purple bong around. It looked handmade and the beaker had interesting, colorful shapes inside like Kagoshima glass. Camel was staring into it, expecting either Bloody Mary or a former life to look back at him.

"Gift from Richard," Remark said, holding his inhalation and speaking around it. "He named it El Kabong."

Later, pleasantly stoned, the three couples sat around on the lawn, which was spacious and soft as Lempster wool, pairing off into new constellations. Camel and Richard moved to a stone bench under a shade tree in the back of the yard. Eedy and Cindy were at the yard's furthermost edge, sitting on a blanket. In the encroaching murk they were all but invisible. Remark and Frankie were on the porch which overlooked the yard like an aerie.

Camel and Richard talked poetry and poets deep into the inky night. They talked William Carlos Williams and Robert Duncan. They talked Yeats and Keats. They talked Eliot and Pound and Emily Dickinson. Neruda and Montale.

"You're poetry reminds me a bit of Dr. Williams," Camel said. "But you're funnier."

"High praise, Camel, thank you." Richard pulled at one side of his mustache, his eyes glazing over with thought. "Listen," he said after an hour or so. "Send me your stuff. Or no, I'll come round for it. Mark'll give me your book. And we'll go drink some wine and read your poems and we'll talk about the scene here, what I know of it, and we'll talk presses. There are a number of good poetry presses springing up like magic mushrooms."

"Yeah, I've been buying as many small press books as possible."

"Tell me about your poems," Richard said. He took a long toke off a mini-joint.

"Pessimistic. Narcissistic."

"Sometimes real pessimism looks like false humility."

"Hm," Camel said. "Yes."

"Gimme another adjective."

"Invisible," Camel said.

"No, no, I've seen it. I saw your Carole Lombard poem in *Sneak*."

"*Sneak*, yeah, yeah, they're great. I met the editor at a Gary Snyder reading."

"Moishe is an old friend. Your poem was the best thing in there."

"Jesus, there was a Rosy Adid poem in there."

"Yeah, Rosy's good. She likes to be on top."

"She's not far to go," Camel said. Only a few days later did Camel realize Richard meant in bed.

"So, yeah, we'll get together and look at your work and I'll show you some new things I've written. I could use the feedback."

"You're kind, Richard," Camel said.

From the darkened corner where Eedy and Cindy were bonding came susurrations as soft as stridulation. The women were whispering now and Camel could just make out their prone figures, which, detail removed by the murk, resembled figures made of sand.

"The sweet voices of women," Richard said. Both men hung their head, meditatively, and listened as if to a prophecy. As if to the sound of the night itself.

Soon the faint murmurs deepened. No more words drifted back from the blanket in the corner. Instead there were sweet animal sounds, a chuffing like an old engine, moans like farewells to Tarwathie.

Then Eedy's voice, thickened cheerleader grunts, "Jesus, Jesus, O Sweet Jesus."

In the morning Remark found the women asleep on the blanket, their bodies, naked as flowers goldened by the rising sun, and Cindy's hand resting like a sleeping bird in the tangled nest of Eedy's pubic hair.

The SDS

Tom Hayden, Phil Booth, Jim Monsonis.

These were names to reckon with. They were the governing body of the Students for a Democratic Society. SDS, one wave of the new tsunami of acronyms. What did they want? A true democratic society? Is that what we all want? Is that *all* what we all want? Is that Utopia?

"I think people are entitled to march without a permit. When you have a few hundred thousand people on the street you have permission," Tom said.

Another acronym was schooling the SDS: The SNCC, or Student Nonviolent Coordinating Committee.

Some folks objected to the word committee.

"What is a government, Nosy? It's a committee of committees and a committee hasn't even got trousers. It's only got a typist, and she's thinking of her young man and next Saturday afternoon at the pictures. If you gave a government imagination, it wouldn't know where to put it. It would pass it on to the cat or leave it out for the charwoman to be taken away with the tea leaves," Joyce Cary said.

The ERAP (Economic Research and Action Project) was the campus arm of the SDS. They sounded so hopeful!

Some folks wanted to burn down the government, start from scratch, the swidden approach. Fresh earth to grow a fresh world.

Some good people thought it was better to work from within the political structure. Camel liked to call these folks the Pep Rally Crowd, or The Peppers, after their acronym, PEP (Political Education Project).

"To the uneducated, an A is just three sticks," said A. A. Milne.

Meanwhile, on the Berkeley campus

The demonstrations were heating up. There was a growing consensus. There was unity. The free speech movement, the anti-war movement, civil rights proponents, were all gaining courage from the size of the crowds. Speakers were motivated by more than seeking renown.

At one headbuster, immediately following Governor Reagan's condemnation of the protests as "that mess in Berkeley," Hondo Minimum had been clubbed, arrested and taken away in a paddy wagon. He was not heard from for many lifetimes. Camel tried numerous times to find him, petitioning all the way up to the mayor's office, but the 'official' word was that he was arrested and released the next day. (Years later, Three Hushpuppy Brown, met an American-born yogi in India, who spoke of his days at Berkeley and his friendship with an enlightened poet from Memphis, Tennessee, whom he said was called Khaki Eros.)

(Later and later, Hondo was in Memphis, alas, for the grieving.)

"Turn on and all will turn to love," Camel said.

"It's the politics of hip," Cindy said. "We're working toward a new world. No governments."

"Turn on and all will turn to love," Camel said.

"But we gotta put our asses out there, Camel."

"I know, Babe. I know. Have I shirked once?"

"No, Camel. There was the first meeting about shutting down the induction center."

"I was reading that night, Babe. I was reading at fucking City Lights!"

"I know, Sweetie."

"I was there a few days later chanting, 'Say no. Don't go,' right alongside you."

"You were. You were, Camel."

These were small cracks in the love affair between Cindy and Camel. Cindy was all about the movement. It's what she ate and breathed. Camel was committed but his poetry—*poetry* in general—put a firmer grip around his internal, Pierian scrotum. He wrote more than he protested. Later, Cindy would have an affair with Bobby Seale, and begin to move away from Camel, emotionally. For now, for a little while longer, they stayed together, over marches, and boo, and books.

And there was the threesome with Eedy Kramer.

The threesome with Eedy Kramer

It was a night of wine and poetry. Camel and Cindy came to a reading by Diane DiPrima at Remark's bookstore, A Buyer's Market. Mark had lowered the bookstore lights and the poet was encased in a soft ball of pungent yellow moonglow. DiPrima was great, still angry, but full of light. Her words were sparks off Hephaestus's anvil.

She read deep into the night and afterward she mingled with the mid-sized crowd, sharing some white wine and cheesy tarts. She seemed to have a coterie of young male poets who wanted to touch her to see if those seriously sinewy words came from that body.

Mark spent a goodly amount of time next to Diane, running interference, standing so close to her that there was more than a dactyl or two passing between them. Diane's husband, Alan, was not there that night.

"Mark seems awfully fond of our poet tonight," Eedy said to Camel and Cindy.

"That bother you, Sister?" Cindy asked. Her voice was gruff but her hand was kind, rubbing Eedy's tanned shoulder, around the strap of her tie-dye summer dress.

Eedy looked at Cindy and then shot Camel a guilty look.

"It's ok, Kid," Cindy said, with a feline smile. "Camel's cool with it."

"Camel, man, Camel, you know about, you know, me and, you know?"

"Of what are you referring?" Camel asked. His catty smile rubbed whiskers with Cindy's.

"Oh, no, I don't know," Eedy said. She crossed her impeccable legs, two bronze columns of desire.

"You've slept together," Camel said. And now he put a placatory hand on Eedy's other shoulder. It felt like high school, sexy, forbidden, *electric*.

"A lot," Eedy said. Then she giggled.

"A lot?" Camel asked.

"Sure," Cindy said. "Afternoons. You've got that class."

"Ah," Camel said. "You guys wanna go off and I'll find my own way home?"

The two women looked at each other with melting constellations in their eyes.

"I guess so," Eedy said, weakly. This was a little outside her ken. "I guess so?" she repeated with a lilt at the end.

"Of course," Cindy said. "But, hey, Camel, baby, don't go home alone. Come with us."

"Ah," Camel said.

"Not at my place," Eedy said quickly.

"Mine," Cindy said.

So, that night, on Cindy's double bed, after shaking the crumbs out of it and making her cat, Felix, stay in the bathroom, the trio unclothed each other, slowly, with deep kissing, and tender words.

"Ahh," Eedy said, when Camel bent his lips to one nipple. "Just like at Trezevant High," she sighed.

"Better," Cindy said, bending her mouth to the other nipple.

While Eedy and Cindy performed an unadulterated 69, Camel sat back and watched. They were really gobbling each other, their mouths lively and their tongues flicking, and their fingers deep in each other's thighs. It was quite a turn-on but Camel sat and watched, concentrating on not concentrating on his own erection. He was trying to close off his 4th chakra.

The women eventually emerged as if from under a dark tarn.

"Camel, Camel," Cindy said, her breath coming in short gasps. "Come here, Baby."

Camel sat still, smiling, the watcher.

Eedy wiped her mouth which was glistening like St. Elmo's fire.

"Camel!" Eedy said. "Your penis wasn't that big in high school!"

A moment of silence and then they all laughed.

"Sorry," Eedy said.

"Penis!" Cindy said, and they all fell out again. "Camel's penis!"

Eedy was laughing but looking from face to face. "What? What?"

"Say dick," Cindy said. She took Eedy's hair in a fist. "Say cock. Say dick."

Eedy laughed a couple more nervous gasps.

"Dick," Eedy said. And another round of laughter convulsed the group.

"Now tell him you want it," Cindy said.

There was a silence now like peace. Strong emotions blew in like a wind from *The Story of O*.

"Camel," Eedy said, her laughter gone now and her voice husky. "Camel, I want to suck your new man-sized dick."

"Alright," Cindy said.

"Alright," Camel said.

And she did. And then Cindy did. And then they tested the outer circles of geometry. In the morning they slept in. Camel missed a class on Blake. Hand-in-hand, Eedy and Cindy walked back to Haigh-Ashbury and, at Eedy's door, Cindy kissed her with passion.

"Good morning, Lover," Cindy said.

Eedy leaned over and whispered into Cindy's small ear.

"I love Camel's dick," she said.

All the way to Memphis

During this entire period in Berkeley and San Francisco, which is delineated here as it if were Camel's whole life, our hero made frequent trips back to Memphis.

Memphis had its own burgeoning hipster scene, its own protestors and hippies and progressive thinkers. Camel had two especial friends at home during this tumultuous time: Three Hushpuppy Brown, so-monickered because he always carried a spare shoe, and Johnny Niagara, the movement's Lothario.

They would get together at Beatnik Manor or The Bitter Lemon and talk all night. It's hard today to glom onto what was happening if you weren't part of it, and why there was so much to say and so few hours to say it in. The whole country was flowering, opening outward like a pod, bodysnatching Amerika and reimagining it as Mindspace.

Inside the doorway to The Bitter Lemon someone had written this in lavender chalk on the floor: *"What is man but a mass of thawing clay? The ball of the human finger is but a drop congealed. The fingers and toes flow to their extent from the thawing mass of the body. Who knows what the human body would expand and flow out to under a more genial heaven? Is not the hand a spreading palm leaf with its lobes and veins?"*

—Hank Thoreau

Underneath that, in canary yellow chalk, someone appended this:

Oh, the day we met, I went astray,
I started rollin' down that lost highway.
--Hank Williams

"Maybe we shouldn't have taken that windowpane with this rotgut wine. I feel like I've a red balloon inside me, expanding, pushing my innards this way and that," Hushpuppy said.

"You've got lightning bolts in your eyes and beams coming out of your afro," Johnny Niagara said, as he was signaling a young devotchka, who had just entered The Bitter Lemon through its make-believe door.

The young devotchka wore a miniskirt made out of an Indian blanket and a fringe vest that did little to hide her crescent moon curves.

"Owsley said this was South American witch doctor medicine," Camel said. His mustache was painted magenta.

"Which doctor?"

"Doctor Who."

"Who's on first?"

"First the advisors, then the soldiers."

"First in our hearts."

"Which we wear on our sleeves like badges."

"We don't need no stinking badgers."

"Don't badger me, man. Just walk with me in the rain."

"Billie."

"What?"

"That's from Billie Holiday, right?"

"I thought it was Doc Holiday."

"Which doctor?"

"Did you wink at me?" the young devotchka inquired as she settled her considerable behind onto Johnny's considerate lap.

"A nod's as good as a swink," Camel said.

"Yeah, and your buddy is nodding off," she said, nodding and winking toward Three Hushpuppy Brown, who was indeed asleep like a Buddha in the sun.

"The man is cool as a mountain in its star-pitched tent. Can fall asleep with cannons going off in his encephalon."

"Is he Arthur Lee?" she then asked.

"He's all Love, Baby," Johnny said.

"You seem to do alright yourself," she said, shaking her long mane of coppery hair. "Lahna Darling," she added, putting out a downy hand, festooned with magic rings.

"I like it when you call me darling, but, darling, we are way beyond the hand-shaking phase," Johnny said, and put his tongue inside her mouth. Lahna Darling sucked on that tongue while Camel and the now-awakened Hushpuppy began to write haikus on their napkins.

"Good," Camel said, reading Hushpuppy's running verse. "What's scrapple?"

"I'll teach you how to play scrapple," Hushpuppy said.

Some new folks entered. Camel knew them all. There was College Herpes, Jenny Lamb and the drummer for the newly reformed Bambam Five (they had six members, but no one complained), a beautiful black woman Camel thought was called Pharaoh Moans. Eye contact was made, more nods and winks.

"Didn't know you were in town," College shouted over the music, which was "Flying Saucer Rock and Roll."

"Back and forth, Baby," Camel said. "Got two homes like a turtle."

Much later in the evening College would lean toward Pharaoh Moans and inquire, "Why does a turtle have two homes?"

"I'm not good at those word puzzles," Pharaoh said, adding silver lipstick to her fulsome lips.

It was on this night, or another, that the plot to blow up the Doughboy Statue in Overton Park was launched. It was these six or another six. It was here or there, now or later, true and false, as outside, encompassing all, the Big Blue Ball rolled in its mercury bath, and filled space with radio waves that had nothing to do with radios. Women and men died. Babies were born. God was in the house.

Also this trip back

A letter arrived. It went this way.

Dear Camel,

I'm hoping you remember your old teacher. And I'm hoping you remember me fondly. I read your book, Camel. It's so good. I'm so proud to have had you as a student. And I did have you, didn't I?

Listen, The Beatles are playing the Coliseum on August 19. I want like all holy hell to see them and I want to see them with someone who appreciates them. My husband calls them racket. Long and short, can you come back to Memphis and escort your old teacher to the concert? The Beatles, Camel! We can have a good time. Maybe dinner afterwards. Maybe, I don't know.

Please write back soon. I'm going way out on a limb here. Please don't saw it off.

love,

Eileen Goff.

She signed it 'love,' Camel thought. He wrote back.

Dear Eileen,

Have bought ticket. Arrive Memphis August 18, 8:15 in evening. Can you pick me up?

access and ooze,

Mr. Eros.

When Camel deplaned and entered the concourse of the Memphis airport he spotted Eileen Goff in the small gaggle of people greeting passengers. Her hair was blonder than before, almost white, and she wore a mini-skirt which accentuated her shapely legs.

"Camel," she screamed like one of the teens greeting the Fab Four at every airport the world over.

Camel bent to buss her cheek and Eileen Goff wrapped her arms around him and put her tongue in his mouth. They hung there like a stud horse for several minutes. Camel's brain was awash in electric nostalgia, mixed with a little sinsemilla.

"You hungry?" Eileen said, when they broke their clasp. "Wanna go to Shoney's or something?"

"Sure, sure," Camel said.

"I loved your book, Camel. It was so—you," Mrs. Goff exclaimed.

"Thanks, Mrs.—Eileen. You're very kind."

"And you're very tall. Were you always this tall?

"Some."

"And the mustache?"

"Longer."

"Tell me right away. I'm mad with trepidation. How do I look? Have I aged badly? Do you think I'm old and ugly now?"

"My dear," Camel said, taking a courtly step backwards and eyeing her. "You look even more like Catherine Deneuve. Age sits on you like an eagle on an aerie."

"Camel. Flatterer. Kiss me again."

They made this kind of silly prattle in the car on the way to Shoney's and then through the meal and then again in the car on the way to the Eros' house. Eileen parked the car in front of Camel's parents' home and turned the engine off.

"Ah the air of Frayser, tinged with wistfulness and toxic miasma."

"This is strange, isn't it?"

"Strange, yes," Camel said. "Unexpected. But life is almost always that."

"Not for me, Camel. Not for me. This is the most— *unexpected* thing I've ever done. Rob—that's my husband— Rob thinks I'm nuts."

"You told him you were taking me to the concert?"

"Yes, of course. He doesn't care."

"Ok."

"Camel—through the years—"

"Eileen, I understand. Relax. This is lovely."

"You are," Eileen said, and put a hand to Camel's cheek. She leaned in and the kiss was more chaste this time.

"Should I drive tomorrow?" Camel asked. Then he laughed: "I can borrow my dad's car."

"No, I'll pick you up. Goodnight, Dear."

"Goodnight, Eileen. Thanks."

"Have a good date?" Camel's dad asked that evening.

"The date's tomorrow night."

"What date?"

"August 19."

"Ok. Goodnight, Son."

Eileen was almost 45 minutes early. She parked the car and honked.

Camel put a hand out the front door and held up one finger.

"This one is anxious," Camel's dad said. "Who is this again?"

Camel gave him a made-up name. "Gladys Pinch-Nerf," he said. "From Trezevant."

"Of course," Camel's dad said.

"I'm sorry I'm so early. I got ready and, well, I just drove here."

"That's ok," Camel said, getting in. Eileen Goff was dressed in an even shorter skirt this time. It was knit and tight and spackled with tiny openings through which one could see white skin, white panties. She was trying to approximate the garb of the young hipsters she'd seen on Consecrated TV, the new Teen Nation.

The drive to the Coliseum was quieter than the previous night's car rides.

"I'm nervous," Eileen said as they neared the Fairgrounds where the Coliseum squatted like a mushroom cloud.

"Nonsense," Camel said. "It's only the best rock band in the world."

He grinned his Camel grin.

Eileen Goff hit him on the arm. "You know what I mean." They were walking toward the glass doors on the Southern Avenue side where there was a long line of young people, many without tickets. What did they expect to see? The line swayed and shimmered like a Dayglo Elvis.

There was also a contingent of Lennon haters with signs that damned him to hell for his comments about a Jewish carpenter many folks believed was the true son of God. And a few ragged Klansmen for good measure. They trudged around in a sad circle, occasionally waving their signs scrawled with inarticulate sloganeering. Camel was tempted to confront them but instead he put an arm around his date and they walked into the Roundhouse in a cozy embrace.

Their seats were not on the floor, not in the loge. They were upper tier.

"Shit, I thought these would be better," Eileen Goff said.

"This is great," Camel assured her.

The Beatles took the stage. Around their heads nimbi smoldered and sparked. The crowd din, 10,000 high-pitched voices, was like the heavens opening at the final trumpet.

"Jesus," Eileen said. "Will we be able to hear the music?"

Camel beamed and put his hand in hers. She smiled with gratitude.

They opened with "Rock and Roll Music."

"Wow," Eileen said, screaming in Camel's ear. "I didn't know they wrote that."

"Chuck Berry," Camel shouted back.

"What did you call me?"

"Berry!"

"Fuck Berry? I want to be your little fuck berry."

"What?" Camel shouted.

"I think I love you," Eileen shouted just as the song finished and the group launched right into "She's a Woman."

Eileen began to rummage in her purse. She was looking for cigarettes. In the dark her fingers closed around a cylinder and she put it in her mouth.

"Light me," she said.

Camel reached into his pocket for his lighter. The swell around them was like an aural sea. The Beatles bopped around like lustrous imp/deities in their white spotlights.

"Would you rather smoke a jay?" he shouted.

"What?"

Camel cracked a flame off his flint and held it to Eileen's mouth. What he lit was not a cigarette but a jumbo Black Cat firecracker.

"Jesus," he said, plucking it from her mouth and flicking it down at their feet. The explosion was magnified by the metallic seats around them. It sounded like a gunshot.

"Damn near blew my lips off! Hell, I took that off Curtis Branson 5th period," Eileen shouted. "He's a miscreant."

Camel didn't hear much of what she said. He was staring at the stage. Had he seen Lennon and McCartney lock eyes at the bang? Are they that sensitive to the roar around them?

After the concert, which lasted all of thirty minutes, finishing with a bashing "Long Tall Sally," there was much talk eddying around them, as they fought their way carward. They now held each other in companionable affection.

"Someone took a shot at Lennon," a gaunt young fellow said.

"I saw it," his friend replied. "The cops let the guy go. They want Lennon dead, too."

Once inside Eileen's Buick LeSabre they sat and looked at each other.

"Camel," Eileen said. "I'm so happy we shared that."

"They're sublime," Camel said.

"I've thought a lot about you, you know? You were my favorite student. Best I've ever had."

"In class you mean?"

Eileen thought for a moment. "Oh!" she said. And she laughed and Camel laughed.

"Motel room or parking?" Camel asked and there was the Camel smile again.

"Both," Eileen said. "I've never been parking in my life."

So, they drove down Southern Avenue until they found a cul-de-sac that seemed dark and inviting. Eileen's hands were sweating. The LeSabre bumped up onto the curb.

"Oops," she said.

After some passionate preliminaries, hands over every softly clad surface, tongues into all facial orifices, Camel ran his hand up his ex-teacher's smooth thighs, under her ridiculously short skirt, and pulled her panties down with one steady pull.

"Oh, Camel," Mrs. Goff sighed as his fingers found her.

She came right away.

"Camel, darling," she stopped and used her serious classroom voice. "I think you must have had the biggest dick in high school."

Camel laughed. "You try many?"

"No, Stupid."

"You're memory is kind," Camel said.

Eileen smirked, fixing Camel with a saucy moue.

Eileen Goff unzipped Camel's jeans. After some clumsy maneuvers to get all the material out of the way, Camel's doohickey breathed the night air.

"Jesus, Camel," she said. "It's so big."

She wrapped her hand around it.

"A parking blowjob," she said. "That's what I want to try! How I've dreamed of it."

"Then let your dreams come true," Camel said, gallantly.

After sucking Camel off and swallowing his cum with exaggerated sounds Eileen Goff raised her still pretty face and put her cheek on Camel's chest.

"I said I love you," she said, quietly.

"What?"

"At the concert. I said I love you but it was too noisy."

"Ok," Camel said. He stroked her nitid hair.

"I don't mean I want you to be my husband instead of my husband. I just mean, well, I've always relished my memory of you and now, having re-consummated my fantasies, I still do. Love you, I mean."

"You're a lovely woman, Eileen Goff. You still want to go to a motel."

"I don't know," she answered, dreamily.

"Kiss me again."

She did. She tasted spermy.

"We can just go home. It's been a fantastic evening," she said.

"Ok," Camel said.

"Though I've never fucked in a car."

"It's overrated," Camel assured her. "Especially at my length."

"You are long," she said.

"My height, my concupiscent ex-teacher."

She laughed and started the car. They kissed one more time and she pulled away. Camel's pants were still undone, his long, limp willy resting on a sticky thigh; he had Eileen's panties in his hands and was, absent-mindedly, stretching their filmy fabric into cat's cradles.

Then Camel moved one restless hand onto her bare thigh. On the radio "Have You Seen Your Mother, Baby, Standing in the Shadows."

"Camel," Eileen said, after a while. "I'm horny again."

Camel smiled and his hump rose once more.

"Street or motel?" Camel asked.

"Motel."

"Summer Avenue."

"Of course."

And so they spent the night together. Before they denuded each other Eileen took a scrap of paper out of her pocket. On it she had written a scrap of verse.

"I brought this for you. In case this happened," she said, solemnly. "May I read it to you?"

"Of course," Camel's face was soft with ardor.

"It's from the poet Ai. Do you say Ay?"

Camel shrugged.

"Fill my tunnel with the howl

you keep zipped in your pants

and when it's over, don't worry, I'll stand."

Camel put his hand to his chin in thought.

"Yes," he said.

In the morning Eileen dropped Camel off at his parent's house and, kissing him lightly on
the lips, said, "Camel, every once in a while…"

"Of course."

She drove home with God knows what story for her husband. Three hours later Camel was on a plane bound for the West Coast.

Meanwhile Camel was publishing

Meanwhile Camel was publishing poems here and there, there and here. As the end of his UC-Berkeley days neared (which, academically, he had stretched as far as he could, lingering to garner numerous degrees, assistant professorships, etc.) Camel found himself with a nice little body of work, growing like grain in wood, plus the respect of his peers. His events at Sinkers and Joe became legendary. There was the night Gregory Corso took his clothes off, a slow strip-tease while a young female poet read, until she could read no further, and fled the café in tears. There was the night Zebo Poncy read his entire book, *After the Zookeeper Set the Animals Free*, a performance that began at 8:30 in the p.m., and continued into the white hours of 2-3 a.m. There was Gary Snyder's reading, on a crisp September evening, which Richard Brautigan proclaimed the 'establishment of the godhead in Goddamn.'

And, with this inchoate success, there grew a coolness between Camel and Cindy, as if too much going well was never part of God's plan. Not long after the publication of Camel's first full-length book Cindy was long gone, leaving California, all together, with a roadie from Dino Valenti's band. It was rumored that they had settled in Montana and had started a commune which they called 'Space for the Spaced.' It was further rumored that a young folk singer named Charlie Manson had stopped there for one night on his way to Los Angeles. Folk singer tales, folk tales, mythos.

"He had eyes like Dwight Fry," the purveyor of this tale declared.

More on this later.

With Camel's fame growing he never hurt for female companionship but love remained an elusive butterfly. He and Richard became very close and occasionally shared the same woman, and the same taste in women.

Still, Camel found it hard to cut his ties with UC-Berkeley. He no longer lived on campus, holing up instead in a hovel near Portsmouth Square, an apartment Remark called Chalet Eros. He kept his contacts within the movement and the movement's artists, writers and musicians. He was there when Joan Baez said, "Action is the antidote to despair." He was there when Hugh Romney spoke, calling for "the construction, by all the Beautiful People, of the first Spaceship to Bliss." And it was there that he met a young street performer, singer/songwriter, and activist named Peter Coyote.

Peter would become friend, fellow-traveler, confessor.

And, around this same time, Camel was part of the construction project that came to be known as...People's Park.

The adventure of the movement, Memphis style

In late March, 1968, a tetrad of conspirators met at The Lemon to hone their strategy. A bomb was taking shape. The pipe was hollowed, filed down, an empty vesicle just waiting to be filled with combustible promise. The four men could not quite bring themselves to pack it with powder, the powder which sat in a flour tin on College Herpes' kitchen counter, a baking substance of infernal power. But the pieces lay spread out on newspaper like a high school science project, close to each other, cylinder, caps, fuse, in an approximation of the design of a pipe bomb. If one squinted and the gaps between the parts blurred it was possible to imagine one was looking at a bona fide piece of ordnance.

Somewhere a longhaired cat sat caterwauling a bluesy number, which may or may not have been "A Day in the Life." Johnny thought it was "Sad-Eyed Lady of the Lowlands," and sang along with that in mind and sometimes, as if by magic, the words coincided. There was a message there. It all meant something.

Camel (a supporting spirit if not a street solder, this time round) was there, scribbling on a pad of paper, presumably working on a new poem, but he just as easily could have been writing a letter to editor Gordon Hanna of The Commercial Appeal, voicing his support for the striking garbage men, a letter which surely would never be printed, given Camel's penchant for poesifying even in his most prosaic attempts at communication. He was just as likely, in his missives, to allude to the Book of the Dead, Jorge Borges, Donald Barthelme's *Snow White*, the new Christ Cardiac Hero or Water-Elf Disease as he was to Stokely Carmichael or Rap Brown. His intentions were pure. Let that be said, now.

Near his table was Creole Myers', another scribe who sat with eraser and number 2 scratching out LP reviews for underground papers.

"I'm getting impatient," Hushpuppy said, and he banged a heel on the Formica in unconscious imitation of his

Red counterpart. "My people saying 'burn, baby, burn' and I'm sitting around watching the riot on my TV and listening to some crispy-fried psychedelia at The Lemon."

"I hear you," College said, and he nodded and nodded. He was lost in thought. His thought was: yes, it is time.

"I'd like to tie this in somehow to the brothers in the street," Three Hushpuppy continued. "Make a show for the nation to know not only 'I Am a Man,'" but 'I am a man, who will not go fight your white-ass war, who will not sit by while we kill women and children so American business concerns' —"

"Right, right," College said, coming out of his sleepy torpor.

"But we gotta stick to our original message, man. Blow up the big stone military man to say, 'War is for pigs'," Johnny said.

The group sat in pensive silence for a while. Sweetness plumped her tired face onto her palm. Late nights at the clubs were taking their toll on her. She wasn't quite her clear-headed revolutionary self this evening.

Across the street they watched as a car pulled up in front of Boyden's Melody Music and two guys got out, one with a crowbar in his hand. They calmly walked to the shop's front door, pried it open and moments later re-emerged with two large amplifiers, which they put into the backseat of their Buick and slowly drove away. Johnny thought he recognized them as members of a band he'd heard once called Peregrine Trampoline. Or maybe it was Limelight Sunflower.

"I guess we set a date," College said, finally.

Over in poet's corner, Camel let out a loud self-satisfied sigh. He stretched his arms heavenward, as if from there he had received communication. "The wind is rattling the cyclone fence," he said out loud and looked around at whosoever's eye he could catch, a grin on his goofy face like a dog scratching its ear.

"We got our gear," Sweetness said, from her sleepy, slobbery lips.

"What gear?" Hushpuppy said, an edge to his voice he didn't intend. Whoever spoke harshly to Sweetness?

"College thought we should have a little protection, so I procured us some things, mostly from Army surplus. M-1 Helmets, shoulder pads, rib-guards. Um, some heavy duty gloves."

"We're not going into battle," Johnny offered.

"Oh, but we are," Hushpuppy said, again with the shoe banging.

"It's best to be prepared, protected. I don't want anyone hurt from this," College said.

"Ok, sure, sure," Johnny said. "I got a motorcycle helmet already. Alright?"

"Sure."

"Ok. Let's set a date," Three Hushpuppy Brown said, swinging one long leg over another, kicking his size ten foot out into the narrow aisle of The Bitter Lemon.

"How about April 1st?" Johnny said.

"Naw, somebody'll think it's some goddam Krappa Sigma stunt, some April fool's joke."

"Right."

"April's birthstone is the diamond," Sweetness said, sparkling.

"The symbol of innocence," College replied, somewhat ruefully.

Another silence, like a spadeful of earth, descended.

"How about April 4th?" College added.

The other three looked at each other. Camel peered up from his notebook as if lightning had flashed across the interior of the coffee bar.

"Ok."

The afternoon of April 4th, at The Bitter Lemon, found Johnny Niagara, Sweetness Enlight and College Herpes, gathered around a small central table, anxious Catilinarians. At their sides were schoolkids' backpacks containing ingeniously plated outerwear and three pipe bombs. It had been determined—College had asked someone at State who knew someone who knew how the Doughboy was constructed—that three strategically placed bombs would more than do the trick. The first two, at its base detonated simultaneously, would unstructure it, topple it like a bad government and the third, set to go off as closely after the first two as possible, would decapitate the anonymous World War I fighting man. It would point up the mindlessness of the military. It would send the heavy sconce aflying, to land in People's Park, Memphis' Peoples Park, people, to be picked up by raggle-taggle gypsies and carried off to some oppressed nation's leader, the Woodstock nation (anon...patience), perhaps, to be placed, metaphorically speaking, on a pike.

Camel came in about five-thirty, tipped a chin at the three conspirators as if to say hello from deep within his well of inspiration, a greeting from the ether. Somewhere, from a scratchy LP came a voice as sinuous as sin, intoning to the assembled, "Are you gonna be there, at the Love-in?" The beat was Cimmerian, dangerous; it tickled the heart's ventricles with arrhythmia.

"Where's Hush?" Sweetness said, her placid surface for once betraying a bit of a sunderance, like a crack in fine porcelain.

"I told him we'd be here early, I'm not sure I said a specific time. I assumed he knew I meant before dark," College said. He was sober as a portmanteau.

As the sky outside drained of color, turning first a sort of tie-dye mix of blood and saffron, then the hue of College's eyes, the atmosphere in The Lemon felt wrong. It felt like a tip of the axis had occurred, like gravity had increased slightly, like Nixon's collywobbles were spoiling everyone's fun. It felt bad.

About six-thirty the manager of the club came in, wearing a home-stenciled sweatshirt which said "Yankees and Niggerlovers," a phrase often thrown the way of The Lemon. In his hands he held two burlap bags. His smile was an eldritch smile, one from the End-time, and College was not happy to see that smile. He grimaced even before the man turned his bags upside down.

College grimaced even before the dozen or so rattlesnakes spilled out onto the floor of The Bitter Lemon, sending patrons scattering, tables and chairs flying every which way, a frantic Exodus to the musical accompaniment of The Hombres and the herpetological manager's insane cackle, which carried out onto Poplar Avenue, which bounced off the walls of every bar and music shop and head shop in midtown Memphis, which hummed in the glass window of the Yellow Submarine blocks away, which tingled in the genitalia of the young and restless roaming the Highland strip miles away, which drove the three conspirators further down Poplar, upwards via the viaduct, west, toward the river, into which the sun had already fallen.

This is surely a bad sign, College thought. But he tried to keep his face passive, as if the snakes had not upset him, as if the absence of Hushpuppy Brown did not upset him, as if the fact that he had a bag full of heavy duty explosives clutched to his side like an unpublishable novel did not upset him. He saw himself as the leader of this lunatic mission and he would not let his cohorts down.

"Jesus," Johnny was the first to speak.

"I wet my drawers," Sweetness drawled. She stepped between two bars and slipped her panties off with a deftness which would have surprised the unschooled. She handed the soiled garment to Johnny with a waggish grin and Johnny secreted them in his jacket pocket. And, children, Johnny, wherever he his, still has this artifact to this day; of course he does.

"Should we proceed without Hush?" Sweetness asked to anyone who was listening.

"I don't know," College whispered. "Let me think."

Time passed there on the sidewalk of Poplar Avenue in Memphis, Tennessee, on April 4th, 1968, much like it passed elsewhere in the world at that particular moment, perhaps. Perhaps it did. But, for these three crusaders, time felt glutinous, as unreasonable as a June bug.

And then, from the west, from out of the west, from the carmine background of that clear shot down Poplar which makes one feel one can see into the future, came a figure, moving down the center of the street, like a drunken gunfighter, noctilucent. His gait was unsteady, loose like the movements of a leviathan. The figure approached. Progress of a sort was being made.

The figure materialized as if from a transporter into the familiar dusky outlines of their friend, Three Hushpuppy Brown. Hushpuppy moved as if zombied. He was walking, but his eyes were reflecting nothing, a dead slate.

"Hush!" College fairly shouted. "What is it?"

Sweetness put her sweet hand on Hushpuppy's forearm. They all stood uncertainly by. They stood by.

"They killed him," Three Hushpuppy Brown said with the soul-less voice of a telephone customer service representative. "They gone and killed him."

"Who, Hush?" Johnny said, a franticness creeping into his bravado.

"Who's dead?" College added.

"Martin. They shot him. The fuckers killed Dr. King."

*

Months later, over heavily sweetened espressos at The Bitter Lemon, while around them the coffeehouse was visibly falling into ruin, people coming now, not to partake of any kind of tribal attachment or community, but to make trouble, to buy drugs and seek rough trade, to revel in the dying light of a once bright dreamtime, the four one-time conspirators re-met. They sought sustenance from a kinship that was splintered but not severed. They sought warmth from a flame that was either flickering erratically or still burning so brightly it was not apparent to their naked eyes.

They would sit for hours in what felt like the rubble of Rome and the music was still sometime Lee or Sid or some of the old crowd but they knew the magic was gone. It was gone but it had been. It had been, once. And sometimes that was enough for them.

And they thought about the time they had made an attempt at taking a stand, at striking out against something baneful and sinister and insidious. And sometimes they felt good about that intention and sometimes they felt foolish. Human nature is pretty silly stuff, is pretty silly putty.

And, years later, after The Bitter Lemon had closed and a more upscale restaurant opened in the neighborhood where their sensible friends now went for food and drinks and to talk about the old days, and after Nixon, that bastard, had ended the war, the four former freedom fighters, met in

College Herpes' kitchen. They met in his kitchen and carefully, reverently, with a sort of prayerful quietude, there they dismantled three homemade pipe bombs.

People's Park

The Battle of People's Park. Who remembers it now?

1969 was a very unco time, a good year for labor and a bad year for wine.

The counterculture believed the movement could be revolutionary, a vision of Utopia Sir Thomas More could not have posited. And they meant to build it in the middle of The City. The City. San Francisco—City by the Bay, City of Assisi and fog, Ethereal City of Tectonic Unsteadiness. Our City. Their City. Just one block, two blocks, which could represent Eden. A space free from odium not opium, from divisions and subtractions, from hate and not hash, from negative head space.

Production for use—not profit.

Jentri Anders brought a nascent idea: equality for all races and genders. Imagine.

Ruth Rosen brought the 'will to love, a belief in a positive peace bloc.'

Camel brought some narcotic cigarettes. A pocketful of poesy. New verse. Universe.

Huey and Bobby stood by and watched the erection of a garden in Cityspace, nodded their jazz nods. Country Joe brought "I Feel-Like-I'm-Fixing-to-Die Rag."

Telegraph Avenue to Haste and Bowditch Streets to Dwight Way. All they wanted was a symbolic garden, a breach in the Wall of Deceit and Capitalism Gone Amok. They wanted it builded there among the dark Satanic Mills.

Briefly, ah briefly, there flourished this Concept Garden in the center of the city. Children played there; music was made; Love was crowned Emperor; poems were written; governments were toppled, if only symbolically (like the raising of The Pentagon, unless you believe Mailer who said, "I was there, Goddamit. I saw the fugging Fort Fumble hover.")

Then it was taken away from them by, what came to be called, The Man. The Man was a committee, a suit, a woman with her bun wound too tight, a devil, a dust bunny.

Ronald Reagan said the park was built by pinkos and imps of the apocalypse. On May 15, 1969, at 4:30 *ante meridiem*, storm troopers from the Berkeley Police and the California Highway Patrol moved in like locusts. They removed all impedimenta; they tore up crops (there's no such thing as a free lunch); they, despite an assurance from Chancellor Heyn, leveled People's Park, recreated it as Death Valley. They scorched the earth.

By noon the protestors had gathered thousands strong. Their Eden had been snaked out from under them. What followed was a bloody confrontation, comparable to the riot on the Sunset Strip ("Something's happening here…"), with tear gas and firehoses and nightsticks, which soon escalated to shotguns and buckshot. ("It was only birdshot," the Republican mayor, wearing a Caligula mask, lied.)

Alan Blanchard was blinded by buckshot. James Rector, student at UC-B, who was only a bystander, died from shotgun wounds.

Ronnie Rayguns said, "It's very naive to assume that you should send anyone into that kind of conflict with a flyswatter."

Built upon the impetus of the 'success' of this way of handling things, RR sent in the National Guard, declared a state of emergency, and 'took the streets back,' meaning the streets were no place for people, citizens, hippies and dreamers.

Camel said, later, "People's Park was an end and a beginning. Things followed that bore both the seeds of dissent and hope, and the seeds of destruction and malice. Woodstock, then Altamount. Buffalo Springfield, then Manson. But something undying was also born. It's in me, now. I can feel it as surely as I feel my spleen. A new organ, one of peace and poetry."

Manson, unfortunately, will appear here anon. But today let's tell the story of Camel's Woodstock.

Camel's Afternoon with poem (almost)

Camel sat with paper in his lap.
A poem was stuck inside his pen.
He looked for a time at the workaday
world weltering past his window.
He looked for a time inward, his
soul filled with air like a sail.
Then the postman arrived with letters
from old friends, almost forgotten.
The poem would have to wait.
In the kitchen Camel's lover put water
on to make some tea. The world
outside the window began to fade like
an old t-shirt. Camel rose and spoke
softly to his lover, I have letters from
old friends to read. And, later, perhaps,
I need to shake the poem from my pen.

Richard and Camel take a trip

We may change rôles
through the rainbow of music
—Bei Dao

Poet Camel Jeremy Eros of Memphis, Tennessee, the Bard of Bluestown, and his friend Richard Brautigan, packed Camel's microbus with as much of their shit as the bus could accommodate to set off Northward on the great American highway, their ultimate destination a farm in upstate New York where they had heard the godhead would be descending. The Garden of Eden was being reconstructed out of scaffolding and wires and mud under the watchful eye of Melpomene. The Beatles were going to be there, Dylan, The Stones, The Dead. It was a pilgrimage then and any hitchhiker along the way may as well have been the Wife of Bath.

It was almost exactly one month since Mankind had giant-stepped onto the surface of Spaceship Earth's only Moon, raping her, impregnating her with man-magic and a poorly utilitarian future. Was there a connection? In our Aquarian minds, yes.

Camel had a reasonably unsettling thought: People's Park redux, but on a scale the size of all outdoors.

The van walls bulged like a Christmas stocking. Camel almost said something when Richard brought his trout fishing gear but Camel was a live-and-let-live sort of spirit. Fishing was the furthest thing from his poetic mind. He wanted to take a lot of drugs, have sex outdoors with women from all areas of the United States, and groove to the sounds of Sly and the Family Stone.

Case in point: Camel looked askance at Richard's 30:40 Krag rifle but said not word one. And Camel hated guns, hated them like hell pains. *Gemütlichkeit* reigned.

They both kissed Richard's daughter Ianthe on her pretty little cheeks and left her with Lahna Darling, who lived near the fairgrounds in Midtown Memphis, Tennessee.

"Bye, Ianthe," Camel said. "Bye, La."

"Bye, Angel," Richard said and Lahna answered, "Goodbye, Richard."

And they were on their way.

"Woad twip," Camel said, early on, as a sugar cube laced with lysergic acid melted on his tongue. The case full of medicinals they carried would hold the average family for a decade or more.

A bottle of Stoli vodka, from which they took periodic swallows, sat in the space between them.

"Obviously," Richard Brautigan answered.

"Further," Camel said.

"As always."

"Half the birds flying north rely on nothing but dumb luck."

"Yet we are lame ducks."

"True."

"As true as the trembling of fiery light on crisped streams."

Camel thought about fishing again and, briefly, a small dark cloud the size of a dollhouse rolled over his consciousness.

"How far away is this place?" he asked Richard just to keep talk flowing and flowing away from flowing water.

"Miles to go before we dream," Richard said.

"Past NYC."

"Decidedly."

"Woodstock."

"Saugerties."

"Saugerties."

"Where it is."

"I thought Woodstock."

"Close."

"Dylan lives there now. He'll just stroll over and blow our minds."

"Leopard Skin Pill Box Hat"

"Stuck Inside of Mobile with like the Memphis Blues Again."

"Ramona."

"Motorpsycho Nightmare."

"Too Much of Nothing."

"Don't know that one."

"Tapes. Some tapes circulating around the city. Heard them at Marty Balin's. Heavy dada stuff. Maybe his best."

"Shit. We get nothing in Memphis. We get a small percentage of nothing."

"You got Stax."

"We got Stax."

"No small juju."

"Say it again."

"No small juju."

"Right."

"You writing?"

"Yeah. Sure."

"Talk."

"Working on long story-poem about Abbie Hoffman."

"Saw Abbie back home. He'll be at the festival."

"Man. Couldn't actually talk to him. Not actually talk."

"Abbie's cool man. No prima donna shit."

"I believe you. Still."

"Right."

"You?"

"New novel. Poems raining down like serpent's teeth."

"Call the novel to me."

"About an abortion. Sort of."

"Uh huh."

"And a library. A liminal library. The library of my dreams."

"I'm hearing you."

Up ahead a blue cloud rolled onto the highway like tumbleweed from Oz. It cartwheeled its way toward the car, sometimes becoming a Meanie with eyes keen, cruel, reptilian, stinging.

Camel gripped the steering wheel like it was his mother's breast. The blue cloud dissipated and opened up a diner at the side of the road. The diner's sign said, "Eats. Or not. Death to all those who would whimper and cry."

Camel smiled at the overarching firmament. Turned again to his companion who seemed to have noticed none of this. Richard sat there humming a tune from a musical from the thirties, the kind of thing Richard knew which Camel didn't understand how. Richard was Richard, a smoking gun, a friendly ghost.

"Where are we now?" Camel said, his paranoia breaking up like phlegm.

"On the road," Richard said and took a hold of his own mustache as if it were a control yoke and he the co-pilot.

"A library," Camel said, his eyes narrowing as if he were unduly busy with this stretch of road, undulating as it was, roiling like the boundaries of dream.

"Where anyone can have a book. Idea I had. No elitist bullshit. Anyone can put a book there. Handmade, written on notebook paper, stapled, drawn with crayon, you get the idea."

"Wonderful."

"Pure democracy."

"Nothing democratic is ever pure. Nothing pure is ever democratic."

"Yes."

"And poems too."

"Some"

"Good, good."

"And yours on Abbie."

"Yeah. I was envisioning something like a 'Paul Revere's Ride' for our time."

"We need it. Heroes."

"Maybe. I thought about telling it from a fireman's perspective."

"Why?"

"I don't know."

"Better stay away from those who carry round a firehose."

"Yeah. Maybe a garbageman, a striking garbageman."

"Right."

"Is that Lana Turner?"

"Where?"

"Alongside the road there, with the whippet?"

"Don't think so."

"Naw."

The car slid on through the broad day, a hot knife through the yellow butter of the sunlight. More vodka, more windowpane.

"Wow," Camel said after hours of silence.

"I know."

"We gotta be close."

"How fast are we going?"

Camel chanced a look at the speedometer, quickly, as if it would turn him to salt.

"32."

"Hm," Richard Brautigan said. "Maybe we could go faster."

"Not in this ice," Camel said.

Richard looked at him. He looked at the road, the sky. Above them Thor stood with his hammer ableeding.

"Ok," Richard said.

A couple of months of silence passed again. Concentration became everything. They entered tunnel after tunnel, each one narrower than the one before. Soon there would be no room for their microbus, tunnels as small as the mouths of stars.

Up ahead a conflagration of penguins rallied roadside, cars and trucks and buses and motorcycles and campers and hovercraft and tugboats massed together in a tangle of transportive modes, deadly inert in the Stygian stillness, closed in their purpose as if frozen by a stopwatch. Miles of snarl, acres of vulgi. The penguins became businessmen and then penguins again briefly and then policemen with riot clubs and the faces of wolves.

Then everything was alright. It was a crowd and there was a tent and the vehicles lining the macadam were as peacefully quiet as bankrupt beggars.

"We're here," Camel said.

"Finally. It feels like home already," Richard Brautigan said.

"I hear music."

"Sounds like The Band warming up."

"That rolling organ, ah sweet minstrelsy."

"And there's Monty Clift walking with Janis."

"Lot of people here."

"Stop the bus," Richard said.

"It is stopped."

"Get it off the road."

"Right."

Camel pulled the loaded microbus onto a grassy patch in the middle of the highway and the rhymesters tumbled out like shicker angels onto the ground as eighteen-wheelers bullhorned past them. The music in the air now sounded soul-deep and inspiring, voices as rich as platters of gravy. They were singing to God and God was singing back in his *basso profundo* and love flowed like the deluding mist of a mirage.

They were in Hopkinsville, Kentucky.

Camel and Richard joined the crowd under the tent and lent their voices to the throng.

"What a friend I have in Jesus," they sang.

"And I walked with him and I talked with him," they sang.

"Onward Christian soldiers," they sang.

And at the end of three days they got back in the bus, sore in joints and pinions from sleeping on the ground and whiskery of voice from so much mantra and palaver. They had made friends with folks from all over, from Hot Point, Arkansas and Bucksnort, Tennessee. They had been sanctified. Sometimes, even, during the weekend, they had preached, opened up for the throngs with the phonation of skalds. Now, tired in their very protoplasm, they turned the microbus around and pointed it back toward Memphis, Tennessee and the home of pork barbecue and the blues.

Years later, when they related their Woodstock experience, listeners furrowed their brows and studied the elements of the storytelling as if reading the leaves of tea in the bottoms of the poets' cups. The tale-spinners said they heard Hendrix do the National Anthem, backed only by a church organ and it was a holy experience. God, they said, they saw God.

And who can doubt them, who here can doubt what they saw, what they heard, what they experienced on that side road of Heaven, on the poets' vacation near the end of the summer in the terminal year of the nineteen sixties?

August 9, 1969

Camel heard it first from Bob Weir of The Dead at a party at Remark's bookstore.

"Steve Stills told me. Said Neil knew the bastard."

"Shit," Camel said.

"Helter Skelter, what's that about?" a young blond in a leather fringe vest asked.

"Blood everywhere," someone else said.

"Shit," Camel said.

"This is L.A. as opposed to The Bay. They're crazy there. The line between peaceniks and crazies is thin as onion skin."

"They're gonna come down hard on long-hairs. Hippie will become a pejorative term."

"Shit," Camel said.

"I knew one of the women," a black dude with running-back shoulders said.

"I met Manson once. He talked shit. I thought he was just tripping on some bad stuff."

"Steve says Neil says he had some talent. He was easy to follow if you wanted to follow. There was a—a *quality* about him."

"Shit," Camel said.

"Camel, baby," Eedy said, slipping her arm around his waist.

"Poetry is dead," Camel said.

"Oh Camel. Oh, Camel, no."

PART THREE: THE ADVENTURES OF THE HEART

The adventure of when Camel met Allen

Mixing in naked passion,/Those who naked new life fashion
Are themselves reborn in naked grace.
    —Stephen Spender

Time is not the main thought from under the rain wrought from roots
that brought us coots to hoot and haul us all back to the prime ordeal.
    —Van Dyke Parks

Few know the story of how Camel and Allen met. Allen, his paramour of the impossibly slim waist. Allen of the Callipygian tabernacle. And Allen of the poems. Their romance is the stuff of romp and myth, Eurydice and Orpheus, Adam and Lilith, Ulysses and Penelope, Isis and Osiris, Patti and George, Patti and Eric. Stiller and Meara.

Camel and Allen.

Now, at this time, Allen Fermor was a witchy and willowy art student at the U of M; she had yet to achieve fame as a sculptress and potter. She was boy-chested and winsomely hipped, with a cheerful face, which reminded some of the Cat in the Hat. There *was* something feline about her, the way she moved, her legs insinuating a slithery theology.

At this time also, children, Camel was already celebrated, both for his singular, surrealistic-goofball poems and his righteous revolutionary activities, alongside his potent partisans, Johnny Niagara, Three Hushpuppy Brown, Sweetness Enlight (the ecdysiast) and Memphis' answer to Jimi Hendrix, the young guitar god, Buddy "Slipshod" Gardner. Their tales were (mostly) told and told (mostly) truly in that seminal underground text, *We are Billion-Year-Old Carbon.* Yet, in that cryptic codex, there is no mention of how Camel met Allen, how the two became One, one might say. Hence, here we redress, as if formerly we were naked, or poorly clad.

The fated encounter took place at the Overton Park Shell Epiphenomenal Be-in and Aquarian Bazaar and Free Market, circa 1970, the 970th year of the 2nd millennium, the 70th year of the 20th century, and the 1st year of the 1970s decade. This event, already the stuff of legend, was in favor of the Trimurti descending, Southern style. The Shell was enveloped in violet light, either from the approaching gloaming or from reflections off the nimbi thereabouts. Everyone was there. Buddy played; Sid and Jim played. Dick Delisi sat in with The Expanding Head Band. Jojo Self, the poet and filmmaker, read her singular verse and showed her short film, *Some Identity Problems*, for the first time. Abbie was there, and one or two Beatles, a couple Stones, Grace and

Janis and Booker T. Joan and David, Andy and Edie, Mark and Eedy, Leonard and Suzanne, Boyce and Hart. Wavy (and Howdy Dogood Tomahawk Truckstop Gravy, his son), Kesey, Sly, Tuli, Vonnegut, Tim Leary, Emmet Grogan and Isaac Hayes. Neil Cassady, who, for all intents and purposes was dead dead, so it was rumored, still managed to sit in on conga when Santana played—Jorge Santana, that is, *el hermano*. And, even off stage, in the audience, which expanded like a gas as the weekend went on, until it flowed into the surrounding park and woodlands, there were pilgrims and seekers and seers, all intermixed like a cosmological experiment in human interaction and estrus. It was the time of Free Love, children, and it was never more evident—the *concept*, the happening *happening*--than during that weekend in the park.

No one talked, yet, of The End.

Now, Camel knew of Allen and Allen certainly knew of Camel, before these august proceedings in August in Memphis. Camel had had his eye on the laconic, slow-mouthed sculptress for months, ever since her friend, College Herpes, pointed her out at a reading at the Bitter Lemon, coffee shop and revolutionary hermatocrit. And, Allen, nothing being coincidental as Doc Jung would say, had already sort of set her beret for him, for Camel, yes.

So, that afternoon, already empurpling into evening, she bee-lined to him and danced around him the way fairies dance around a dolmen. She was wearing a caftan made of butterfly-wings, as see-through as the Warren Report. Camel was dressed as a sagittary, a costume rigged up for him by puppeteer Jimmy Crosswaith, a visage both comic and fearsome. So it goes. Allen began a mating dance heretofore unknown in courting rituals. She danced like Delilah. She danced like Sadie Hawkins. She danced like Sweetness Enlight. She danced like an enchanted nautch, all sinuous deadman curves and limbs like a willow's. Her dance wove a spell around rooted Camel; it whistled through his short hairs.

Camel smiled and that smile, even from the depths of his centaur costume, said, *I will follow you anywhere*. Allen held out a pretty hand. In its soft-as-a-petal palm, the size of a small oasis, was a hit of windowpane. Camel licked her palm, slowly, like a drinking faun. He allowed his tongue to linger there.

When he stood back erect Allen was already dancing away, was already many yards away as if by sorcery, and she was looking back over her shoulder with the glint in her eye, like the light off Joni Mitchell's hair. Her glints said, yes, follow me. *Anywhere.*

She danced into the woods. Camel trailed her, a tattered train. The music began to fade behind them. The last song they heard was "Enos is Enough," Buddy Gardner's guitar ringing like Eden's last bell. The woods were dark, like the ragged end of mystery. Camel could just make out the dancing white form in front of him. Meanwhile, a psychedelia was ablooming in his brain, half-acid and half cacoethes. He shed some of the heavier accouterments of his costume as he tripped along.

When he caught up to Allen she was standing in a small clearing. They were deep in the Old Forest, so deep they might as well have been in Birnam Wood. They were far away, their tethers severed, yet they feared not. It was 60s abracadabra, children, still working, amaranthine sorcery. They were held in spectral suspension. woodnotes echoed around them.

As Camel's eyes began to focus he realized that they were not alone. Standing in front of Allen was a small, indistinct figure, impish, seemingly made of matted fur and glop. And Camel realized that the silence of the Forest Primeval had been replaced by the soft soughing of sincere sobbing. Allen turned her lovely Cheshire face toward Camel and there were tears there, too. But it was not Allen's crying which Camel heard, like music from melodic sprites, it was the squonk's. It was the squonk crying, standing there in the pine-sweet opening in the Old Forest. Its sorrow was infectious for Camel felt like weeping, suddenly, also.

Then--and this is important, children, for it presages much of the future relationship of Camel and Allen--then, with a grace and earthmother tenderness born as natural as Mama Cass's appetite, Allen knelt on the soft earth and put her arms around the squonk, who continued to sob, though now with a syncopation that seemed almost dulcet and agreeable. Its cheerless, furry face peered at Camel over Allen's consoling shoulder. After a while Allen rose and the squonk wiped its cheeks, not quite smiling, and Allen dug deep into her Fortunatus purse, and handed the squonk her last Thai stick. The squonk, on this evening anyway, would not, as Brother Ray so eloquently put it, drown in its own tears. Not this evening. Instead it slowly backpedaled, keeping its glistening eyes on the couple, and then—poof!-- it evanesced like smoke. It became, simply, part of the shadows of the wood.

"That was a lovely thing you did," Camel said.

Allen wiped dry her own cheeks. "I didn't know they were *so sad*," she said.

Camel pondered this for a while.

"You know the way of squonks?" he asked.

"I do now," she said. "A little better." And that was the last word they said about the squonk. This is not the story of How Allen Saved the Squonk, except tangentially, you dig?

Allen looked her pursuer over as if he had just arrived at the pearly gates with a resume that seemed too good to be true.

"You wrote 'The Plot to Kidnap Stonehenge'," Allen said, naming one of Camel's more obscure poems.

"I did," he said, and he dropped one more leaden piece of costuming. He was almost returned as a man.

"For that alone you deserve the last word in blowjobs," Allen said, with a sly smile.

"We poets get so little in return," Camel joshed back.

Allen slipped out of her clothes so smoothly it was as if the forest had absorbed them, like it had the crying creature. She stood before Camel as naked as a heron's wing. Her body was lovely, slim shoulders sprinkled with an admixture of freckles and tiny pimples, breasts the size of seashells and the color of a conch's pearl with attention-getting nipples, a waist Camel was sure he could engirdle with two hands, legs as shapely as a fountain's spume, and a patch of pubic hair as mysterious as the Gordian knot. Camel wanted to try to untie it.

Instead he did encircle that waist with his two hands, which filled him with wonder.

"A perfect fit," he said.

"Made for them," Allen countered.

Now Allen reknelt in the leafrot and loam, her hands running down the front of him, hickorydickory. Camel noticed that the part in her hair resembled the Road to Jericho. She unbuckled Camel's complex trousers and they fell from him like the wings of fallen angels. He wore no underwear so that his pizzle now sprang into Allen's adroit and silky hands. She sighed as she pulled on it, using all eight fingers and both thumbs, and Camel's sigh in return was the air escaping from his earthliness.

"For that poem," Allen said, glancing upward briefly, before sliding her yearning mouth onto him. Her gracious, slick, Cheshire mouth. Her beautiful, lipsome, practiced, crackerjack mouth. She took him in, took him in.

"Oh, Gawd," Camel said.

Allen's eyes looked into Camel's even as she kept that rigid dojigger enmouthed. Her eyes said, you can do better than that, *Poet.*

"Oh, Kirke! Oh, Ouranos! Oh, Ikkyu, oh, Buddy Holly!" Camel intoned, challenged.

Which excited Allen all the more. Her ministrations took on a noisy enthusiasm. Camel felt a surge building in him and the desire was great to let it fly into that place from whence Allen brought forth her sweet speech. But, another longing, older, more consecrated, cried within him, also. He wanted to enter her whole, to be within her. So he bade her stand.

She reluctantly gave up her all-day sucker.

And, first, he kissed her for a long time. Their first kiss. Their tongues entwined and made friends, their saliva mixed and formed a third substance, a cosmic goo. They kissed, children I repeat, for a long time.

Then, Allen understanding what was to come next, what *must* come next, turned and backed up against the tall, now stripped versifier. She ground herself against him. And, listen, I tell you this to make plain: the word above, the conjuring word for Allen, callipygian, means this: having a perfectly shaped bum. Her ass, let's be clear, children, was the First Ass, the Primo Cast, as if God were a sculptor like Allen, and, on this day, he had done his finest work in human clay. Camel could only die a little inside to feel it pressed to his now insistent erection.

Allen took one step away and Camel felt the loss, though only temporary, of that warmth, that smooth fleshly impression. Allen took one step away and then bent slowly, oh slowly, from the waist, until her hands were on the ground, like a randy Agnes DeMille. Her legs were parted. Her head lowered, so that the blood rushed there to see what all the commotion was about, her hash brown hair mingled with the earth's smallest denizens. She resembled a triangle, such mink geometry for the first time germinated. Camel was mighty stirred.

Now it was Camel's turn to kneel and worship. He reverently placed his tongue along the valley of her elegant hills, pulling the tongue downward like a soft-bladed plow. Till he found the two entrances below, both of which he slavered with the attention he normally reserved for a quatrain.

Allen said, "Ah, ah, ah."

Camel re-stood. He took a moment—a human moment—to relish the sight, Allen's perfect backside, now shimmering with lickspittle in the moonlight. And, as the clouds had just parted, Camel parted her cheeks, rested his prick there in its deep fold, felt it close around him like the sea rushing back, and then Camel took his prick on the journey his tongue had advance-scouted. For a second, for two seconds, he pushed it tenderly against the first opening. The smaller, tighter, more restricted.

Allen said, "Ah, ah, ah."

Now he entered her below. He sank deeply into her vaginal syrupiness. He pushed his weight against that perfect ass, his prick now bathed in heat, in wet heat. And he began to work her, to move in and out, side to side, round and round. He used his engorged prick to pleasure her, to make her move beyond inarticulacy. He wanted to hear her words of passion, for he was a word man, a lover of *lingua franca* (though Allen's kinesics spoke volumes). Now, he fucked her, just like that, simple and firm, and with a dilution and depth he did not know he possessed.

Now Allen spoke.

She said, "Oh, Camel, my sweet Camel, do fuck me hard. Do. Fuck. Me. Hard. Your prick, your cock, your licorice stick, your Polyphemus, your popeye, your stiffness, your lovemeat, your probang, your shaft, your linga, your phallus, your willie, your rockoon, your hard dickdickdick!" She sang, she fairly sang the names that now drove Camel to furious feats, and to sing his own salty song.

"Oh my, Allen (or was it My Allen)," Camel harmonized. "Push your ass against me. Never take your ass from me. Never. Take. Your. Ass. From. Me. Your ass, your fundament, your neat nates, your buttery butt. Your kerf, your pussy, your kaze, your beaver, your delubrum, your Lucy, your churn, your bush, your delta, your honey pot, your ringerrangerroo, your hot wet cuntcuntcunt!"

And this song, this daring, drooling duet, rose from the Forest Primeval, rose toward that pallid mirror in the sky, recently raped by mankind's rocket cock, and it spread like the stain of weak light emanating from above. It rose as Allen and Camel howled like wolf pups, and seeded the shredded clouds now regathering, and it brought forth upon them and the surrounding Be-in a silvery rain, a pizzle drizzle, bright and shining like mercury.

And, children, Camel exploded into Allen, pulling her so close to him that briefly, aflame, they were one flesh, literally, he entered her and she entered him and they were Camelallen. They were Allencamel. And he came and came and she came and came and then they collapsed onto the forest carpet and slept like Adam and Eve right after the rib-pilfering, and before their sons invented murder. They slept innocent and blissful and hallowed and full of a new light that was all theirs. A light called Love.

And, it is said, that the rain that fell that night, silently and like a benevolence over the crowd at the Be-in, was a sortilege rain, a beatific, enchanted, mystic rain. It is said that anyone in attendance who was not pubic suddenly achieved puberty. It is said that men who had not had erections in years suddenly sprouted them, confident, cocky and full of life. It is said that women, who thought themselves frigid, suddenly discovered in themselves a new wanting, a hunger that both made them happy and tormented them. And it is said that childless couples who had longed for offspring that night were made pregnant. In the nearby zoo, it is said, chimps and emus and peafowl and bonobos and capybaras rutted. Cattle (and icebergs) calved. Dogs made it with cats.

All, all under the zestful and jazzy and argentiferous and munificent and amorous rain engendered by the forceful and ardent coupling and coming together, like Peace and Light and Eros, of Camel and Allen, deep in the squonk-haunted Old Forest, lovers now and forevermore. Lovers always, before time and after time.

And that, children, is the story of When Camel met Allen, which happened in a little fuscy corner of the Dayglo Overton Park Shell Epiphenomenal Be-in and Aquarian Bazaar and Free Market, in a small fiefdom called Memphis Tennessee, in an Overlord Empire called America, Before the Fall, in the appropriately monickered time period, post Summer of Love.

Again, say it with me, children. Of Love.

And Camel and Allen begat their own era of love. This era will be with us for the remainder of the tale told here, *The Adventures of Camel Jeremy Eros*, so appointed.

Camel Ruminates Further

This kind of fucking occurs at the very limit of what is possible. Everything had been transformed into orgasm and visible, chattering oceans of elf language."
—Terence McKenna, from *True Hallucinations*

Camel found himself (though he was never quite lost) the happiest man from Frayser, Tennessee. He had fallen into the freaking lap of luxury. And what a luxurious lap his paramour had. Camel was smitten, no doubt.

He pondered his new situation.

Though his black dog had often sat squarely upon his brightest joys (had he pushed Cindy away because he felt he did not deserve happiness? Had he Eedy?) These were questions that became comfortable to ponder from the vantage point of his romantic high ground.

How did he know that Allen Fermor, willowy sculptress from his hometown, was the one, the ultimate One, the one that all others pointed toward? Allen True North.

He did, friends. He just did.

The gears meshed. The tooth bit. The pea fell into the pod. The hand went into the pocket. The vel crowed.

Camel said to himself, "My stars have aligned. The planets have spoken. My heart has begun negotiations with the rest of my organs, even that splenetic spleen. All signs point to Alice's Restaurant. All roads lead to Coca-Cola."

And then this slight corrective:

"Dear Camel,

The universe is neither stacked for nor against you.

love,

Camel."

The free store

So, this is a love story. Starring Camel Jeremy Eros and Allen Fermor. The journey from here on will include both Man ♂ (Mars) and Woman ♀ (Venus).

Shortly after (mere hours!) the primeval pranks Camel and Allen moved into her apartment, a small 3-roomer across from Overton Park. Camel, who owned few things save his writing implements and books, traveled light and arrived even lighter, having given some of his esoteric tomes to Hushpuppy Brown, who was in the throes of self-education. "I want to read them all," Hushpuppy said. "Books, you know?"

And shortly after this cohabitation began Camel and Allen threw a couple duffle bags full of apparels and accoutrement under the front hood of Allen's paisley VW Bug and headed westward. Camel wanted Allen to meet his friends, Richard and Remark, and he had also been invited to help Peter Coyote and his group, The Diggers, with a little anti-enterprise they had concocted in Berkeley. They were calling it The Free Store.

"Free store?" Camel asked. "What's for sale?"

"Nothing," Peter Coyote said. "It's all free."

"What is?"

"Food, clothes, necessaries. You know, stuff."

"Beautiful," Camel said. "I think I'll dig the Diggers, eh?"

"Those of us who sought to place our lives on a more stable and sustainable footing created alliances with other like-minded groups and the Diggers evolved into a large confederation of autonomous communities that became known as the Free Family," Peter replied.

A week later Pete wrote Camel a postcard. On one side was a picture of Cocteau. On the other: "The Diggers are an anarchist experiment dedicated to creating distinctions between society's business-as-usual and our own imaginings of what-it-might-be, in the most potent way we can devise. It is a feature of youth, I suppose, to distinguish itself and its values from the domination of adults they are soon to become. Each generation attempts to find a style too outré to be co-opted by the majority culture."

Camel wrote back, on a small postcard with the face of Jean Arp on one side: "Coming. With wife."

Camel and Allen were married en-route in Eureka Springs, Arkansas, in a great glass cathedral called Thorncrown, attended by squirrels, gefs (talking mongeese), eagles, jackelopes, rabbits, chipmunks, minks, armadillos, doves, allocameli, axe-handle hounds, white-tailed deer, fauns, blue tigers, black bears and Northern Scarlet Snakes, and officiated by The Christ of the Ozarks (or a prophet, named Ohem Jee, who was working in His stead).

"In the name of Emmet Sullivan and his Christ, and his Dinosaur World, and his Share the Wealth Program, and in the presence of Buddha, Siddhartha, Gaea, Crow, Xerxes, Odin, Fearless Leader, all Lamas and llamas, all Mamas and Papas, and the complete Peterson's Guide to the Creatures of the Forest, I now pronounce you male and female versions of the same thing. In other words, dig, you're married," Ohem Jee intoned.

Afterwards they had a mud bath in the spa, picked up a little bobble-head Quick Draw McGraw for the dashboard, a crystal hash pipe, and an ounce of Arkansas Whoopee Grass, and drove on, 48 hours straight, until, at the border of California, they stopped at a Native American Sweat Lodge, and consummated, with the complete gamut of body humours, *and how*, their hallowed wedlock.

The love song of Camel Jeremy Eros

Reader, he loves her.

This love lasts longer than red bricks. It lasts longer than the passage of numberless ages in slumberless song (Swinburne). It lasts longer than a Devonshire lane or a Christmas Day sermon.

Reader, it lasts longer than life.

The adventure in San Francisco with the Diggers

Cultivate poverty like a garden herb, like sage. Do not trouble yourself much to get new things, whether clothes or friends. Turn the old; return to them. Things do not change: we change. Sell your clothes and keep your thoughts.
—*Henry David Thoreau*

Richard Brautigan found the newlyweds a small apartment in Telegraph Hill. The shadow of Coit Tower fell over their building and, as if they needed it, spurred our lovers to new heights of concupiscence.

After their first energetic rut in their new pad, Allen settled her plush rear end, onto Camel's briefly soft but retted penile area, and whispered, "Is it really called Coit Tower or were you just trying to turn me on?"

"Which would you prefer?" Camel asked and he smiled that smile he had, the one with Fruit Loops and sunshine in it.

And Allen whispered, "My Camel."

And he filled again and entered her once in her gunny sack and once through the rear door and then they went for

Thai food and to meet up with Peter Coyote at his house, a convening place for the hip scene, still vibrant even though the Summer of Love had become the Summer of Pause.

"Pete, this is Allen. God knows I love her," Camel said.

"I can understand why," Peter said, with that voice that was part cigarette, part whiskey, part Buddha.

"Your voice," Allen said, and pretended to swoon into his arms.

"I love her, too," Pete said, grabbing Camel and hugging him, making sure his heart snugged up against Camel's. "You guys hungry?"

"We just had Thai," Allen said, now leaning into Camel as if they were part of each other. 'Snick' went the sound of her body snugging into his.

"Best khao phat I've had in years," Camel said.

"You went to Family Thais." Pete said. "Their nam phrik could be used for rocket fuel. It rearranges your chromosomes."

"So, what's the agenda?" Camel said.

"No agendas," Pete said.

"Right."

"I wanna see the free stores. I wanna help if allowed," Allen said, a bit shyly. She ducked her pretty chin into her pretty neck, a subtle gesture that had some swan in it.

"The stores have done their job, more provocation than charity, perhaps. A slap at consumerism, at Capital C Capitalism. They're running out of steam now, but let's go there," Peter Coyote said.

"Car or cable?" Camel said.

"Cable. One's not far. Page Street."

The building was unexceptional. From the outside one would never guess that a revolution was going on inside. Except as you drew near you noticed the empty picture frames tacked along the outer walls.

"What's that?" Allen said. "Art?"

"Our Free Frames of Reference," Pete said.

Inside the shop was as generic as the outside except for the groovy people within. There were tables stacked high with distaff clothing and racks along one wall. There were a dozen or so people going through the clothing. In one corner sat a heavy-set woman, with a wild afro and eyes like cocoa nuts, giving out free homemade cashew butter. There was a sign on one wall advertising the Free Medical Clinic, and a framed photograph of Peter and the Diggers performing their street theater piece, "The Death of Money."

"Ah, Janis is working," Pete said, rushing over to hug a woman with long dendrites of complicated hair and granny glasses.

"Is that Janis Joplin?" Allen said into Camel's ear.

"It is." Camel smiled at his awe-struck love.

"I mean, really, I was just listening to 'Piece of my Heart'."

"They might be playing tonight, though her band has sort of split up and scattered. Jerry's coming later. I'm pretty sure the Dead are playing later. A lot of the money for the stores comes from the groups, the Dead, the Airplane."

Janis hugged both Camel and Allen.

"Great, great," she said, in her husky voice. "Beautiful people." She hooked her arm in Allen's.

"I wanna help," Allen said.

"Baby, you're helping. I can feel the love off you," Janis said.

Later that night, around a campfire at Pete's place, Allen told Camel that this was the best day of her life. And, later still, mere months later, when they found Janis Joplin's body, gone now to Ghostville, Allen wept for three straight days.

"She was so fucking young," she kept saying, over and over, while Camel held her and patted her shoulder, and let his own tears fall like a broken necklace of pearls.

The next morning

The party at Peter Coyote's lasted most of the night. Janis came (Allen spent much of the evening practically in her lap), Emmett Grogan (Digger #1, he was introduced as), Peter Fonda, all the Dead, some of the Airplane, most of Fever Tree, Mimi Farina, Jimi Hendrix ("You used to play in Pigpen's first band, didn't you?" he asked Camel more than once), Richard Brautigan, Judy Goldhaft, Ron Thelin, Sweet William (*Hell's Angels*, Janis whispered to Allen), Ohem Jee (in from the Ozarks), Pete's gal Sam (who spent much of the evening naked [she said to all in hailing distance, "I'm just gonna be naked for a while"]), George Harrison (dressed as Wild Bill Cody), Lenore Kandel, Remark and Eedy ("I didn't know you knew Pete," Camel said. "We don't," Mark said. "Eedy wanted to crash it."), Phil Jackson (who challenged Camel to a game of one-on-one at the nearby playground hoop), and some weird looking cat, whip-thin and whelked, with great wide glasses like Mr. Magoo might wear, who sat on the floor, backed into a corner, with a sketchbook in his sweaty hands.

"Who is that?" Allen asked Camel.

"Crumb. The artist."

"Jesus Fuck. Who did Big Brother's album cover?"

"Yeah. Don't talk to him though. He says people make him nervous."

The next morning Allen and Camel awoke in their temporary digs near Coit Tower with no memory of how they got home. It was around ten a.m. and the sunshine through the windows and white lace curtains was the color of an iron butterfly.

The newlyweds woke and exchanged bad breath kisses, lying naked in each other's arms, enjoying the quiet solitude.

"You want breakfast?" Camel asked, kissing Allen's temple. "There's a place near here does a quite passable Mexican breakfast."

"Aw, Camel Baby, can we stay in and make our own breakfast and then play board games?"

Camel laughed the kind of laugh that sneaks out around a toke.

"Of course, my love."

And so they did. In the kitchen, still naked, they searched the fridge and cupboards. They found eggs and butter and bread and made themselves some scrambled eggs with dill and dope. Camel called them Pickled and High Eggs. And toast with butter spots and large tumblers of fresh orange juice. And, still naked, they played Scrabble, then Parcheesi, then Clue (Camel's guesses included Charles Manson with the paper cutter, Dr. Crippen with the can of Raid, and Lizzie Borden with a pointed stick, to which Allen said, Baby, you're as stoned as Judas's Chariot, to which Camel said, What?), and finally, a protracted game of Monopoly, where Allen owned every single piece of property except the Utilities ("I love the Utilities," Camel told her, "because you never know"), and probably won but neither of them wanted to count their filthy lucre.

"We all win," Allen said. "Me, you, Sweet William, Robin Hood and even Pat Nixon."

"Even Pat Nixon, Baby?" Camel groaned.

"Sugar, she is an innocent. She is born of the blood."

"Ok, Baby. You want dinner now?"

"Jesus, look how late it is. How long ago did we eat that entire massive bag of cheap cheese puffs?"

Camel looked at the empty bag, painted inside with orange shrapnel. He looked into his love's swirly eyes. "You want to go out?"

"I guess so, Sweet. I don't think I could handle another round of Higgled and Pied Eggs."

"Pickles and Herb," Camel corrected her.

"Peaches," Allen said.

"What?" Camel said.

"What kind of food can we have? I am really hungry."

"We can have anything, Baby. This is San Francisco."

"Crumpets?"

Camel laughed that laugh again, like air escaping an inner tube held under water to find the leak.

"Do we have to get dressed, Baby?" Allen asked.

Camel looked himself and his beautiful wife over.

"We're still completely naked," he said.

"100%."

"I guess we have to get dressed to go out. Unless you want food delivered."

"Ooh, yeah. Let's get Krystal burgers. 50 Krystal burgers."

"I don't think they deliver."

"Chinese it is then."

And lo it came to pass. A young dark-eyed son of Siam arrived with mu shoo and fried rice and soft noodles. Allen answered the door wearing only her change purse.

"How much, Sweetie?" she crooned.

"You're gorgeous," the lad said, his eyes full of sloe gin.

"Aw, thanks, Sweetie. You wanna come in?"

He did.

And so they toiled and played on into the nights

Allen loved San Francisco, its ambience, its artists, its soul. But she missed Memphis, whose soul was a solid thing like a red wagon. She pined for Memphis, as did Camel. Soon, they told each other, we shall return to the City by the River, the city which beats in our blood. They made this vow even as they partied with writers and musicians and artists of all stripe. Maybe not all stripe but a good 75% of the available stripe. Even, hush child, some polka dots instead of stripe; some paisley.

Allen also missed her art. She wanted to return to Memphis and set up a studio. Camel said he thought the garage could be converted. Allen had a sculpture in mind, a Duchamp influenced construction of car parts and Mississippi red clay. She made some sketches but she longed for a studio, the infinite space of a studio, the place where her art could expand like a gas.

Meanwhile, in the shadow of Coit Tower, their little hideaway had become a gathering place for West Coast artists and provocateurs. Peter was there most nights, accompanied by some Diggers like Emmett and Peter Berg. Howard Hesseman and some members of The Committee, some members of the San Francisco Mime Troupe. Gary Snyder, Richard and his new current woman, a Cherokee poet named Soft Wind, Remark and Eedy. Sometimes Lawrence Ferlinghetti, who was rightly treated like the royalty he was and is. Janis, Nick Gravenites, Pigpen, Bob Weir, Hugh Romney, Ginger Baker (surly and mean, Allen called him), Melanie, Bill Graham. Some strangers showed up, some strange strangers. It was usually all alright.

They made music (Richard had a soft, almost feminine contralto that made Camel beam), drank wine, shouted poems at each other, plotted strategies for street theater and street protest. They made love, smoked pot, chewed mushrooms. It was a good time.

"I wanna be high as Tim Leary and drunk as Crazy Googenheim," Richard crowed.

At one point, on one such night, Camel found himself in a back bedroom with Melanie. She had cheeks like crab apples and a mouth that looked so kissable Camel sat and stared at it. It might have been the mushrooms but Camel imagined that her mouth was Arnie Saknussemm's entranceway to Snæfellsjökull.

"What are you doing, Camel Eros? Hey, did you know your name means Love?" Melanie cooed.

"Your mouth," said dazey Camel.

"Looks like Arnie Saknussemm's entranceway, doesn't it?" Melanie said.

"Oh Holy Christ," Camel said. "Oh, God's Holy Trousers!"

"What is it, Baby?" Melanie said. And then she softly sang, "Then in a quiet room apart from the everyday far from the in and out of breathing I turn down the noise in my head."

"You're as beautiful as a toy cowboy."

"Camel, Baby, you woo nice, man. Come here."

And she placed the entranceway to the center of the earth over Camel's whiskey and whiskery mouth. Their tongues made a knot that could not be undone for some time. So they sat, entangled at the lingual septum. Melanie slipped her guitar-calloused fingers into Camel's loose-fitting trousers and pulled his pizzle out. She just held it there in her hand while they slowly tried to figure out the knot's configuration. Oh, so slowly.

And, in recompense, Camel slipped his own hand under Melanie's short, lutestring skirt and found the central heating of the troubadour's delightful body. He slid a finger inside where it was warm.

"Uh huh," Melanie said, using only her glottis, a deft oral movement that Camel admired then and later.

Finally, their tongues found their way back to their own mouths and yet they kept their hands in place.

"You're hung like a…camel, Camel."

"And you're soft and wet as Eden."

"You're a beautiful person, Camel."

So Melanie gave Camel a divine handjob and Camel made Melanie come with two fingers and a thumb.

"Where were you?" Allen asked later in the evening.

"Fingering Melanie Safka," Camel said.

"I fucking LOVE her," Allen said.

"I know," Camel said. "I did it for you."

The adventure of the drive back to Memphis

And so our intrepid heroes gathered their few belongings, one more time, and piled into a VW microbus that Camel bought from Michael McClure. It was lime green and on its side, in purple, gothic script it said, "Beauty will be convulsive, or it will not be."

They sold the bug to a guy standing on a street corner shouting his poems into the wind. Richard knew him and said his name was Larry Fischer. He paid for the car with a crumpled handful of bills, handbills and poems. Allen kissed him on the cheek and they never counted how much money he'd given them. Once back in Memphis they framed one of his poems called "Merry-Go-Round," and hung it in their bedroom.

They smooched and embraced every sentient being in the Bay Area before heading Easterly. The van broke down 111 miles outside of San Francisco. There they met a young mechanic named Antonioni who fixed the van for a half ounce of Mississippi Thunderfuck.

"It's the best dope I've ever doped," Camel told him.

Antonioni took a small pinch and put it inside his upper gum, ala snuff.

"Mm hm," Antonioni said. "Oh. Mm hm."

"Thank you, Antonioni," Allen said and kissed his potty mouth, wet and sloppy. "I love you, man," she finished.

Allen was full of love and her kisses were as precious as blue roses.

"God speed," Antonioni said, as they pulled away. And then he remembered the end of the joke as the lime green rear of the van disappeared over a brick-red rise in the road, "But you don't have to."

They slept the first night in Albuquerque, New Mexico.

"I know this place," Camel said, exiting the bus and stretching his small-forward frame. "This place talks to me."

"Beautiful," Allen said.

When Camel looked in her direction he saw she was not talking about the snow-capped mountains or the indigo sky or the fiery desert which lay just east of the motel. Allen was looking at her husband.

"You're a beautiful man, Baby," she said.

"And you're pretty as a pepper-laced omelet from the Hilltop Café in Truth or Consequences, New Mexico."

"You're also a nutty nut," Allen said. "And now you've made me hungry."

"Can we get omelets?"

"We can but ask."

And so they wandered away from their shitbox motel in search of Southwestern omelets as hot as a just-lugged bear. Allen wore a mini-skirt that rode the crest of her perfect ass like a hodaddy. Camel wore jeans and a "Save Overton Park" t-shirt.

Later, sated and sleepy as pythons, stomachs rumbling like Krakatoa, they watched *Bonanza* on the TV in their room whose décor was an odd mix of pumpkin orange and Delta dirt brown. At least they thought it was *Bonanza*; the reception created a picture that was half oater and half Jackson Pollock.

"Little Joe, your fiancé, I don't know how to say this," someone said.

"It is *Bonanza*," Allen said.

"And another dead fiancé," Camel said.

The next morning, they smoked a bowl before heading out. Once on the highway heading east, a long grey ribbon on the typewriter of their tale, they made small talk, the kind of talk lovers make when they are happy and young and the world looks like a Joe's Special Milkshake from Wiles Drug Store on Union Avenue in Memphis.

"Camel, darling, what's the best book you've ever read?" Allen inquired in a dreamy voice. She was looking straight ahead.

"Oh, hm, oh my," Camel said. Silence fell like a bell jar.

"It's something one should know about one's husband."

"Yes," Camel said. "Yes, I see that."

"*To Kill a Mockingbird,*" Allen said.

"That's yours?"

"Uh huh. Not good?"

"Oh, hm, mm. Yes, I guess so. Yes."

"Have you read it?"

Camel glanced at his new wife out of the corner of his slitty, gunslinger eyes.

"I'm in the minority, Baby."

"Oh, damn. You hate it and now you think I'm a literary light-weight. I was nervous, you know? Talking to all those writers you love and who love you. I was just waiting for someone to try and talk poetry with me. It made me nervous as hell."

"Oh, Kitten. No. You can't be nervous about that. No."

"What is your favorite book?" Allen was on the verge of embarrassing tears.

"*The House at Pooh Corner,*" Camel said.

"Oh, Camel."

"I'm serious. It's a beautiful book. I wish I could write a book that beautiful."

"Really, Camel? Your books are so—so—what? So lucid, like looking into sea water. You know?"

"Yes, Baby. Thank you."

That night, while Allen was in the shower of yet another shitbox motel room, Camel wrote this poem in ballpoint on yellow legal paper:

For Allen

Even if this poem
does not concern you,
here you are
behind a rhythmical pause,
underneath
a particularly
well-placed adverb.
I take your rib
for the poem's humor, your
smile for its grace.
And in the evening
when I read this to you
you will see yourself in it
as if it were your best and most
personal mirror.

And when they made love the poem lay underneath their sacred wilding thrashing and was reduced to smudges and wrinkles and crumples, dampened by the oil of catechumens. Camel was able to rescue it from its decrepitude, ironing the page with the side of his hand and re-writing it on a fresh sheet. In so doing, he changed the word 'evening' to 'gloaming.' And this made him unaccountably happy.

Further on down the road

The radio was playing a Ricky Nelson song and Camel was singing softly underneath the lyrics his own version, an aural pentimento.

"Who's this, darling?" Allen asked, behind sunglasses and a sleepy mien, a small drop of spittle on the edge of her half-smile, like a glistening drop of dandelion wine.

"Nelson Rockefeller," Camel said.

"I thought he was a rich politico."

"He was. After the TV series."

"What TV series, darling?"

"*Jeff's Collie.*"

"I don't know that show."

"Pre-Lassie Lassie."

"It was about Lassie."

"I think so," Camel said, and he gave his bride a James Coburn grin.

"You smile pretty, my Pyramus," Allen said. "I like it when you call me lassie."

"You make me smile, Turtle-dove. 'Millions of eyes have looked at this landscape, and for me it is like the first smile of the world'."

"What's that? A new poem?"

"Al Camus."

"I always hated his comic strip."

"That's Al Capp. I hate his comic strip, too."

"What's Al Capp?"

"I'm not sure. I prefer lower case, as the case may be."

And so they drove on, sozzled on their own bond, their cupboard love, riding the back of the highway snake the way Pecos Bill rode once upon a time a twister. The day bloomed, faded, fell, and they stopped at another highway public house.

The inn in Oklahoma City

"Richard has some special affinity for Oklahoma City," Camel said, his long legs stretched out upon the abrasive counterpane of the inn's cheap bed. "I'm not sure what it is."

"What did he say?"

"He said he had a special affinity for Oklahoma City but he could not explain it. He said it made his aura wiggle just to see the name on a map."

"You make my aura wiggle," Allen said, snugging up next to him. She was wearing only a pair of men's white briefs. The little nipples on her almost not-there breasts looked like the helmets for very small soldiers.

"Show me," Camel said.

The TV was on. *The Price is Right* was on, its music and gaiety almost that of a porn film.

Allen laughed her little Allen laugh and stood up on the bed. She straddled Camel's long legs, facing away from him, eyeing Bill Cullen who seemed to glow like the star of a porn film, and she danced to the pinging outer space music of the game show. Her perfect hips wiggled like loosened melody.

"Groan," Camel said. "My beautiful Allen."

Allen laughed once more her Allen laugh. She now shook her fanny at her fancy-man, lowering herself gradually, her balance the balance like light, like veins in a leaf. Her white-clad moon set over Camel's smiling horizon, so close to his face he could smell the baby powder on her fundament.

He gently placed a hand on each cheek, half-arresting the dance, so that her ass still shook lightly in his large hands. He slipped a hand under each hem. Allen sighed. She reached around, still in mid-squat like a brooding hen, and lowered her briefs. Then she lowered her Allen-self, and, as her bottommost point rested lightly on her husband's face, her husband slipped the sharp arrow of his tongue inside her quivering quim.

"I love you, Camel," she said.

Then she said this: "Ahhhhhhhhh...."

The adventure of the newlyweds on the last stretch of road to Memphis

Before taking to the last stretch of road to Memphis our lovers breakfasted in the motel's restaurant, a small remarkably comfortable eatery with morning sunshine aplenty pouring in large plate glass windows.

"I love motel restaurants," Camel said, studying the menu as if it were an ur-text.

The waitress approached in sullen slouch, a plump brunette wearing a striped uniform and cap, and a nametag that read 'Bradamante.' She also wore a countenance as grim as a government mule.

"Bradamante!" Camel boomed. "Warrior maiden! Feed us for we have a large hunger gained from a night of lovemaking as few humans have e'er accomplished in the palliasses of your fine establishment."

Despite herself a smile spread across the ample cheeks of their waitress who looked as if she had climbed out of an overactive bed this very hour.

"You crazy fella," she said.

"As Carroll's man of a hundred caps."

"You're mixing your literature in dangerous quantities," Allen gently chided him.

"A rasher of bacon, toast triangles and four eggs mooning me like ludic imps," Camel now said. "And my bride shall have pancakes with M&Ms in them. A stack this high, like seven LPs on the changer."

Allen laughed and Bradamante laughed. The latter also failed to write anything down.

"You crazy fella," she said again, her chuckling barely ebbing and a small slime of bat-mucus appearing in her left cave.

"I do want pancakes," Allen said. "I like the ones the size of silver dollars. What do you call them?"

"Silver dollar pancakes," Bradamante said. Then she laughed at herself.

"You two have made my morning. I was feeling really crappy when I came in this morning. My boyfriend left me."

"Bradamante," Camel said, now more gently. "Can you sit and have breakfast with us?"

"You're sweet—"

"Camel."

"What?"

"Camel, my name is Camel. And this, The First Lady of Memphis, the Sculptress of Fortuity, is my wife, Allen.'

"You guys are sweet. What do you want to eat?'

They repeated their orders and Bradamante practically skipped off.

"You made her happy," Allen said.

"Sweet young thing."

Then Bradamante returned, a sheepish grin on her round face.

"What's wrong, Dear one?" Camel asked. "Out of M&Ms?"

"The cook asked me to ask you if this ain't you."

From behind her back she brought forth a slim paperback copy of *Jokes my Kidnappers Told Me*. She pointed to the rubbed picture of a younger Camel on the rear cover.

"He's nuts for poetry," she added.

"What's his name?" Camel asked, genuinely touched.

"Ruggiero," she said. "He is, was, my boyfriend."

"Ah," Camel said. He took the book from her hand and inscribed it, boldly, "Pay attention to the Axis Bold as Love. For my new friends, Bradamante and Ruggiero."

"Take this back to him."

When Bradamante brought their breakfast her fry-cook boyfriend came too.

"Thank you, Mr. Eros," the rosaceous boy said, thin and stooped as Barney Fife, staring at his own greasy tennis-shoes.

"Stick with her," Camel said, then tucked into his eggs, whose moons were as bright and round as Norval's shield.

"I will, Mr. Eros," Ruggiero said, and the couple joined hands and walked back to the kitchen, heads together like conferring lawyers.

"Nice," Allen said.

"This bacon is perfect," Camel said. "The boy has a gift."

"Oh! Camel! Look," Allen said, just now looking at her plate. "M&Ms! And, O Propitious Divinities, a red one!"

Thus fueled they drove the last leg home.

"Are you sleepy? Do you want me to drive?" Allen asked a heavy-lidded Camel.

"I'm more hollow than sleepy. No, wait, I am more sleepy."

They switched places. Camel pulled his floppy hat, a gift from Richard Brautigan, over his eyes.

As they crossed into Tennessee Allen stuck one hand way out in front of her, fingers resting against the dusty dashboard, pressed against the dusty windshield.

"Two states!" she crowed.

"Allen, my love, what are you on about?"

"I made it back to Tennessee first."

"Ah," Camel said. "If you are the first to Tennessee you will shortly be the first in Memphis. Wake me when you cross that Rubicon."

As I40 began to slope down into the city proper, to the north the dingy storefronts and warehouses of Summer Avenue began to take shape like an unreal city emerging from a brown fog. Allen poked Camel gently in the ribs.

"Memphis, baby," she said, softly.

Camel stirred. He repositioned his hat and tugged both sides of his mustache, a waking ritual Allen still found tenderly sweet.

"Mf," Camel grunted. "Summer Avenue."

"Welcome home, Mr. Eros. Camel Jeremy Fermor Eros."

Camel smiled at the reference to John and Yoko. He touched his own lips and then passed the kiss, via his pointer finger, to Allen's lips. She smiled and licked the tip of the delivery finger. Camel nodded to the south and Allen turned.

Amid some non-descript, capitalist billboards (Meineke Mufflers! Ernie's Supper Club! Piggly Wiggly!) one stood out. It was a bright, colorful representation of a young long-haired man, wearing a shirt that was partly a peace sign and partly an American flag. And the message in large black, block read: "DON'T LIKE THE COPS? NEXT TIME YOU'RE IN TROUBLE CALL A HIPPIE."

Give me Memphis Tennessee

Once back in their apartment fatigue took them like a sneak thief and they threw their bags into a corner and collapsed on the bed which was covered with myriad quilts and tie-dyed sheets. It looked like it hadn't been made in ages because it hadn't been made in ages.

They slept for 14 hours exactly and woke simultaneously. Turning toward each other they smiled, mixed morning breaths, and exited the bed in search of sustenance.

In the refrigerator they found a tomato almost reduced to paste, a half loaf of Wonder Bread (which they kept in the fridge so the Rodentia did not partake), a half stick of butter, orange juice and a chocolate bar.

"Breakfast," Camel said. "I'll make. You shower first."

So a little later they sat down to toast and juice and black instant coffee, through the musty window a peevish light leaked, and they asked of each other whether a plan was necessary.

"There is the making of money to consider," Camel said.

"I'm not going back to teaching. The girls at Miss Hutchison's don't want to know the difference between papier-mâché and plaster of paris and I don't want to tell them."

"I could teach, I guess," Camel said, and looked contemplatively into his coffee cup. Finally he added, "This would be better with a little milk."

"You'd be a good teacher," Allen said, and stretched her long feline arms skyward.

"I would be," Camel said, smiling at his wife.

"Maybe I'll have an open house at my studio. I've got a crapload of finished stuff there."

And so that came to pass, Allen's Open House.

Allen's open house

Camel's friends attended. Three Hushpuppy Brown, Lahna Darling, Buddy Gardner (who brought along a beautiful young model named Cybill), Jenny Lamb, Creole Myers (the reviewer), College Herpes, Memphis poet, Etheridge Knight (here for a visit stretching between jail stretches), Pharaoh Moans, Sweetness Enlight and a wannabe filmmaker named Billy Ass, newly arrived from Indianola,

Mississippi (he had made a ten minute documentary about Elvis Presley's barber that was well-received in certain high-faluting filmic circles).

Camel's parents came early. Axel was dressed in an old Brooks Brothers suit Camel knew he'd bought at Goodwill on Highland. He was also sporting an apricot ascot, a sartorial touch that surprised the younger Eros. *His dad owned an ascot? More than one?*

Maya looked beautiful in a shimmering white dress. She kissed Allen's cheeks, French-style, left, right. "So proud of you," Maya said.

Many of Allen's fellow artists, the ones she was close to, attended. Carroll and Pat Cloar, Dolph and Jessie Smith, Fess and Linley America (the pair worked in mud, good rich Southern mud), Bill Eggleston, John McIntyre (whose date was a woman dressed as Urania, or perhaps it *was* Urania, some said), Burton Callicott. Potters Lee and Pup McCarty came up from Merigold, Mississippi. And a new, young painter, Jeri Ledbettter, whose Twombly-like abstracts were about to become celebrated by the cognoscenti and the uncognoscenti alike.

There were also East Memphis nabobs with money.

Afterward a smaller clutch of friends gathered at The Bitter Lemon for late night java and conversation. They were joined there by another new cat in town, though word of his arrival had preceded him. His name was Stinging Nettles and he could blow a sax make Bird leave his nest. He had played with Coleman Hawkins and Stuff Smith.

"I made $2600," Allen whispered to Camel.

"Baby, you're a rich man."

"I'm paying tonight," she whispered again. "Then tomorrow we can talk about what we want to do with the rest, if we want to do anything."

"We're only in it for the money," Camel said, smiling with his entire mustache.

"Money for food. Money for music. Money for books."

"Exactly, my darling."

"You Camel?" the stately Mr. Nettles said as he approached the table where they all sat.

"I am," Camel said. "You're Stanley Nettles."

"Call me Stinging."

"Stinging. Nice to have you in town, man. My buddy Buddy's been heralding your arrival."

"I'm looking forward to playing with the young guitar whiz. He here tonight?"

Buddy looked up. He was almost shy, but it might have been awe.

"I'm Buddy," Buddy said, and presented a hand at half-mast, not knowing whether the black sax man wanted the soul shake or the white man's. He chose the white man's and wrung Buddy's hand.

"Honored, brother," Stinging said. "In town to play on a session with The Relatives, you dig? Never heard them before but while I'm here I'd like to feel the Memphis mojo, you dig?"

"Wanna play some?"

"Sure, sure, yeah" Nettles said. "Anxious to. You get some other cats together with us?"

"As many as you want, whenever you want."

"Man, I knew Memphis was gonna be good for me. When, when. What are you doing now?"

"About to make some puredee Memphis jam music, baby." Buddy rose and Pharoah Moans rose and before they left the Bitter Lemon they had an octet.

Before he sauntered away with his inchoate makeshift band, Nettles leaned over and said to Camel, "Played with your dad once. That cat can cook. He still with us or he join Gabe's band?"

"Still here. He'd love to see you, I'm sure."

"We'll do it, we'll do it," and he tipped his porkpie to the table.

Another book

Camel's next book of poetry appeared in 1973. It happened like this.

"Camel, there's someone on the phone for you," Allen said. She was making empanadas for dinner.

"I'll get it in here," Camel shouted back.

A few minutes later Camel came into the kitchen wearing a smile as broad as human thought.

"That was Harry Ford."

"From high school?"

"What?"

"Didn't you go to—oh no, wait. I went to high school with a Harry Ford. Or was it Henry? No, certainly not Henry Ford. Henry though. Henry Chevrolet. I think that's right."

"Allen, sweetheart."

Allen looked up. She had flour on the end of her turned up nose.

"Harry Ford is an editor at Atheneum. They've accepted *Asleep at the Verso and Recto.*"

"Jesus, that's good, right. They're big?"

"They're poetry central right now. They publish Merwin."

"You love Merwin!"

"I do. I love Atheneum."

"And they, apparently, love you."

"Harry said so. They're looking at spring."

"That's fucking fantastic, baby. Kiss me. My hands are greasy."

Camel kissed his beautiful wife as if he were giving her the sacrament. It was quite a kiss.

"That was quite a kiss," Allen said. "Whew."

"You really want to fuck me right now, don't you?" Camel said. "I'm being published by Atheneum."

"I really do. Atheneum makes my knees weak."

"And my john-thomas hard."

"Jesus, Camel, let's hurry. Unsnap my overalls and let them drop right here."

Camel did as instructed. Allen's letter-perfect caboose was swathed in thin cotton, panties, as brief as a sigh. Camel sighed.

He entered her before she even took her hands out of the dough.

The adventure of Camel's first death

Johnny Niagara had built a bomb lab underneath the streets of an old Memphis neighborhood. It was a mythic place, half Sheol, half alchemist's lab.

Camel and Allen were at home when the explosion rippled under their own floorboards. Camel knew what it meant right away. He had no sixth sense but his five were as finely tuned as the strings of Yoyo Ma.

Camel and Three-Hushpuppy Brown found Johnny's charred remains amid the acrid smoke in the converted sewer. Johnny was hoisted by his own petard. Johnny was fricasseed. The two men held each other and wept. Johnny's extirpated body, a mass of cloth, bone, blood and torn flesh, lay a few yards from the table. Their worst nightmares became reality: Johnny had been "tinkering" when the explosion occurred. It must have set off a chain reaction, igniting every still usable explosive in the cockeyed lab. It blew Johnny a good twenty feet from his workspace. It blew him into pieces. It blew him, foul wind, into Gehenna.

"My first death," Camel said.

"My-my-my," Hushpuppy said, tears like gold on his dark mocha cheeks.

Back at Camel's they began planning Johnny's send-off event. College Herpes wanted to build a floating pyre, piled high with kindling, books by The Beats, and Johnny's entire collection of Miles Davis and John Coltrane LPs, Johnny's body covered with marijuana leaves, set afire and set adrift on the brown, forgiving wavelets of the Father of Waters.

They settled for a party, a shindig, a hullabaloo, a throwdown, a shivaree, a clambake. They called it on the invitations: The Party of Special Things to Do.

That night, alone in their oversized bed, Camel and Allen held each other by their soft parts (the sexual embrace as a symbol for this condition of psychic unity is also found frequently in Tibetan thangkas.) Camel's mustache was still damp with tears.

"My first death," Camel whispered to his paramour.

"Sh, sh," Allen said. "Come inside me."

In the studio

I have gladly given my life to Memphis music, and it has given me back a hundred-fold. It has been my fortune to know truly great men and hear the music of the spheres. May we meet again at the end of the trail.
—Jim Dickinson

Buddy Gardner had a jackleg studio in the basement of the apartment building he lived in on Madison Avenue. The landlord allowed them to play and record there in exchange for keeping the water level and the rat population low.

"Nice, nice," Nettles said, as the troupe trooped in.

The basement was long and narrow, like a churchgoer's conscience. The walls seemed sweaty, the air musty with a hint of cooking grease. But there was room for a small orchestra so the musicians gathered at one end where there was already a piano and drumkit.

Camel, Etheridge, Allen and Cybill Shepherd found a couch at the far end. There they could talk comfortably while the players noodled around and learned each other's best and worst habits. Music was forming like a cloud inside the Astrodome.

Another young woman joined them, from they knew not where.

"Ellie," she said, shaking hands all the way around. "Ellie Masonry. You're Camel Eros, right?"

"I am," Etheridge said.

"Funny. You and I know each other, Etheridge."

"I wish that were so," Etheridge said.

"I took an impromptu class of yours once in the Pipkin Building at the Fairground."

While Etheridge tried to recollect if that were true Camel found an old sprung chair in one corner and dragged it toward the couch so that Ellie could join them.

"Thank you," Ellie said.

"What brings you here tonight?" Allen asked. Allen was eyeing the lissome brunette, who was spattered with freckles as if she had been misted by the skin blemish truck. She wore her hair in a Sylvia Plath flip. In fact she looked a little like the late poet.

"I followed you guys from the coffeeshop."

"Bold," Allen said.

"Did I sleep with you once?" Cybill said.

"Me?" Ellie asked and blushed like Eos. "No, I mean, I'm straight."

"Mm," Cybill said and began rummaging around in her purse.

"I'm a poet, too," Ellie said now.

"That's a fine thing," Camel said.

"Etheridge inspired me."

"You from East Memphis," Etheridge said, sitting up straight now. "You're a St. Mary's girl, come from money, from way out east money."

"My parents are rich," Ellie said. Did she duck her chin genteelly? "I'm trying to live that down."

"And you brought some poems tonight?" Allen asked.

Ellie looked at her oversized bag. Allen looked at it, too.

"It's ok, honey. You wanna read some for us?"

"Oh no, no," Ellie Masonry said. "I wanted to give them to Camel. Just as, you know, a gift."

"You're a wonder," Camel said. "Pleased to have them.'

Now, emboldened, Ellie reached into her carpetbag and brought forth a stapled stack of foolscap. Typed in fine pica print on the first sheet it read, *A Weekend with Thanatos, and Other Poems,* by Ellie Masonry. And underneath her address and phone number.

"This is very nice," Camel said. "I will treasure them." He patted her knee with his large, knotty hand.

"Lemme tell you a story, Ellie Masonry," Etheridge said. "Don't think I've told you this either, Camel. Harken."

The group relaxed into their seats as if a mage were about to hold forth.

"Years ago I wrote a poem, a fine poem. It was published in a little Southern fascicle called Clap and Trap. Small but eager readership. They took a number of my things but this one, this one poem was special, I thought. Got some good feedback from Tom Pumpking, the editor, maybe you remember him. Never mind.

"So one day I got a letter from a poet in Italy wanted to translate it into Italian. Course I said, sure, sure. And apparently he followed through. Now the story begins and I can only tell it as it was told to me. Someone in Genoa read the Italian version and gave it to a Portuguese poet friend who translated it into Portuguese, and then this was followed by a poet in Romania, Swaziland, Prague, Manilla, France, I don't remember where all. But you get the idea. It had been translated and translated, moving further and further away from the original, as borned on Etheridge's Olivetti . Many languages later it was discovered by an editor at Poetry Magazine in Chicago. I think the version she saw was in Ewe, a west African tongue. This editor happened to speak Ewe and translated the poem back into English. The poet's name had been long ago lost, mistranslated or simply disappeared. My name, that is, was gone, but no matter. The poem was no longer mine. They ran that poem, crediting it to the editor of the West African journal where it appeared. And hence my poem was no longer mine and when I read it I was, you might say, agog at the end results."

"It was your poem word for word," Ellie said.

Etheridge, like a good storyteller, let the Pinter pause elongate.

"No, ma'am," he said, finally. "My poem had become 'Break on Through'."

"What was your original title?"

"Warden Blues." Etheridge gave with an elfin, toothy grin. And he laughed.

"Wait, like The Doors song?" Allen asked.

"Exactly like The Doors song," Etheridge said. "Try to win, try to hide. Break on through to the other side, yeah, doo doo doo doo…"

"That's fantastic!" Ellie said.

"Etheridge is pulling your leg, honey," Cybill Shepherd said.

"I assure you I am not, though that leg is a pretty one."

Ellie Masonry reflexively crossed her legs.

"Meanwhile…listen to those cats cook," Camel said.

Then they all emerged from the bubble and were aware of the heavenly sound around them.

"That might be the sound Buddy's been looking for his whole life," Allen said.

"They're getting it," Etheridge said.

They listened for a while. "Feeling Alright" went by, followed by "Incident at Neshabur," by "Summertime," "Yardbird Suite," and "Third Rock from the Sun." Then something amorphous yet glorious. It resembled nothing previously iterated or sung or dreamed. It was the music of angels nobbing.

"The guy on sax there. I think I fucked him once," Cybill Shepherd said.

And so….

And so Time passed because it didn't have a good hand. Because Time knows no other way of BEING.

Camel wrote up a storm, a freak storm, a Rory Storm. Marriage agreed with him. He and Allen still went out with friends but not as often. They saw a lot of Etheridge until he returned to his cell where he continued to write astonishing poems, many of which he shared with Camel via the seraphim in The United States Postal Service, the only office of government Camel trusted. They saw a lot of Johnny even after his untimely death, sometimes his sketchy visage showing up on their television screen like a staticky death mask. The after-party for Johnny's funeral was as lively as a square dance at the Roundhouse, and has been passed down into Memphis myth.

Camel and Allen made their nest nesty. And, once nesty, they decided to buy a house instead, and make a bigger nesty nest. Allen came into some family money, as it is said, and she wanted a room solely to spin clay and crack rocks and shape plastic in.

Sophrosyne (n), Camel wrote in his notebook: a healthy state of mind, characterized by self-control, moderation, and a deep awareness of one's true self, resulting in happiness. And he began a poem by that wobbly moniker which became a suite of poems called, "Like Bull Connor in a China Shop."

These forge-hot new poems of Camel's became a major component of his subsequent book, now re-titled *Everyone is Missing* (Atheneum, 1970).

It also contained the aforementioned California poem.

California

for AN

In your eyes
oceans.
In your face
skies.
Your cheek is
a stone.
Your nipple is
a cap a
pixie wears
if he is
on the road
to
California.
California
is where the
world ends. It is
where
you are,
sky, sea, stone.

The adventure of Mr. and Mrs. Eros buy a dreamhouse

In the matter of furnishing, I find a certain absence of ugliness far worse than ugliness.
　　　—Colette

It was in the Cooper-Young neighborhood, midway down Young, between Barksdale and Tanglewood, a small white bungalow circa 1910. There was a commanding oak tree in the front yard as large as a figure lengthened on the sand. Little oak embryos littered the grassless yard. Hen-of-the-forest grew about its great root system.

"Ygdrasil," Camel said to it.

"Camel, Allen, welcome" Ygdrasil said back.

They moved their disorder from their cramped apartment into the 1500 square feet of Home and the first night there they celebrated with Champaign and barbecue and some ripe Alaskan Thunderfuck, a gift from Three Hushpuppy Brown. And they made love on their futon, to the sound of The Crickets (of the night, *and* on the spinny), doing a tousled version of "True Love Ways."

They moved in Allen's new baby palm she had named Rootboy.

Last of all the 72 boxes of books.

Camel looked around them, the walls pregnant with purpose, the floors as clean as the birch at Yule.

"We shall call it Camallen Wanigan," Camel said.

"Is that the boo talking, darling," Allen said, running a finger through the sweat around Camel's hairy navel.

"It's the boo of a house haunted by our newly born spirits."

"Talk like that some more."

"You talk, Love."

"Camallen Wanigan, we are yours as you are ours. It is our honor to share this space with your walls and floors which have born the spirits of many of the children of Adam. It is our honor, further, to be born again among you, walls, floors, ceilings, mantels, lintels, chimneys, hearths, valances, fascia, roof, common and principal rafter, overhang, downspout, gables and transoms."

"Beautiful," Camel said. "Beautiful Allen."

"Mailbox. Spigots."

"Ballcock," Camel said and sniggered.

Allen sniggered too. "My magnificent pagan beast," she whispered.

And they made love again.

Having christened Camallen Wanigan

They did not sleep again until he had explored with his body all the sweet crevices of her body.
        —Alasdair Gray

And thus, having christened Camallen Wanigan with their fragrant bodily fluids, they set about the task of arranging and rearranging. Having few possessions this amounted to putting a bookcase in each room, careful not to scratch the immaculate hardwood floors the color of ambergris.

"Poetry in the living room?" Camel inquired.

"Poetry in the bedroom," Allen said, blowing back a sweaty tress.

"Minx."

"Horndog."

One of the three bedrooms, the rear one with a window opening onto a backyard that ran all the way to Cincinnati, became Allen's studio. Potter's wheel, electric kiln, rough work table made of an old door and two small bookcases (housing books of art, Klee, Arp, di Chirico, Henry Moore, Calder, Rivers, Bellmer, Fini, Goldsworthy), upon which lay her tools: blades and chisels, gouges and stones, hammers and clay modelers, pyrometric cones and witness cones.

Camel made the middle bedroom his study, his writing room, his snuggery, his place of worship. Small desk, small bookcase (Blake, Berryman, Ferlinghetti, Plath, Dante, Milton, Petrarch, Pessoa, O'Hara, WCW, Dickinson, Lowell [Robert and Amy]), a stack of foolscap as tall as a Munchkin, a large wastebin, a stand with his beloved *Webster's Third New International Unabridged Dictionary*, and two typewriters, an Underwood and an Olivetti.

"The Olivetti is for poems," Camel explained.

"And the other..." Allen obliged.

"Correspondence."

"Ah."

Because it's a neighborhood there are neighbors

The lovers had been living on Young Avenue, under the protective bumbershoot of Ygdrasil, for a couple months, having only nodded and perhaps offered a muffled "hey" to nearby denizens, when a small committee appeared on their porch.

"Hello!" boomed an amiable Viking with golden beard and eyebrows like gypsy moth caterpillars. "Welcome to Cooper Young!"

He really did speak in exclamation points.

"Rod Master! and this is my wife, Syl! We live in the brown house four doors down!"

"Camel and Allen," Camel said, though Allen was back in her studio, knee deep in a sculpture based on the alien towheads from *Children of the Damned* .

A frowsy overweight woman with a face like a skillet of scrambled eggs and a sour mouth, as if she had ingested alum, spoke in a voice somewhere between a parrot's squawk and a tire's screech. "Melba Tornado," she said. "I live next door. My porch looks upon your garbage can."

Camel sensed a hostility.

"Pleased to meet you," Camel said, and did a half bow.

The other neighbors stood about with complacent smiles, ceding authority obviously to the Viking and the stickybeak Crone.

"Glad to have you in our little Eden!" Rod said. His wife, Syl, looked at her shoes. She was younger than her husband and looked a bit like the actress who played Mary-Ann on *Gilligan's Island.* Right down to her gingham dress.

"Yes, glad," she said.

"My husband, Tooth, has a great lawnmower," Melba Tornado said. "It mulches while it cuts."

"Huh," Camel said. The negative energy this woman enclosed was anathema to Camel. He wanted to be far away from her. Did she say her husband's name was Tooth?

"If you want to borrow it," she finished, her mouth a vinegary twist, her eyes sparking.

"Ah," Camel said. "I get it now. I get you. Groovy people. I'm hip now."

"Just so you know we're here to help," Tornado blew again. "And you know that big tree seems to be dying. You might want to think about taking it out. My husband says—"

Camel cut her off. "Melba, my Quidnunc, you touch Ygdrasil and I shall rain terror down upon your kith and kin, lineage unto lineage."

Melba Tornado's head moved backward as if she'd been slapped.

"Are you a horrible person?" she asked.

"Melba," Rod said, his voice lowering, calming. "Let's not get ahead of ourselves. We want to welcome Camel and Ellen."

"Allen," Camel said, as if making a point.

"Allen, of course."

"Allen," Syl sighed.

"Anyway, Camel. If you'd like us to cut your lawn you'll let us know. We're a community here and we help each other, right, Buddy?"

He called Camel Buddy.

"I like the grass the way it is. If you cut it where will the toads go?"

"Toads?" Rod said.

"Holy Christ," Melba Tornado said.

"I love toads," Syl whispered.

The adventure of the poltergeist

Camel was in the Memphis Room at the library. He was researching Gus Cannon's Jug Stompers. He had in mind an epic poem celebrating the early Memphis music pioneer, perhaps a whole chapbook about early Memphis sounds. One of the librarians recognized Camel and came softly over to him. Softly is how she did everything.

"Hello, Camel," she said, in a girlish whisper.

Camel looked up. The middle-aged librarian had gray eyes. Lovely, Camel thought. He put out his hand.

She took it and placed a soft palm above and below it.

"You don't remember me," she whispered.

"I'm sorry," Camel said. "LSD, you know."

"Phyllis O'Kalia. Phyl. I used to be married to Buddy Gardner's father."

"Phyl, of course," Camel said and started to rise.

"Sit, sit. I just wanted to say hi."

Camel was computing in his head. Surely, she was much younger than Buddy's father, a grizzled, angry ex-Marine Camel remembered with a shudder.

"I was his child bride," Phyl said, as if reading Camel's thoughts.

"Of course. Can you sit?"

"For a sec. How are you? I'd heard you were back living in Memphis again."

"Yes, yes. Just bought a house in Cooper Young. Married Allen Fermor."

"I know Allen," Phyl O'Kalia said, softly.

"Tell me about you."

"Nothing to tell, Camel. Cooper-Young. I lived there briefly in the 60s." Phyl shook her lovely gray head with its lovely gray eyes. "Hippie days. We had a tie-dye flag with Frank Zappa's face on it. We hoisted it every Mother's Day."

Camel's laugh was a tad louder than a library laugh. "Excuse me," he said. "Where was your house? We live on Young."

"We lived on Young, also."

"1954," Camel said.

"Yes," Phyl replied. "How did you know?"

"No, I mean we live at 1954."

Phyl O'Kalia wrinkled her brow and her mouth formed a pucker of concern.

"Oh my," she said.

"What is it?" Camel asked. "You look as if—" The words died on his lips as Phyl's eyes widened.

"You're not gonna tell me there's a ghost there."

"Camel, no, I'm sure she's gone now. She's why we left, though she was benign. It was just---unsettling—to come upon her sometimes. Like having a mouse run along your baseboards suddenly. She loved the bathroom and that was— unsettling, at times."

"Who is she?" Camel asked. The Jug Stompers faded- -again; their glory shall rise another time.

"Well, from what we gathered, her name was Challa. In the 1920s her family lived at 1954. Her father was a druggist and her mother a seamstress at home. There was a brother but I can't remember much about him. Challa was a fifth grader at Idlewild Elementary. You know, when she— passed."

"What happened?"

"Not really clear. There was some talk of abuse, or perhaps just abandonment. The druggist was a brute and a bigot, but she was a willful child, given to pulling the tails of cats and putting pepper in the dog's bowl. Kid's stuff. I don't think she was evil. And she certainly was not an evil poltergeist."

"But, Phyl, why would her spirit still be restless forty years later?"

"Camel," here Phyl placed a hand on his sleeve. "Her parents were atheists."

Camel allowed himself a small smile. He swallowed it quickly, seeing the earnest expression on the librarian's face.

"Anyway, I'm sure she's gone now. I think perhaps forty years is about the limit for how long a spirit can haunt a house, don't you think?"

"I know nothing of the ways of the afterworld. I've never met a preta, unless you count Richard Nixon."

"Yes, yes," Phyl said. Perhaps she was one of those people who do not actually laugh. "At any rate. I'm sorry I bothered you."

"No bother at all, Phyl. It was lovely talking to you. I'll let you know if Challa appears."

A quick cloud passed over the librarian's features and then she smiled and her gray eyes twinkled.

"If you do see her tell her Phyllis O'Kalia is sorry about the baking soda."

Before she could explain, Phyl was gone back behind her desk.

"She threw baking soda on the girl's apparition," Allen said, that night, after Camel related the conversation.

"Why?"

"Supposed to make a ghost ashamed of its pallor so that it cannot return."

"The things you know," Camel said.

Allen sculpted while the city sweated and slept

The family money was nice, the rich aunt Allen only remembered as a fussy, migraine-ridden lady who smelled like spearmint gum and who died from sticking a knife into a toaster, but, since both Allen and Camel believed banks to be corrupt institutions, their stockpile was dwindling. They gave part of it away, too. Friends in need. Black Panthers, CORE, Etheridge's legal fees, PEN, The Hog Farm, Seva Foundation.

So, Allen worked long into the night on new commissions. She got some public commissions from the city, Mayor Loeb loved Allen's small works in concrete ("I feel guilty taking the old bigot's money, but…" Allen said), and her rendering of the lynching of Ell Persons, done in mud, broken glass and plasticine was controversial enough (the Commercial Appeal called it 'tasteless mud-raking') to make her name in town. Her cachet was growing; her work in demand. Like her friend, Carol DeForest, her studio became also a sales showroom, and, like Carol DeForest, she began to be able to pay her way so that Camel could write poetry and teach the odd adult continuing education class. When buyers came to visit Allen's space Camel closed the door to his writing room and turned up his rock and roll. Camel always wrote with loud music playing.

"I learned it from Andy Warhol. Andy told me he painted to the Stones because they drowned out the conscious brain which only gets in the way of creativity."

The two artists lived together in harmony and adoration and tenderness. Camallen Wanigan became a stop on the celestial highway. Some nights friends gathered with musical instruments and wine and ganja and tales of the old days (the 1960s, now gone a few years only, but…), tales of bravery and hubris and Love.

The adventure of the signing and reading for *Everyone is Missing*

At this time in the story there was a little bookstore in the woods. It was created from ticky tacky and sugar and confectionary in the Land of Cockayne. The witchy woods were in the middle of a mystic metropolis called Memphis, Tennessee, a city built on a bluff, beside The Father of Waters, who rolled on and rolled on, some said in search of The Mother of Waters (this may be folk legend and the river may just be moving because there is Music in Memphis that can make dead men dance), and the woods were lovely dark and deep.

This enchanted bookstore was called The Bookstore in the Pines and it was run by an old couple named Aradia and Dianus Pocs, who, some said, had lived in the woods since the days of Magick and fairy-folk. Some said they had moved there from Detroit after Dianus was fired from his job in the auto industry. Some say there were whispers of Wicca, white magic, practiced by Aradia and her circle of suburban housewives.

At any rate, they opened The Bookstore in the Pines (the name of the woods themselves were often called The Pines, though, on some maps they are entitled Pinckney's Woods) with little knowledge of business but a belief in the power of books as transformative objects.

The little shop sat like a toadstool at the end of a loamy path. The nearest parking was about a quarter of a mile away. The doorstep of the shop was carved from the earth and over the lintel was a sign that said, *Art lies because it is Social.* (Fernando Pessoa). The door was decorated with tinctorial sigils and signs. Upon entering you may think you have entered the funhouse at The Mid-South Fair, instead of a bookstore in the woods. The floors tilted this way and that, mostly this way, much like the funland sets of Dr. Caligari. The walls, covered in vines and, where not vines, signs containing quotes from books of ancient vintage, or books of modern vintage, or books not yet written. Sortilege words. For the Pocs they represented a sort of protective spell and gave the bookstore its atmosphere of peace and light.

The bookstore became a zendo, a thingstead in the 1970s, its appellation and its liturgical events passed from hand to hand like a secret society's minutes.

It was in this place that Camel read from *Everyone is Missing,* his newest collection, about which he was right proud; after the reading, he signed 152 copies for the throng which had gathered in the lower floor (entered by ankle-walking down a rickety, skewing wooden staircase, and under an arch upon which was carved the likenesses of Shakespeare, Cervantes and Shelby Foote.)

Camel read as if his heart were on fire. The faces around him seemed to be a heavenly consortium, a gathering of saints and sinners, a crowd of the knowing and ignorant, the loud and the dumb, the eager and the indignant. As his words flowed forth, every head began to blaze like a corona and every mouth opened to receive the communion and every ear grew soft as a newborn's. It was quite an evening.

When Camel read, "Let the Light Stand," (reproduced below) it was as if everyone became naked, their bodies radiating brightness and heat, their third eyes opening to understand that poetry, that undaunted thaumaturgy, was *for* them, was *part of* them, was connecting them as tellurians.

Or maybe this is overstating things.

Let's say it's not.

Let the Light Stand

Let the light stand for nothing
but illumination. Let
the naked man and woman
out for air. Let the curtain hide
only another side of the
curtain. Let the food consumed
be consummated. Let the
consommé be a dish. Let the
dish into the bedroom
because she is there for the
cat. Let the cat be cool as Miles.
Let it all happen again
if you can. Let it happen again
if you can. Let the first word
spoken during intercourse be the
only definition you require. Let
need be need. Let love be need
also, if need be. And let
it all happen again because it can.

The adventure of Ellen Masonry and her boyfriend, Caba Jim

Camel was in the kitchen chopping vegetables when the doorbell rang. It didn't exactly ring but it made a wee buzzing noise that meant electricity was straining, unsuccessfully, to get to the bell and make it ring. Someday I'll have to find out where that chime is hidden in the walls,

Camel thought (for the umpteenth time) as he wiped his hands and went to the door.

On the doorstep stood the lithe young poetess Ellen Masonry and a short fellow with a Moe Howard haircut and a nervous mouth. Ellen was wearing a small cotton dress with tiny seahorses on it. It showed off her thin legs, shapely as moonlight.

"Hi Camel, I wanted to introduce you to my boyfriend, Jim. He was jealous that I actually know you."

"Come in," Camel said, simultaneously trying to shake Jim's hand as he passed, making for an awkward jumble at the threshold.

"I'm in the kitchen. Follow me," Camel said and Ellen smiled and Jim tried to hide behind her as they marched to the kitchen.

"We're disturbing you," Ellen said.

"No, no, I can talk while I chop."

"Oh, good."

"What brings you two scamps here on a Saturday afternoon?"

"I wanted Jim to meet you. Wait, I already said that. And I wanted to ask if you'd read my poems yet." She stuck her jaw out like a small child emulating Jimmy Cagney.

"Jim, you have a last name?" Camel asked, as his knife edge sent a section of zucchini squirting across the room.

"Jim," Jim said.

"Jim Jim?"

"No, Jim is. Ellen," Jim cast his eyes at his paramour as if English was his wobbly second language.

"His full name is Caba Jim. Jim is his family name," Ellen stepped in, placing a hand on Jim's shoulder.

"Ah, of the Philadelphia Jims."

"Sorry?" Jim said, looking up finally.

"Or the Nasium Jims."

"I don't—"

"He's playing with you, Jim, dear."

"Oh," Jim said. His mouth stayed in the small circle he had engaged to create his petite o.

"So, the poems," Camel said. He put down his knife, wiped his hands on a dish towel. "Let's go to the living room and talk. You want wine?"

The two youngsters sat very close on the couch. They held their glasses of cheap red wine as if the wine was a solution to a problem concerning social interaction. Camel sat near in a dilapidated Lazy-Boy, with Ellen's poems in his lap. He scanned them again briefly while the young people sat, afraid to move.

"Yes," Camel said. "Mm hm."

He flipped pages as the youngsters' bones turned to granite.

"Yes," Camel said. "Uh huh. You're going to be a poet."

"Oh!" Ellen squealed. "Oh, I could kiss you, you big kind man!"

"Ha ha," Camel said. He smiled into Ellen's giddy young eyes. Was she going to cry? She now uncrossed her legs and leaned over to hug Jim, her legs akimbo, her white panties shining like a nightlight.

"Wait," Ellen said. Her face crinkled in thought. "You said going to be." A frown threated her smile, joyful tears threated by weeping. "I'm not a poet now?"

"Well, Ellen, dear. Few are at your age. How old are you? 16?"

"I'm 18, Camel. I told you that."

Had she?

"18 then. Poetry is a long apprenticeship. But you have the mind and the sensibility and the puckishness to really produce something meaningful. Stamina is called for, yes? Courage?"

"I see." She sipped her wine.

"What's this?" Allen asked, entering. She had been in her studio and wore a pair of overalls with nothing underneath. Had she breasts they would be making an entrance with her.

"Poetry meeting," Camel said.

"Hi Allen," Ellen said. She rose and pulled Jim up by his elbow. "This is Jim. He's my boyfriend."

"I see. Nice to meet you, Jim. What do you do?"

"Nice to m-meet you. I'm at Tiger High studying literature. But I also play in a band. Well, we're not really a band. We're just having, I don't know. Mostly Renaissance writers, that's my focus. And I'm minoring in philosophy. I like the existentialists."

Camel and Allen's eyes met and said sweet things to each other.

"You two want to stay to dinner?" Allen asked. "Lemme join you with wine." She floated into the kitchen. Sometimes she floated.

"We're horning in," Ellen called.

"Nonsense," Camel said. "Just veggies over brown rice. We'll make a ton."

"Well, sure then," Ellen said. They sat back down. She looked quickly at Jim who was reddening.

Allen returned with wine and a doobie hanging gangster-style from her lip. She toked while she talked.

"Dinner plans set then?"

"Yes, they're staying."

"Cut up more eggplant. I bought too much," Allen said. "The ones at Easy Way were ginormous."

She handed the joint to Caba Jim and sat down in Camel's lap.

"Oh," Jim said. "Thank you." He took a long draw. "Sweet," he squeaked through closed teeth.

"Camel says I can be a poet," Ellen said after one toke.

"Lovely," Allen said. She put her hand in Camel's floppy hair and gave it a friendly tug.

"Allen—Ellen—did not show you her best poem," Caba Jim said at one point.

"And why would that be?" Camel asked. His brain was sitting pretty, like an egg on a throne.

"Jim," Ellen said, softly.

"It's about our sex," Jim said. He had made bold and now he returned his gaze to his lap.

"Ah," Camel said. "I have some poems like that."

"Yes, Camel writes about your sex all the time," Allen said. She smiled her stoned Topcat smile.

This brought on such gales of laughter that Ellen tumbled to the floor on a dusty rug that used to be many colors. Her short dress rode up over her pert little hiney.

"Read it," Jim said, reaching down for Ellen's hand and pulling her back onto the couch.

"Jim."

'You have it with you. You must want to share," Camel said, smiling like Buddha.

"Yes, I must," Ellen said. Jim was handing her a worn sheet of legal paper.

"His Cock," Ellen said. Her voice broke. "Ahem," she cleared and rebegan.

"His Cock. I ride it like a bareback rider. It's tough as leather and when I touch it it blooms. He's my horse and it makes me hoarse, this fucking. His cock is full like a banana in its skin. His cock, when I take it in, whether cunt or mouth, says things to me, no other part dare say. His cock says, I love you, I want you, I want to thrum and shoot you. I want it, too. I want it to shoot in me, his cock, his cocked rifle."

They were quiet. Camel was looking at the floor and rubbing his mustache.

"It's terrible," Ellen said, her voice so soft it might have been smoke.

"It's not," Camel said. "Very good. That is, it's not good right now. I suspect you just wrote it."

"Yes, that's right."

"It needs re-writing and re-writing. But you've got good stuff there. Throw out some of it. If you read it often enough you'll know what has to go."

"Thank you, Camel," Ellen said. She raised her watery young eyes and Camel raised his soft brown eyes and they just gazed at each other.

"It made me horny," Allen said, after a while, watching her husband and this young poet talking with their peepers.

"Yes," Camel said, breaking the gaze. "I'm quite horny myself."

"Oh, well, we can leave," Ellen said. "I mean."

"Stay," Allen said. She rose and moved next to Ellen and reached for her young hand. "Help us celebrate our new friendship," she said.

"Ok," Ellen said.

Allen ran a velvety hand up Ellen's young, hairless leg.

"Oh, wait! You mean, like with sex?" Ellen nearly gasped.

They all laughed, except Jim who looked simply astonished.

"That would be nice, wouldn't it?" Allen said, now rubbing Ellen's palm with a circulating thumb.

"Yes, I guess it would. Yes, I guess so," Ellen said. "I would like that. Jim? Would you like that, Jim? You mean, like group sex?"

"Or in twos, if privacy would make it nicer," Camel said, delicately.

"I guess so," Jim said. His voice was a gnat's. 'If in twos."

"Ellen and me, you and Camel?" Allen said. Her smile was crooked, feline.

"Oh no," Jim said, quickly. "I couldn't, you know, with a man."

"Good enough," Camel said. "You and my beautiful wife. Would you like to use the master bedroom and Ellen and I will take the living room."

So, that's how it happened.

Allen led Jim by his sweaty hand into the bedroom. He was blushing and looked back once, with a sheepish grin. In the bedroom he tried to take it all in.

"Wow," he said. "This room is so—"

"Messy," Allen said.

"Yes," Jim admitted. "I was picturing my parents' room."

"Come here," Allen said, unbuckling the overalls so that they fell loose to her waist.

"Oh," Jim said.

Allen put her lips against his and Jim pressed back, too hard as if trying to penetrate her.

"Sh, sh," Allen said. She put a hand behind his neck and looked into his eyes. Then she licked his nose.

She undressed him slowly as he stood with one hand on her shoulder for balance. When she took his underwear off she noticed they were silk. His family must be moneyed too, rich kids in love.

Jim's cock was not erect.

Allen took her overalls all the way off. She was as naked as Eve. She put her arms around the reluctant young man and ran her hands over his shoulders and back. Underneath her she could feel his erection beginning.

"Ah," she said, as she stepped back and put her hand around it. "That's a nice one," she said.

"Its's," Jim said. He choked slightly on his own saliva.

"Hard," Allen said. "It's making me wet just to hold it."

"Oh God," Jim said.

Allen put her other hand under his balls and began to gently pump him. Four seconds later he shot off on her thighs.

"Oh no," he said. "Oh no. I'm so sorry."

"Sh," Allen said, again.

"I'll clean that up," Jim said. He was near panic.

"Come here, lover boy," Allen said, and led him to the messy bed. They lay down, skin to skin, and Allen began to stroke him lightly and tell him stories about her life. Her words swirled around him like an incantation. Her words were the words gods use to turn clay into birds.

Meanwhile, in the living room:

"Camel," I have something to confess," Ellen said. She was now sitting in his lap where his wife was earlier.

"What's that, Bunky?'

"I've fantasized about this."

"Having sex with old Camel. Well, sure. Tell me about it."

"I can't talk about it. I'd rather just show you."

"I'm all yours."

"I wish that were true," she said, and her lip quivered.

"No, no, now. We don't own others. This is love, but it's free love, free like the Free Store, free like first innocent, free like the circling seas."

"I love the way you talk."

Now she began to unbutton Camels' work shirt and when it was off she removed herself from her perch and knelt next to the chair and undid his buckle and pants. When his johnny was out, she hesitated.

"Oh," she said. It was a strange 'oh.'

"That's a strange oh," Camel said.

"You're, you know, *big*."

"Hmm."

"I think I can do it anyway."

And she bent over him to take him into her mouth, the trick that she must have thought she had invented, or was showing Camel for the first time. His cock banged around inside her little cave for a while. Finally she took her mouth off.

"Whew," she said. "I can't put it all the way in."

Camel stood, shrugged out of his pants, and pulled her to her feet. He was now only wearing a pair of electric green socks. He began to undress his guest.

"Strip me," she said, feigning further boldness. Her knees were wobbly like that last pin before a strike.

Camel took everything off her, which wasn't much. Her lovely supple dress, a pair of sparkly shoes and very white brief panties.

"Your socks!" she said, as she stepped out of her panties.

"A gift from Wavy. You want me to remove them."

"No, I don't think so," she said.

Now Ellen Masonry sat on the couch with her legs spread while Camel knelt before her and began to expertly tongue her young, fresh crotch.

Ellen squeaked and squealed and offered sounds not in the alphabet. Until she said, "Sheeeeeeee, Camel!!!"

Camel pulled her crotch tightly against his mouth, his large hands surrounding her bottom Her orgasm took 4 and

¾ minutes. Afterward Camel raised his head slowly. His mustache glistened.

"Camel," Ellen said, when her breath returned. Her breath had gone all the way to Iceland so this took some time. "I've never. You know, never, had, that, that…"

"Cunnilingus?"

"Right, heh, that. And, you know, the orgasm part."

"Oh Baby," Camel said, and rose and put his arms around her and kissed her hair and neck. "Welcome to the world!"

"Whoosh."

"Exactly. And now you carry wisdom as lightly as an extra poncho."

"Why wisdom?"

"Because, like the magi, you came by Camel."

After a while Ellen began to lick Camel's ear. Camel never had cottoned to that but he did not let on.

"Now you, right?" Ellen said. Her voice was stuck between ages 18 and 35.

"Sure, if you'd like."

"I'm not, you know. I don't. Shit. Which way? You want I should suck you some more. Or you can fuck me. I'm on the pill. I can sit in your lap or you can get behind me, if you'd like, though I've never really done that, you know, but I'd probably like it, if you didn't stick it in my asshole, that is,

I am not sure about that. Well, if you'd like that I guess I could try. I…"

Camel laughed. "Honeybee, what would *you* like?"

"I don't know. I also give a really good handjob."

"Do that," Camel said.

So, with an apprentice printer's concentration, Ellen began to work Camel up and down. It was a little rough, a little too loose, a little painful.

"Here," Camel said, and he put his own hand around himself. "Watch."

She did. She opened her lovely eyes wide.

"Do you want me to help or do you want to shoot off on me?"

"That would be nice," Camel said.

Ellen re-knelt and pushed her breast out like a brave warrior. She was prepared to take the load on her chest and face. Camel watched her rapt face watching him.

It excited him, no fooling.

"Come here," he said. And he placed his hands in her armpits and picked her straight up and placed her on his lap, immediately impaling her on his erection.

"God, Camel!" she said. "God!"

And so Camel did jaculate inside this young poet with the Sylvia Plath hair and the thin, flaming legs. And as he did, Sweet Ellen Masonry came for the second time in her life.

The dinner was excellent. Camel had lightly seasoned the vegetables and he put a bottle of tamari on the table. The conversation was about books and movies and the TV series *Barnaby Jones*. Camel and Caba Jim were both fans.

The next morning

Camel was in the kitchen making buckwheat cakes with M&Ms. Coffee was hot and waiting under Chemex's little carport hood.

"How long you been up?" Allen asked, stretching her lithesome body, exaggerating with excessive arm movements. "Man, did I sleep!"

"You were sleeping the sleep of the just, or the just fucked, so I rambled around for a while, read a little in the living room and then started breakfast."

"Camel, was that ok last night? With the kids I mean?"

"They're adults, Baby.

"Yes, I know."

"Was it bad in the bedroom with Scooter?"

"Caba. I wanted to call him Caba. He was so— frightened."

"That's too bad."

"I imagine the little poet is a hellion. Poets are."

"No, not really. False bravado."

"But you fucked."

"Wayul, sure. Didn't you?"

"No, he shot early. Then I told him about my siblings and my upbringing."

Camel laughed. "Next time," he said.

He went back to his mix and Allen stood quietly beside him, sipping her coffee.

"Camel," she said, after a while.

"M&Ms, Babe," Camel said, smiling like a cowpoke, holding under her gaze a multihued handful.

"Camel."

"What is it, Love?"

"I don't want a next time."

Camel thought about this for a moment.

"Ok, Darling. I'm sorry the young Lothario was de-sworded early."

"No, I mean. What?"

"Tell me."

"I didn't like your having sex with Sylvia, Jr."

"Ok. Too young?"

"No, it's just. It's just, I don't want to do that anymore."

"Fucking."

"Other people."

"Ah. Yes. Well, let's not then."

"Ok."

"Ok, Grimalkin. Want some flapjacks?"

"I do, my Sweet. I want lots of M&Ms."

Eel Within and Stalag Patterson

In those days at Memphis State there was a department of English. This was populated by a diverse group of academicians and readers and loopy dreamers. The head of the department was a stern looking woman with severe hair, a silvered mane somewhat like Susan Sontag's, but without her accompanying soft features and womanly figure. She was short as Pluto's scepter and she carried a small extending pointer in her hand at all times like a riding crop. In this way she also resembled Mussolini. Her name was Eel Within.

Having been summoned by letter to meet with her Camel put on his best floral shirt, a pink satin bowtie Tom Wolfe had given him, and a pair of white painter's pants.

"You look beautiful, my dromedary," Allen said, her hair already spackled with plaster at 8 a.m.

"Dromedary, my mouse, you insult me. Surely I am good for more than one hump."

'Don't start talking like that or you'll be late for your job inter-review. Bactrian."

"Odd that, isn't it? A job interview at my age? My first."

"Huh."

And so Camel arrived on the campus in the middle of the city, a sprawling space of appealing lawns and neat sidewalks, large penitential gray buildings, and the most beautiful population this side of Shangri-La. Youth is beauty, Camel thought, striding with his long legs, toward Patterson Hall, aka The English Building. But beauty is not youth.

"Hello, Mr. Eros," Eel Within said, ushering him into a cheap plastic chair in a large lounge, with corporate tables, blank colorless walls, and coffee and snack machines.

"Call me Camel," Camel said, his impersonation of Mr. Tibbs lost on the overly serious warden of the English department.

"It's rare we get the opportunity to hire a writer of your stature," she said, honestly.

This is going to be a short interview, Camel thought.

"Wayul," Camel began, clearing his throat, before realizing he had no response to that. Then, to cover, he added, "My stature's been with me for some time."

Is he stoned? Eel Within asked herself.

"I'd say we're lucky to have you. But two quick questions."

"Shoot," Camel said, straightening in his chair like a gunslinger.

"Can you commit to 3 classes? It's quite a lot of work I know, for a writer working on his or her own writing."

Did she know this? Was Eel Within a closet poet? Playwright? Librettist? She's a closet something, Camel wagered.

"I will put my queer shoulder to the wheel," Camel said, offering a Camel grin. Then he cautioned himself about his flippancy. This woman is dead serious, if not dead completely.

"Fine then," Eel Within said.

"And the second question?"

"You don't use drugs or sleep with co-eds."

"That's two questions," Camel parried.

"It's neither being no question at all," Eel re-parried. Then she offered him a smile. It was like a slash in a mud wall.

"I shall not use narcotics or sleep with my charges, regardless of the charge I might get out of either. I shall be a good soldier in the army of the university."

Eel Within said nothing but fixed him with a raven eye.

"I mean, of course, that I feel lucky to have landed here," Camel said. "And I appreciate the opportunity to teach."

"Very well then. I'll have the contract sent to you. Classes start September 3rd."

"Very fine," Camel said, rising like a hot air balloon being filled. "If you don't mind I'll just sit here and have a cup of machine-made coffee and read for a while. I'm needing to acclimate myself to the aura here and have the aura acclimate itself to me."

"Of course," Eel Within said, shaking his hand and moving away.

Camel got a coffee, adding all the amenities the machine offered. It tasted like motor oil. Camel loved it in the same way he liked most institutional food: hospitals, convention halls, prisons. He pulled out his copy of Anthony Burgess's *One Hand Clapping* and began to read and sip.

Two men materialized beside him. Camel looked up like a sleeper shaking off a dream.

"Hello," Camel said. "I did not hear you come in."

"We are your welcoming committee," the shorter, fairer one said. "We thought you might like to see friendly faces after being greeted by the commandant."

The other was taller with a kind face, bespectacled like Santa, and a Ginsberg potbelly. He wore a vest festooned with buttons: "War is Good Business, Invest your Son." "Steal this Button." "Free Love." "Pigasus for President."

"And we use the word 'greeted' in the Scottish sense of weeping," the tall one said. He put out a hand. Camel rose to take it.

"Gordon Osing," Gordon Osing said.

"Camel Eros," Camel said.

"We know. I loved your first book," the shorter, light-haired fellow said. His face was young and kind and soft. Camel liked his face immensely. "Ricky Koeppel."

"Hello, Ricky," Camel said, taking the small man's hand in his. "Gordon. This is most kind."

"May we sit?"

"Of course."

All three sat after Ricky got coffee for himself and Gordon.

"So, she's for real?" Camel asked with a sly smile.

"Ha. Yes, she's real. She runs this place with an iron maiden," Gordon said.

"Welcome to Stalag Patterson," Ricky said.

"Pleased to meet my fellow inmates. You guys write? Might I have seen something?"

"Ricky had a poem in *American Poetry Review* last month."

"And Gordon is published often in the best poetry journals. He is also an accomplished essayist and a regular contributor to The New York Review of Books."

"Hm, tall cotton. I see I'm going to have to hold up my end."

"Nonsense. Your books are your ticket to paradise," Ricky said. "If paradise you seek."

"Only to come up snake eyes," Camel said.

"You'll do fine here," Gordon said.

The adventure of Camel among the philistines

When Camel entered Patterson Hall for his first class he embraced the smell, the noise, the rhythm, of the familiar academic surroundings. Though at Berkeley he was distracted by politics, women and his own poetry, he did enjoy many classes and was stimulated easily by talking about the written word.

In the conversation pit in the center of the Hall a droopy gaggle of students lounged, most with coffee and new pens and books. They were an attractive bunch, the Eloi, and Camel smiled thinking some of these fine young people would be his pupils.

In his classroom a dozen students were already seated. Two of them looked eager, hair brushed, smiles stretched like a canvas. They sat in the two chairs closest to his desk. One was a skinny young man who looked a bit like Ernie on *My Three Sons*. The other was a beautiful young woman. Her shoulder-length blond hair was parted in the middle and her cheeks were sharp as cheese, and she had a spiky little nose shaped like the Tin Man's. Her short skirt showed fine, strong thighs. Her smile made Camel saturnine, ringed by grief for the world of beauty.

Other students filed in. By the time the bell rang there were twenty-one of them: the new denizens of Campus Camp Camel. They were not a very diverse group, a couple guys with Kerouac conspicuously in their hands, a girl with a Beatles satchel, another girl with thin, red hair and delicate white skin, about five foot two: she looked like she was thirteen. Still, the front two, were the only ones who looked happy to be there.

Some of them were making their own assessments about their teacher: they took in his shoulder length hair, his vivid mustache, his paisley shirt and thrift-store vest with its peace symbol button, his thin string of multi-hued beads, his beringed fingers, his jeans, faded up to the sky. His huaraches.

"Creative writing," Camel said, once the silence seemed as if it was there for him to break. "Creative. Writing." Camel smiled his James Coburn smile.

A few students sat up straighter. The blond crossed her legs and tried to smile even harder. That glimpse of thigh entered Camel like a flu.

"You are all writers," Camel said. He had prepared no remarks ahead of time. He got off on winging it. "You know writers: pasty, flimsy as reeds, neurotic about their bowel movements, good friends but lousy lovers...." He paused for the cackle that never came. "This semester we'll work on some things, some reasons to write, some ways to do it perhaps."

One boy in the back row was nodding off. A girl near him, her face an upturned bowl, was trying to get hiccups under control.

"To start I'd like to play you this record."

Camel had placed a phonograph on his desk and he pulled an LP out of his bag. "Listen closely," he said, sitting on the desk next to the record player. The LP was John Cage and the piece Camel played was "4'33"."

The silence was like the silence of demons winnowing by.

At the conclusion of the piece Camel reverently removed the needle from the grooves. "That was a live performance by John Cage," Camel said. He looked around. Most students were looking at him. Their faces were as empty as shells.

"I couldn't hear it very well," the Ernie look-alike said.

"You could. You did," Camel said, smiling.

Shifting buttocks. A hiccup.

"So, here's my idea for the first piece of writing we'll do. Let's pretend there are no rules. Let's say, for now, that all the rules of writing that have been gathered and disseminated down through the years, are bushwa. I want you to think about that and I want you to think about this John Cage piece, and write me something. We'll talk about them next time."

Silence.

"Ok then," Camel said. "Class dismissed."

An uneasy tension filled the room.

"We've still got 40 minutes left," the blond said.

"Oh," Camel said. He looked at his wrist and reminded himself that he needed to buy a watch.

"Lemme tell you the story of my highschool English teacher," Camel said, settling one buttock on the edge of his teacher's desk.

"How was it?" Allen asked that evening at the dinner table. They were eating tabouleh and drinking sake (Peter had sent them home with a bottle which had gotten squirreled away and forgotten until this evening.)

"I don't know. I guess I have to win their trust or something."

"It's creative writing. How far could it go wrong?"

"That's true," Camel said.

Two days later the class met again. Camel had met with his other classes also but the creative writing class was the one he was ginned up about. Not that he didn't like talking about Alexander Pope.

"Got some things to show me?" Camel said.

When the papers were gathered Camel held up a finger, meaning 'gimme a minute' and sat on the desk scanning the pages before him. The inmates sat in stiff repose, the caesura before the electric shock treatment.

Most were incredibly dull stories about family, or lost lovers (an even dozen about lost lovers, calling them names like bastards and limp-dicks and whiners), or drugs, or what they did that summer. One was a reworking of Camel's monologue about Eileen Goff. That was dispiriting.

But one student had written one long sentence which did not end. Or more precisely the sentence ended off the edge of the page. The end read like this: "In this way peace came, in this way a sm." The name on this paper was Percy Fledge.

Another student had turned in a blank sheet of paper. On the reverse side a name was written in white ink, which reminded the teacher of the cover of *The White Album*. The name was Clam Tennen.

"Not bad for a first paper in your freshman year," Camel said. "I'd like to single out two papers though which I think perhaps reached a bit higher. Would Percy raise his or her hand?"

It was a small surprise when Percy Fledge turned out to be Front Row Ernie Douglas. He was blushing.

"Nicely done, Ernie," Camel said. "Pat yourself on the back."

Percy, instinctually stretched one hand toward his shoulder. Then, realizing it was probably not meant *literally*, he smiled sheepishly, and put his hand inside his other hand, as if to restrain it.

"Percy," he whispered.

"And Clam Tennen?"

It was the blond of course. She beamed like she had made the final three in a beauty pageant.

"Nice, Clam," Camel said. "Nice."

Clam turned her head slightly left, slightly right. Then she nodded toward her teacher.

"Today I'd like to read some Whitman and I want you to listen to the sentences. There's music in Whitman, which may not be apparent initially."

"Is it music like that John Cage crap?" a stocky fellow near the windows asked. The class laughed and Camel laughed too.

"You decide," Camel said, and began reading.

"How was it this time out?" Allen asked. Camel had found her in the studio putting the last touches on a head of Che Guevara.

"I've got two students," Camel said. "The rest are sleepwalking."

There's a party tonight at Camel's and Allen's

The party spilled out the back door, like vines seeking sunlight. The backyard, as long as death, was scrubby and dirt-pocked, a rusted swingset sat in the Northeast corner, jetsam from the family who owned it before Camel and Allen.

Allen had strung Christmas tree lights from the overhanging lamp in the shed. The bright and colorful strands ran from house to tree to fence. In addition to this she had hooked up two revolving color wheels, borrowed from her parents' house, where they still put up their aluminum tree every year. The revolving, changing hues reminded Camel of some of the light shows at Janis' concerts. Janis gone now, gone the way of all flash.

Stinging Nettles, Buddy, Crafty Connor (from Buddy's band) and Pharoah Moans had set up a combo on the patio. They were jamming to a slow motion version of Buddy's "Blues for Sandra Leathers." Camel had already had two of the neighbors over to chat with him about the music. He had invited them in for wine and pot-laced Rice Krispies squares and Rod and Syl Master had come in (they stayed the entire evening even later than the musicians, Syl stoned as an owl, had removed her shirt and bra and was dancing with Pharoah for much of the party); Melba Tornado, the hex next door, had threatened Camel with the cops. God bless her pointed little head.

Among the great unwashed dozens, Lahna Darling came and sang a few numbers with the band, her sweet, wobbly contralto making a church hymn out of "Sugar, Sugar." Caba and Ellie came, somewhat red-faced initially, but soon part of the swing and sway. Hondo Minimum and Destiny Dingle were in town from the West Coast, because Hondo, now a recording engineer for Dot Records, was meeting with Jim Dickinson about cutting a new Sha Na Na record in Memphis. And, there was a striking pair of curvy, identical twins, friends of the late Johnny Niagara, who were dressed like Tweedledee and Tweedledum.

"Who's that dressed like Tweedledee and Tweedledum?" Camel asked Allen.

"Friends of Johnny's," she said. "Came to meet those who had been close to him, they told me."

"Huh."

"They apologized for the costumes. Someone told them it was a Halloween party."

"This is August," Camel said.

"I know. You're looking at more than their costumes."

"They're striking women. Bonnie as Bardot."

"Right. Good to see full bodies again. But don't get any ideas, Bucko," Allen said, elbowing her husband.

"I've always got ideas," Camel smiled back at her.

"Me, too, my Cucumber. Me, too."

"Imagine the four of us."

"That would be delicious, of course."

"But we don't."

"We don't."

"Do they have real names or are they really Tweedledee and Tweedledum?"

"Sarah and Vera Money."

"Ok," Camel said.

At the end of the evening, right before they shooed Rod and the topless, small-breasted Syl home, Camel saw Allen dancing to Stinging Nettle's original composition, "Old Hob," with one of the twins, Allen's sleepy, moist mouth resting against the newcomer's sweaty neck, the newcomer's hands gripping Allen's textbook ass as if it were a life preserver. Camel got a growth. It was one of the prettiest things he saw that night, or any other.

Allen's new friend

Camel came home from his intro to English lit class (yes, Beowulf is the hero, not the monster, Camel said more than once, just as Frankenstein is not the creature's name) to find Allen and one of the twins in her studio on the spattered and legless couch, drinking peppermint tea and talking amiably, their pretty heads, one thin like Lincoln's without the beard, and one round like Scarlett's Mammy, close together, a complot of femaleness.

"Hello, beautiful women," Camel said.

"Hello, Camel, darling, you remember Sarah?"

"I do, though I would have had no idea which twin this is."

"Hello Camel, darling," Sarah said, with a snigger. "You won't have to worry about that much. Vera lives in Boston."

"Ah," Camel said. "Well, the apple doesn't fall too far from, um, the other apple." He ran a finger along his mustache, a tic of his that Allen loved but never told him she did. "Which twin were you entwined with at the end of last week's clamdig?"

"I have no idea," Allen said.

"I'll never tell," Sarah said, and laughed a laugh that was full and as melodious as a choir of golden, nesting birds.

"Tease," Camel said.

"All I know is your wife kisses better than my boyfriend."

And both women laughed their laughs.

Camel took off his hat, scratched his scalp, and started toward the door.

"Carry on," he said. "I need a smoke."

"Aw, Camel, come here, honey. You're not pouting are you?" Allen said. She waved her hands to indicate that he should return to them.

"Pouting no. But I still need a few tokes. The children, oh the children in their bright school clothes and closed minds!"

"C'mere," Sarah Money said. She was singing, almost inaudibly, "The Girls Want to be with the Girls." She patted the place between them on the spattered, legless couch.

Camel dropped between them. Allen put her hand on his chin and turned his face toward hers. She kissed him with the kind of kiss they usually saved for bedtime. It took a long time.

"Excuse us," Camel said, breathing again.

Sarah Money put a finger on Camel's chin and gently raised her mouth to his. She kissed him softly, with full lips and a wet, mobile tongue.

"Thank you," Camel said.

"Is it horny in here, or is it just me?" Sarah asked.

Camel and Allen looked at each other.

"We don't do that anymore," Allen said.

"Oh," Sarah said, nonplussed and embarrassed.

"Kiss me again," Camel said to Sarah.

This time the kiss lasted a little longer.

"Thank you again," Camel said and rose. He tipped his hat to them and exited.

"That was embarrassing," Sarah said.

"Naw," Allen countered. "Now take off your clothes and let me sketch you. You are going to make one dynamite sculpture. Your hips could shape the hands of Atlas."

The adventure of copulation for the furtherance of the race

"Camel," Allen said, one morning when they both found themselves at the kitchen table with eggs and hash browns and coffee. "You want a little Camel?"

"Allen-o-Dale, whatever do you mean?" Camel said. "Are these hash browns from scratch."

"Yes," Allen said. "A little Camel, a little Allen, a little Eros?"

"A child?" Camel said. He put down his knife and ran a finger around his facial hair.

"Bad idea?"

"No," Camel said. "Not a bad *idea.*"

"But it would be a bad reality?"

Camel was now in reverie and his potatoes cooled on his plate. A sundog snuffled through the kitchen window, bounced around the blue glass bottles Allen had placed on the ledge, and entered the room, a study in cerulean. Cerulean cats danced on the ceiling, chased by the sundog, and Camel, staring into his coffee cup was disturbed by rain clouds reflected there. Bluish-brown clouds the color of the Gulf of Mexico.

"I think we owe the world a child," he said at last.

"Yes," Allen said, as if Camel had brought it up. "Yes, I think you're right."

"We gotta stop dropping," Allen added.

"Yes, we can do that."

"This kid's gonna be far-out. Camel, do we need to stop weed?"

"Nope, I don't think so. Look at Grace's kid, God."

"Grace took acid while she was pregnant."

"Did she? I'm not sure."

"I'm not sure either, but let's not do acid."

"Let's trip on getting pregnant."

So they began fucking for offspring. This is a different kind of fucking. While play is still essential, behind the play there is a curtain of seriousness, a duty taken on, a mission, a *strategy*.

"Like this," Allen said, her head on the pillow, her face facing the face of Camel, her knees drawn up to her chest, a cannonball making a splash in Camel's heart and a pulse in Camel's wang. "I have to tilt my vagina toward my cervix. Of course. And when you come help me stay tilted upward. Oh, and keep your dick in me after you shoot."

"Look at your little hairy love box, squeezed up tight between your divine thighs. Look at that mouth asking me in. Look, lovers and friends, at my wife's fuzzy cookie, a treat for the eye, tongue and dingus."

"Dingus?" Allen said, her serious face now scribbled with a smirk.

"Tinkle pipe?" Camel said.

Here Allen laughed so hard she let go of her knees and her legs fell akimbo, opening her blind entrance for Camel's hungry gaze.

"T-tinkle pipe?" she snorted.

"What my mother called it when I was a pup," Camel said, now mirth spreading in him like warmth.

"Your m-mother," Allen snorted harder. "Tinkle pipe!"

It was a good ten minutes before Allen was able to resume her position, her flawless ass tilting upward so that her cave was all downhill.

"The sperms don't have to swim so hard," she explained.

Camel mounted her in that position. His sweet and handsome face hung over his bride like a moon.

"Ahhh," he said as he slipped into her like a Cutty Sark gliding over the Gulf of Mexico.

"Ahhh," Allen said, too.

Soon they were saying it together like a hymn. Or a her.

Supplements

"This reminds me of being at Kesey's house," Camel said, perusing the gathering of bottles and little fanciful bags of herbs tied with hair from horses' manes, spread out like the king's gold on his kitchen counter.

"They're vitamins and supplements. I doubt you could get off on them. But you can try."

"Drop a little folic acid."

"That's the ticket," Allen said, tilting her head back and throwing in a handful of vitamins C and E, zinc and a prenatal vitamin the size of a Matchbox car, washing them down with some kind of green witch's brew she had concocted in the blender.

"Sarah turned me onto her herbalist. He lives in Midtown in a castle, you should see this place. The yard looks like the Hirschhorn Gardens by way of the junkyard. And he has this strange orange dog named Fritz who can sing but only Tommy James and the Shondells. And, you enter his house through the fruit cellar because years ago the police nailed his front door shut and he discovered he liked it better that way. You step down into this earthy odor, redolent of old potatoes and earthworm dung, and, once your eyes adjust you find yourself in this lab, no kidding, it looks like Dr. Frankenstein's, in *The Bride of Frankenstein*, not in *Frankenstein*, and he's a short little Croatian with a bald head and whiskers like a demented Rutherford B. Hayes. His eyes sparkle like gemstones and his smile, it like tunnels into you, into your heart, your spleen, your guts. He placed his hand on my belly and said, mm, mm, mm, I think so, yes I think so. And, whew, he asked me a lot of questions about us, our religious beliefs, our sexual habits, what kind of poetry you write. He asked what kind of poetry you write! It was crazy, Camel, crazy. But I loved him and he has convinced me that these fey concoctions and roots and herbs will speed us toward our destination, in other words, a new Camelallen! Whoosh!"

Camel tugged at his face hair.

"The dog only sang Tommy James?"

"Yes. Fritz. He's the color of Cheetos."

"What is this mage's name?" Camel asked.

"Oh, yes. His name, ha ha. His name is Al Chemist."

They talk about names

The three of them—Camel, Allen and Sarah Money—were situated on the Eros's living room floor, with pillows, a beanbag chair and a joint the size of the horn of plenty. There was a fire in the fireplace, which surely needed cleaning, because it sent some of the rich, piney smoke out into the room where it danced with the scarlet vapor from the Maryjane, a foggy ridotto.

"This kid is gonna be cool as a river in shadow," Sarah said, her pretty cheeks sucked in, holding a hit. "You gotta name it something—apropos to its heritage."

"What heritage is that, Sarah Money?" Camel asked. His head was in Sarah's lap, his long gold-red hair spread over her like a prayer rug.

"Memphis mojo hipster chill," Sarah said, tugging on one of Camel's gold-red strands of hair.

"Orpheus," Allen says. "Orpheus Eros."

"That's not bad," Camel says. "Hrothgar."

"What's that?" Sarah asks. "It sounds like a sneeze."

"The kindly king in Beowulf. Camel loves Beowulf," Allen says.

"Goffredo for a boy, Irena for a girl," Sarah says.

"Or vice versa," Allen says.

"Vice Versa," Camel squeaks around a hit. "Vice Versa Eros."

"It's got something."

"Too much sibilance," Camel says. "But, still—"

"This joint is as big as a horn of plenty," Allen says. "Who rolled this? And who's writing down these names. We certainly won't remember them in the morning."

"Sore," Sarah says. "Sore Eros. Get it."

"We had a friend in Berkeley named Remark Kramer."

"Ah," Sarah says. "Camel your hair's making me sweaty."

"I once owned a camelhair sweater," Camel said. "I think I did."

"Undine. Justine. Mignon."

"Horn Aplenty Eros," Camel says. "Baconetta"

"Baconetta?"

"I love bacon."

"Rancho Doritos."

"Stop."

"Rocky Raccoon Eros. Semolina Pilchard Eros."

"Jethro Bodine Eros. Jethro Tull Eros."

"Challa," Camel said, with an imp's grin.

"Best not tempt the spirits of Ancient Memphis," Allen said.

"Glumdalclitch."

"What the hell?"

"Mary Ann," Sarah says. "Like the Dylan song. I love that song."

"No, not Mary Ann, Ginger," Camel says. "Ginger Eros. Yeah."

"To match your hair?" Sarah asks.

"No, you said Mary Ann. So Camel said Ginger."

"I still don't get it."

"*Gilligan's Island.* Camel loves *Gilligan's Island.*"

"Jesus," Sarah says.

"Too religious," Camel says. "Pope Joan," he adds. "If it's a girl."

"Pope if it's a boy," Allen says.

Camel sits straight up as if drawn upward by empyrean wires. "Pope Eros! Pope Eros!" he says, holding the joint skyward like a torch. "Pope Eros!"

The women broke down in a fit of toppling laughter. They laughed like a twister, like a game of Twister, like a rainbow coming in colors everywhere, like a speedboat's wake, like a waking dream. They laughed until they stopped, winding down like a monkey playing tiny, tinny cymbals.

"Heh, heh," Allen said, catching her breath. "First, Camel. First, Sarah. First, Allen-myself, I must get pregnant."

"Yeah. It's imminent," Sarah said. She kissed Allen tenderly on the mouth. "You're gonna make the best mama since Mama Thornton, since Mama Cass."

"I love you, Sarah, baby," Allen said, petting her friend's hair.

"Pope Eros," Camel said, softly. His head was in dreamspace now. He was lost to the waking world. He was in a poem.

Class

"In the 60s," Camel was saying to his writing class, "there was a recognition, an eye-to-eye thing, between hippies and other hippies, between hippies and blacks and freedom fighters and libbers and all the disenfranchised. It wasn't overt. It was just a commonness that passed among us, a bond that didn't need words. If I passed another man with long hair we acknowledged each other. Perhaps it said, I am not a banker. I am not a politician. I am not an insurance shill. I am just who I am."

"It was a coolness thing?" Clam Tennen asked.

"It was a vibe thing. We weren't necessarily cooler. We were viber."

"Is that a word?"

"Everyone needs more viber in their daily diet," Camel said, straight-faced.

"You make it sound like a secret society," the red-haired woman said.

"A society anyway," Camel said, solemnly. "The secret was that there are no secrets."

He met their blank faces with his stoned hippie smile.

"I love you," Camel said, looking down at his own hands. "Go home and write a new bible. Class dismissed."

The adventure of Camel at the fertility clinic

Properly called The Infertility and Reproduction Clinic.

Camel in waiting room, reading *Diary of a Nobody*. His long legs splayed out in front of him, vaquero-style.

"Mr., um, *Eros*?" a bleach-blond voice says into the room, which is empty of human life except Camel's.

"Present and rarin' to go," Camel says, in his best mock-Gene Autry voice.

"This way," the nice woman says. She's about 50, heavy-set with an arabesque of hair that threatens to tumble to the linoleum.

"This room here," she says.

It's a cubicle, about the size of most doctors' inner rooms, except not as antiseptic. There's a chair, a stool, a small table that belongs in pre-school. On the table are magazines which decidedly do not belong in pre-school. *Playboy, Hustler, Jugs Aplenty, Studs* (the all-male cowboy theme appeals to Camel in an odd way, though he is and always has been exceptionally heterosexual—except for one night with the guitarist for one of the West Coast psych bands), *Esquire*.

"*Esquire*?" Camel says, and pulls at his mustache.

"Here's a cup," she says, handing Camel a morning-coffee-sized plastic cup with a screw top.

"I'm gonna need something much bigger than this," Camel dead-pans.

She smiles a tight smile. "First time I've heard that one," she pans deadly back.

"Ok," abashed Camel says. Now he's embarrassed, now that she's shut the door and he is left alone with porn and cheap furniture. There is no lock on the door. This doesn't disturb Camel—hell, he'd jack off for someone if they wanted to watch—but it's a detail that would show up in a later poem.

Camel drops his bemired jeans and his Yellow Submarine underwear and sits on the chair, legs akimbo, his fruit dangling. He picks up *Hustler*.

The pictures are stimulating enough even if the beavers have been reddened with formaldehyde. (Where had he read that?) He flips through. Nothing.

He tries *Playboy, Jugs, Stud*. Nothing. He eschews *Esquire*.

Instead he tilts his head back and closes his eyes and lets the soft music of memory enter his sensorium. His first mental instinct—the direction an awkward leap—was toward Cybill Shepherd, then Mary Ann, then Daisy Duck (those thick ass-feathers!). Decisively then, his mind knows what to seek. He finds his wife in a sylvan setting, days before she became his wife. He espies again in memory her perfect fundament. Spanker, he.

"Allen," he sighs as he throws enough jism into the cup to procreate a Third-World nation. And a splatter or two on the linoleum for Nurse Ratched.

"All done," Camel shouts down the hall.

Nurse Ratched appears from out of nowhere. Camel wonders for the first time how stimulating this is for her. He hands her the cup and she deigns to look inside.

"We'll be in touch," she says.

"Aren't you even going to sneak a peek?" Camel asks, with a sideways grin. "I peaked so you could peek, or does that pique you?"

Nurse Ratched holds his eye for a moment. Then she looks into the cup and takes her time studying his output.

"Hm," she says. "It's the wrong hue."

Camel starts. "Wrong hue? You say wrong hue?"

She smiles tenderly now and moves away.

"Got me," he calls after her. And now he feels restless. He wants to find Hushpuppy or Johnny and smoke a reefer. He remembers Johnny is dead.

In the fertility clinic I think of death, Camel writes on the pad in his head.

Well, it's not me

"Shit, that means it's me," Allen says. "Shit."

"I don't know. Are these tests 100% reliable? It's been my experience that no test is 100% reliable. Except the Test of the D'Urbervilles. Nor no doctor, nor no absolutes," Camel says. "Lemme see that report again."

"Shit, Camel. It says you're able to father generations unto generations and that your sperm is probably Superman's sperm and that with any other female, human or animal or plant, you'd be fathering up to your beautiful floppy mustache."

"I didn't know it said all that."

"I guess it's my turn to go to the doctor or clinic or whatever. I should have assumed that this is usually the woman's fault."

"Forget it. Let's go to Coletta's and then come back here, stuffed like Pooh bear, and ball all night. If Coletta's barbecue pizza can't make babies I'll move to another town."

So that is what they did. The pizza was excellent, though Allen ate more salad than meat. And the lovemaking, under the influence of cheese and grease and Van Morrison's *Astral Weeks* was slow and groovy and as erotic as the moaning of chafed spirits.

In the morning they both woke up sure that the previous night's rutting had produced a zygote to match anyone's zygote. They were sure Little Pope Hrothgar Eros was on his or her way.

Galley pages

"What are those, Camel, my favorite hump?" Allen asked, sliding into the living room in her stocking feet, wearing only one of Camel's oversized sweaters and his rolled down gym socks.

"Galley pages, proofs, they're called. I think. Poofs. Goofs. Roofs. I need some roofs."

"You don't."

"I don't."

"Okay."

"Today I took a comma out and an hour later I put it back. This was my day's work."

"That's fine."

"It is. It's a good day's work. What is this that floats before me?"

"It's your new book, Jughead?" Allen's kittycat face opened up a rident glow few women engender.

"Yes, my love," Camel said. "In inchoate form."

"May I see?"

"Of course."

Allen picked up the bound pages and riffled through them.

"Not pretty yet," she said.

"Right. Not pretty yet. Waiting for Camel's final edits. Waiting for Camel to okay them and send them out into the world to do his bidding."

"What is his bidding?" Allen said.

"Hearts. No trump."

"You don't even know what that is."

"I don't. Shall I say two queens?"

"Yes, you can have two queens. Just let me take the jack off."

The adventure of Camel's new book

Camel called his new book *Beautiful Goddamned Infinity* (Atheneum, 1977) causing some mild consternation on the publisher's part, though Harry Ford at Atheneum stood resolutely behind Camel. "They won't stock this at Waldenbooks," the publisher's sales staff warned. "Has Waldenbooks really ever sold much poetry?" Ford countered.

Camel gave them an alternate title: *The Winter of my Discotheque.*

It had been a long time between books for Camel (he was almost constipative about releasing new work, revising and revising, going over each poem with his fine toothed editorial mind) and there was a part of the public ready for new words from the 'hippie poet.' Hence, a small tour was planned, during the summer school break. This pleased the hippie poet and his wife. They thought a break from Memphis (where they spent too many nights with friends with bongs, where they worked privately in their separate garrets, where they were tempted by movies and music and their wild society, where they continued to try and fuck the future into human shape) and from worrying about their reproductive systems, would do them a world of good.

(Time slipped by, slipped by, while Allen avoided the medical profession and concentrated her soul's power on creating a fertile garden within her own unplumbable plumbing.)

Camel was most excited at the prospect of returning to San Francisco and their friends there. Remark and Eedy had already booked a reading and party the night after the day they were to arrive.

But, first, they had the launch party at The Bookstore in the Pines, with Aradia and Dianus spending a lavish amount of money on advertising and on the spread of food (Another Roadside Attraction Catering) which took up a large table in an adjoining room. The cheeses alone could have fed a small African nation. ("What is this, brie?" Camel asked of one particular cheese, which had brie's consistency but an earthier flavor. The answer was lost as Hushpuppy grabbed his friend from behind and whispered in his ear, "Your night,

Poet. I love you. Later at my place hash brownies, so go easy on the cheeses.")

That evening Camel read his poem "My Cock," a Ginsberg-like recitative chant that sent some of the women (and men) into sweats and at least three couples out into the country dark night to rut in the bushes. It took him seven minutes to read it and later Dianus dubbed it 'your seven minutes in heaven poem.'

The Eroses did not get home till 5 in the morning. Neither had to get up the next morning since their flight to the West Coast was at 6 pm. By the time they boarded they were rested and high again.

High and on high.

At San Francisco International Airport Remark and Eedy were waiting at their gate with a horse collar festooned with multicolored flowers. Remark hung it about Camel's neck.

"Our visiting High Mucketymuck," Remark said, with mock, if not muck, solemnity.

"Is this some kind of Dada leis?" Camel asked.

"Does Dada need to get laid?" Eedy whispered in Camel's ear, as she pulled his neck down to hug it. She added, as an unnecessary gratuity, a quick tongue to his anti-helix.

Camel wore the horse collar to his reading the next night. It was accepted by most of the crowd as either (a) a wry comment on the celebrity status of some writers, or (b) some kind of Memphis hoodoo thing (the rest of the U.S. assumed Southerners were a romantic mixture of Faulkner novels and Val Lewton films), (c) a modern art performance appurtenance, or (d) a new affectation. At any rate, in California style, it was excellent via whatever motivation.

The room was packed. Peter Coyote brought a new young woman (possibly an actress, some said she looked familiar—was she in that thing with Jimmy Caan? or that foreign thriller with Jon Voigt?). Gary Snyder, Ginsberg, Corso, Zebo Poncy, Diana DiPrima, Ferlinghetti (even though Camel was signing at City Lights the following evening), all the jivey musicians who loved poets, all the strippers who loved bookstores, all the criminals in their coats and ties, all the young dudes, holy men and seers, Sears and Roebuck, Roebuck and Mavis Staples, country gentlemen and town mice.

Camel read from the new book. After every poem there was the snapping of fingers, the gentle palms onto palms, the sighs of the besotted. Camel was still a master at the podium, a figure of high learning and animal sex appeal.

At the party afterwards at Doragon Restaurant in Japantown, where they commandeered an entire room, there were faces young and old, familiar and unfamiliar. Eedy kept purposely bumping into her old paramour, especially when

Allen wasn't near. She was wearing a very short organdy dress that showed off her commanding legs. On one thigh she wore a new tattoo, a vivid Ouroboros.

"Swallowing his own tail," Camel remarked when Eedy pushed him into a corner and raised her already high hem. "There's a metaphor a poet understands."

"Look closer," Eedy said. Her breath on Camel's cheek was hot and boozy.

Camel hesitated. Eedy put a hand on his neck to gently push him closer.

"Ah," Camel said, rising back to his full, impressive height. "That's not his tail."

"Hee hee," Eedy tittered. "It's his big dragon cock," she slurred. She now was leaning against Camel's tall frame, in what might have been feigned tipsiness.

"Big. Dragon. Cock," she repeated unnecessarily.

"I get it."

"You got it."

"Ha ha, Eedy. You hot little otter."

"Oh Camel you mean it. You wanna go someplace and ball? You know Mark won't care."

"I otter. Eedy, nothing would please me more."

"Oh Camel, baby. I want your big dragon cock. It's been so long. So LONG!" Her voice rose and her cackle drew some half-stoned interest from others at the party. Where is my Allen? Camel was fretting.

"Eedy. You suck and fuck like an Amazon but, well, Allen and I don't do that anymore."

"You don't suck and fuck. Camel, you really do need me." She slipped a hand down the back of Camel's pants and her finger went straight to his anus.

"Oof," Camel offed. "We do suck and fuck, eh, Eedy, darling, but just each other."

"I don't believe that."

"It is God's truth."

"Aw, Camel. Come on. For old long zine."

"Jesus, Eedy, keep your finger there a bit longer, just a bit, and then we must part, to my regret."

Eedy put her finger further inside Camel.

"Camel, I see the bulge. I see it and here and in my mind's eye." She seemed cold sober now.

"Kiss me once, Eedy, fill me with song." Camel bent toward her.

And there, in the corner of the back room of Doragon Restaurant, on this still summer night in Japantown, San Francisco, Camel kissed Eedy time-consumingly and soggy, while she wiggled a finger inside his caboose. When they broke Camel gently, like the gentleman poet he is, but reluctantly, lifted Eedy's slim arm from the back of his trousers.

"I love you, Baby," Camel said. "I want you to go cornhole someone else now."

"Alright, Camel," Eedy said, in mock-pout. She made a beeline for Peter Coyote.

(Later Allen asked of Camel: "Did Eedy fuck Peter Coyote?" To which Camel replied, "Eedy fucks everyone. It's her superpower.")

*

In NYC Camel read at St. Mark's Bookshop. Harry Ford came and brought with him practically his entire stable of poets: Merwin, Marvin Bell, Merrill, Mona Van Duyn, Anthony Hecht. Camel was treated royally and, royally, he read his works, crowned by his acceptance in New York. He had always thought of himself as strictly a West Coast writer, by way of Memphis. At the after party, there appeared from the shadows a young rock singer named Patti Smith who approached Camel and, without a word, handed him a cassette tape. On it was written "This tape kills fascists."

"Don't get off on self-love," Camel told himself, "wear the love like heaven." At the end of the night of the last reading Camel rode away on his silver bike (metaphorically, you know, speaking), before they rode

Translove Airways back back back to their home, their town, their hometown.

In class

"Dr. Eros," the rusty-colored, whelked boy in the rear, spoke from his personal murk.

"Camel, please."

"Sir?"

"I'm not a doctor. I just play one in my boudoir."

"Professor?"

"Camel"

"Ok. Mr. Eros," he rebegan. "This story you had us read bothered me."

"That's good, right?"

"Sir?"

"Camel."

"It's good? To be bothered by what we read?"

"I think so. Don't you?" Here Camel opened his hands, spreading wide his long fingers, a gesture meaning the question is open for all to discuss.

The boy went on. "The story has a character with the same name as the author."

"This is what bothers you?"

"Yes, Doc—Camel, Mr. Eros."

"Because it breaks the fourth wall?"

"I don't understand that either."

"Ok, listen. Why is the author in his own story? Anyone?"

Clam Tennen was looking at Camel with her melting cluster eyes. She had an answer. Of course she did. Camel smiled his half-mast smile at her. Though this was a new semester, and a new class, The American Novel, she was back, in the front row, in her provocative attire, with both her radiant, spheral legs. Camel hoped, prayed, that she would only bring one leg this year. He was but a man of flesh and blood.

"Lemme just say this. Do you know the word verisimilitude?"

Clam almost raised her hand but Camel hurried on.

"If nothing else perhaps you'll take this word away with you from your years here at Tiger High. Verisimilitude means, vaguely, adding reality to fiction, employing it in your fiction, to create a heightened sense of believability. It's been used as long as humans have made things up for the enjoyment of the other apes. In this case, the author inserts himself into his story for a similar reason. But, ah, also for its opposite."

The class was a mass of white and brown masks. It was a Noh play.

No play.

"By inserting himself into the story he is both saying that this is perhaps part of his life, our life, hence believable, and that, contradictorily, friends, readers, countrymen, it's also only a story. I'm making it up. See, he has it both ways."

The audience of Noh was figuratively scratching their figurative heads.

"So you want us to use reality in our stories? In our poems?" This from the tall Caucasian fellow who was a small forward on the Tiger basketball team. "In our *papers?*"

"Reality should be one of the cards in your deck but not your ace. Maybe a queen or knave. No, Reality should be the joker in the deck and you should never entrust too much to the joker." Camel smiled, pleased with himself.

One fellow laughed. Maybe he was listening. Maybe he was remembering something he'd heard on *Crazylegs Crane* the night before.

After the silence a voice from the wilderness: "You're sexist."

Camel sniffed as if a bad odor had wafted by. He was trying to imagine what he'd said was sexist.

A round-faced young woman was glaring with red eyes.

"You said, 'countrymen.' You're implying that only men would understand."

"Ok," Camel said, as if had just traversed the desert with a fat man (or woman) on his hunched, humped spine.

A phone call

"Yes, hello, this is Camel."

"..."

"Oh, Jesus, thanks. No, really."

"..."

"Yeah, I get that. I'm not sure. The angels, you know? Yeah, yeah. I know."

"..."

"Really? Groovy. Sure, whenever, I'm out that way. Yes, Allen, too. Thanks, man. I mean it."

"..."

"Ok, goodbye. I'll keep in touch."

"Who was that?" Allen asked, entering the room in her white-spackled white coveralls.

Camel smiled. He smoothed his mustache. Put his index finger in his mouth biting its nail, lost in thought. He looked up slowly into his wife's eyes.

"Camel? Bad news?"

"Hm?"

"Bad news on the phone?"

"Oh, no no. Just made me think is all."

"Who was it?"

"Leonard Cohen calling from Nashville."

"Leonard Cohen."

Camel smiled.

"Leonard Fucking Cohen, whose first album has been our soundtrack for years."

"I know."

"What did he want?"

"He praised a poem from *Beautiful Goddamned Infinity*."

"Which poem?"

"Hm. 'Jesus Was a Proper Noun'."

"I love that poem! Oh, of course, of course, he loved it. I get it."

"Yeah, I know."

"Now what?"

"He invited us to visit him. He thought Nashville was as close as our backyard."

"I'm packing my bags."

"Ha, funny grimalkin."

"When?"

"Oh I doubt he meant it. He relishes his privacy."

"Leonard Cohen."

"I know."

"Now what?"

"Now what. I'm going to go write some new poems."

"Because now you've been sanctified."

"Yes. Where is the album?"

"In my studio. Want me to get it?"

"Hm, no. I'm going to write a poem. I'm thinking some Big Brother for this poem."

"Ok, baby."

"Ball and Chain."

"Ok. Ok, baby."

August 17, 1977

Camel's father called. It was early in the morning and Camel hated when the phone rang that early. It could only mean someone died. Or worse.

"Good morning, Son," his father began. His tone was sepulchral, alright, too formal for their usual banter.

"What is it, Dad?" Camel had to clear his throat. He wanted coffee.

"Elvis, Son."

"Shit, really? How? He wasn't shot, was he?"

"That's an odd leap, Camel. Why would you think someone would shoot a pop singer? I remember once in Harlem. Echh, never mind. I thought you'd like to know. How are things?"

"Fine, Dad, really fine. Working well. Got a couple new poems that are distracting me from life."

"Don't wander too far from it, Son."

"Of course, Dad. Of course, you're right."

After he hung up he found Allen in the bathroom. She was sitting on the toilet, flossing her teeth. Her long, lithe legs turned a key in Camel's heart.

"Why are you flossing at 5 a.m.?"

"Hm? Oh, I don't know. Suddenly I wanted a strong piece of floss in my hand. What was the phone call?"

"Dad. Elvis died."

"Elvis Presley?" Allen had a piece of floss stuck in her teeth.

"Allen."

"Right, of course Presley. What happened?"

"Oh. I don't know. I got sidetracked. I'll bring the paper in."

"You met him once, didn't you?"

"Yes, a long time ago. Backstage at the Shell. He was warm and friendly. I liked him immediately. I was a punk hanging around musicians so I could score pot."

"That was it?"

"No, I talked to him later on. He was at Jim Dickinson's ranch and I told him about the other time and he didn't feign that he remembered. I liked him for that. He asked me about a poem of mine. It was the damnedest thing. He kept up with Memphis people, his people. He was true to the city."

"You wanna make love, Jughead?"

"Should I get the paper first?"

"Your call."

"Let's make love first."

In bed Allen whispered in her husband's ear. "We could name him Elvis."

Subsequently, one of the new poems...

Leonard Cohen

Leonard Cohen sits
in a house in Greece.
Its walls are white
and outside his window
the sea is a blue never
used before. In the
next room a woman
sleeps, a stranger.
Leonard Cohen puts his
fingers on his typewriter.
The room hums.
He begins by typing a
single word: *lonely*.

"I love this," Allen said. "It's Cohenesque."

"I don't know. I'm happy with most of it. There are a couple words I'm not sure of."

"Which ones?"

"Oh, I'm not sure. Never sure."

Dinner with the Pocs

"Today, friends, I have received the gold standard of strange phone calls. You know, retail is interesting because it involves converse with the great unread masses, and, over the years, I have had the strangest phone calls since 'Watson, come here, I need you'."

"That's saying something," Dianus added, in support of her husband's proclamation, "that this is THE strangest. Stranger than the guy who called ahead, asked for you and wanted to know if he could borrow a piece of tape?"

"Stranger. *One Step Beyond* strange."

The couples had met for dinner at Grisanti's, an Italian restaurant with atmosphere and the best ravioli in Memphis. Camel had been surprised at the invitation. They did not know the Pocs well, but had always enjoyed their hospitality at the bookstore.

"Leonard Cohen called Camel," Allen said.

"What? Holy shit. Leonard Cohen?"

"Sorry," Allen said. "It just came out. I am not trying to upstage your call. Tell us, please."

"Ok, but then tell me what the Canadian pietist had to say."

"Sure, sure," Camel said. "This ravioli. Damn, it's the best in Memphis."

"Perhaps in the entire South."

"Perhaps in the U.S."

"Perhaps—oh never mind. Talk, Aradia."

"Ok. It's a woman and she says, 'Do you have any books on how to get dried placenta out of fabric?'."

Allen snorted wine through one nostril.

"Wait, it gets better. Then she says, 'And how do I tell if my daughter is dead? She just had a baby'."

"Oh, fuck. That's not funny," Allen said.

"And: One more thing she wanted. 'Do you have *The Poky Little Puppy?*'"

"Jesus God, what did you say?" Camel asked, putting his fork down and tenting his hands in front of his face. He seemed to be praying for this poor woman's lost soul.

"What could I say? I told her of course we have *The Poky Little Puppy.*"

"Seriously?"

"No, no. I said, 'Ma'am, please first call the police'."

"What did she say?"

"She said she'd call The Book Shelf instead."

Much time has passed

So, readers, we return now to the continuing drama entitled, *We Want a Child.* The last we saw of our heroes they had determined that Camel's love juice was not the problem, that indeed, his love juice carried enough impregnating agents to repopulate Angola, if Angola needed repopulating, which we assume it didn't.

The Eroses, as if to talk about it somehow jinxed them further, had not discussed the problem for months, and then years. Camel did not want to push his wife, who feared doctors and their power and their pronouncements. They continued to swive as if any encounter would produce the second wave of Camallen. The swiving, so attuned to each other, was the good part. But, finally, Allen went to see a gynecologist that Sarah Money had recommended.

Dr. Ole Worm had a private practice, a converted house, which sat on a small hill like a cake topper, in Midtown, among the poor and hip. The interior still bore some of the charm of its original home, brown wood on the mantle of a working fireplace and around the doorways, wallpaper that hadn't been sold for decades, a thick Persian rug. Dr. Worm was in his sixties, a kind-faced man who resembled the actor Richard Farnsworth. He spoke in comforting whispers and his warm hand settled many a nervous stomach. Allen had a nervous stomach.

"How are you feeling, in general?" he asked Allen, after she had settled into an easy chair beside his desk.

"Good, real good. Eating healthy, working well. Sleeping well."

"Intercourse."

"We fuck like hyperkinetic sea lions. And often."

Dr. Ole Worm laughed.

"That's good, good. Let's go ahead and get you into the stirrups and see what's what. When was your last exam?"

"This is like confession," Allen gave a short laugh. "It's been a while."

"Nervous about it?"

"Yes. Some."

That night at home

That night at home, after a dinner of clams over linguine, Camel and Allen snugged up under an ancient quilt on the couch in the living room, and watched Woody Allen's *Annie Hall* for the eleventh time. Their VHS was a home-recording that was wearing thin and in places jumped like Godard.

"Comfort movie," Allen said.

"Not that we need it," Camel said, petting his wife's thigh which was slung over his. "The tests will show nothing and we will continue our rambunctious nocturnal thrashings until one of your eggs gives up her prick tease and accepts one of my slimy little swimmers."

""I-I'm gonna buy you these books, I think, because I think you should read them, you know, instead of that cat book....cuz, you know, I'm obsessed with-with, uh, death, I think," Woody Allen said.

"Death fixation. Ugh. Glad you don't have that, my Mr. Goodbar," Allen Eros said.

"Come here, Grimalkin," Camel Eros said, while running his hand up his wife's smooth thigh and under her flippy skirt.

"Camel," Allen sighed into her husband's mouth. She followed her exhalation with her pulpy tongue, and then a slow leak of a moan, as Camel's hand surrounded her vulva, clad only in thin, white cotton.

"Oh, baby," Allen said, as their mouths disconnected. "I'm wet as the caves wherein earth's thunders groan."

"Poe," Camel said. "Poet. Who's the poet?" Camel was panting a bit himself as his wife began to grind against his hand. He slipped a finger inside her panties and inside her groaning cave.

"Jesus," Allen said.

"I want and I want and I want," Camel said.

"What do you want, my Camel? I'll give you anything. Any—huh—thing."

Camel made with the wide eyes, the waggling eyebrows.

"My imagination."

"Is the heart of us."

"What do I want?" Camel asked, with feigned seriousness, still scratching his wife's inner itch.

"Think fast because I'm aching for it."

"Stand up," Camel said.

Allen looked into her husband's mischievous eyes. She removed the quilt and defingered herself. She rose slowly, like a dancer, and stood astride Camel's long legs, each of hers planted firmly, a Colossus. She lifted the hem of her skirt so Camel could see the damp spot.

"What do you want, Lover Mine?"

"Remember the park."

"Our first coupling? Like I remember my own name."

"First look at this." Camel unbuckled his pants and pulled his pizzle out.

"Jehoshaphat, husband! That's a mighty big log you got there. That's a Captain's log! Pull it a few times for me."

Camel did. Eyes on the prize.

"Dammit, man."

"You remember what I want."

Allen gave him a sly look. "It's coming back to me."

She turned her back on her seated husband and pulled her cream-colored sweater over her head, tossing it onto the floor. She unhooked her skirt and let it fall, kicking it, expertly, onto her sweater. Now only her thin, white panties, a flag of surrender, stood between Camel and his favorite work of God's.

Allen slipped a thumb in each side of her panties and slowly, slowly, rolled them downward. She heard Camel moan and pump his cock harder. Letting the panties drop she was naked as dawn.

"The cordate ass upon which the world rests," Camel said. "My rosy-cheeked winter apple. My wine-ripe redemption, my primitive prize."

"You wanna write about it or take care of me?" Allen said, looking over one shoulder.

Camel needed no more invitation. He placed his hands gently on each heavenly hip of his callipygian wife, and scooting forward, kissed each cheek a dozen times.

"Eat me, Camel," she said, her voice so breathy it was almost melancholy.

Camel did. ("It tastes like happy," he said.) And, when he stood and his pants made a ridiculous puddle around his ankles, and he entered her with his lengthy erection, they both hummed a song that they had been singing together since the dawn of time. It was their song. It was the song of the choirs of The Elementals, the song Adamandeve sang before knowledge condemned them. And Camel came inside her with long-lasting hot streams, hours of pale lava flow which they were both sure was the elixir needed. Afterward, naked as vapor, under their sheets and coverlet, they again sang names back and forth into the night air, names that led eventually to fantast, names that Adamandeve had inadvertently left out: Tangerine, Triamond, Phyrne, Abelard, Nomy, Suzanne, Noel, Sanjaya, Swilda, Hamlet, Grace, Pigeon, Dandie, Zoe, Hank, Delia, softly, softly, fading into whispers, and then noiselessness.

Back on Earth, in Hell

While Camel was out he bought his paramour a present he spotted in the window of a junk store in Cooper-Young: a pair of ancient, yellowed ivory dice, large as golf-balls, set in a small cardboard box, with its snake-eyes outward, an Edenic watchful pair. He wrote on a piece of colored paper, "We are par-a-dies," and placed that azure missive on top of the dice, placing the lid back on the box.

Camel wanted only to get home and show Allen his corny gift. Camel loved Corny.

However, Allen never saw the dice.

She was sitting at the kitchen table and her grass-green eyes were full and as red as drops of blood from a wounded heart.

"O Camel," she said.

Camel knelt beside her chair. He put his head in her lap, and his hair covered her knees like a comforter.

And they were quiet for a long time.

The diagnosis

Endometrial cancer. Endometrioid carcinoma. Cancer of the uterus. Spread too far. Gone on too long. Stronger than life, large as death.

Death.

The diagnosis is death.

Allen is going to die.

"This is why we couldn't get pregnant?" Camel whispered. He could only whisper. His voice was wee because the pain was vast.

"Only a coincidence, Dr. Worm says. Some funny coincidence, eh, Camel my love?"

Camel answered with tears. Uxorious Camel stroked Allen's stomach and lower abdomen. He told the demons there to depart. He told them to go back to whatever cesspool of hell had spawned them. His tears dropped, one, two, three, on Allen's stomach, a rainmaker's cure. Allen could not die, Camel said to himself. Though he knew he was foolish, a child-man. If Allen dies I die, too, he amended, which was not much better.

And after the rain of tears the petrichor was as sour as mash.

First you cry

Camel didn't teach for two weeks. Allen did not make art. They stayed in bed, ate small quick meals, toast and broths and cheese. They smoked dope and held each other and made love as if one or both of them might disintegrate in the process.

They turned the phone off. Some days they never turned the lights on. They turned the television on only to watch old movies, *Arsenic and Old Lace*, *The Letter* with Bette Davis, Chaplin, *Rules of the Game*, *The Apartment*, *The Seventh Seal* (they wept), *The Miracle of Morgan's Creek*, *My Man Godfrey*, *The Passion of Joan of Arc*. Sometimes Camel watched the castaways and sometimes the castaways made him feel frustrated and hopeless and outside the world in a bleak and terrifying manner and he had to return to Allen's bed and Allen's arms.

Eventually they re-entered the world, gradually, reluctantly.

They plugged the phone back in and no one called.

Camel talked to Ricky Koeppel, at the university, kind Ricky Koeppel, who assured him that his position would be waiting for him. Camel returned to work, after getting reassurances from his wife that she would be fine, that she was anxious to start making art again, that she could not think of any emergency situation that would involve her having to find him immediately.

"Go, go," she said. "Camel, my only love. I need space to expand, to take formlessness into my hands and remake it as form. I need Art, Love."

Schooling

O golden bodies of lasting fire.
—Mark Strand

When Camel returned to teaching his face looked as sad as midnight's awful treasure. His students grew restless in their seats. His pronouncements were gnomic and sometimes incoherent. Only when he read a poem aloud did the old teacher's voice come through. Only then was there a faint electric crepitation, like a fire that *almost* ignites.

Clam Tennen wore an expression as full of love as Camel's was of grief and fear. She looked like a Madonna, if a Madonna could wear miniskirts and lacy shirts and still be a Madonna. (Of course a Madonna could.) Every time Camel's gaze raked across hers it was like wind blowing wheat and wheat tried to caress the wind.

Leaving class one day Clam caught up with him as he trudged toward his car.

"Hey, hey, Camel," she called in her honeyed voice. "Teacher, stop."

Camel aversely turned. Clam's tender beauty looked like Mother Mary's. She slipped her hand under Camel's arm.

"You wanna get a beer or something?" she asked. Her face strained toward his. Her expression was nearly desperate. It said, you cannot refuse me; you cannot turn from my succor now.

"I can't," Camel said. He managed a smile as weak as a flicker. He put a hand to her young, downy cheek. It was downy.

"*Camel*," she said. It was a one-word supplication.

Camel shifted from one foot to another. Had he four feet Camel would have gone on shifting, circularly, time ticking.

He said, "Yes, Clam. Ok. Where do you students drink?"

"I hate the student hangout. Hey, you hungry? We could go down to Buntyn's for a meat and three."

"Hungry, no. I don't think I'm hungry."

"We could have coffee and pie. Great pies there. Whaddya say?"

Camel still hesitated. The sun ducked inside a neighboring cloud. "Yes, ok. Pie and coffee."

"Let's take my car."

Clam Tennen's old Vega had seen better days. One could see the road through the floorboard and the whole car smelled like an old saddle. They also had to move mounds of papers to clear the passenger's seat. Had Camel been noticing anything he would have wondered how a person, so meticulous in her personal appearance, could drive such a sty.

Going west on Southern they drove right past Buntyn's without slowing down. Camel looked up, literally up; he looked at the cold, blue sky. Where had the clouds gone? Someplace where clouds were needed.

"Ok if I run into my apartment first?" Clam asked out of the side of her mouth. "Just another block."

Clam Tennen's apartment, on the south side of Southern, was a college dorm's older sibling. It was almost as messy as her car and smelled of cat litter and cigarettes.

267

"Gimme a minute," she said, disappearing into a bedroom.

Camel sat on the couch. The 11-inch television was about 15 inches from the couch, on a TV tray. A brindled cat came from somewhere and quickly found Camel's lap. Camel stroked its fur and heard its purr as the grinding of the world's cogs someplace far away and Stygian. Black cogs.

"That's Pyewacket," Clam called from the bedroom.

Camel petted Pyewacket a long time. Time stretched and thinned and snapped back a few snaps before Camel moved anything but his hand in the cat's rich fur. The apartment was as still as a mausoleum. There were two magazines on the floor: a *New Yorker*, and a *Poetry* from 1946.

He rose and walked back toward the bedroom. He didn't care if the executioner awaited him there. The door was cracked open a few dreadful inches.

He stood and listened for a while.

"Camel?" came a voice from inside. "Are you by the door?"

Camel didn't move. He knew this play. He hated this play and its author.

Yet his fingers gently pushed the door open.

Clam Tennen was stretched out on the bed face down and facing away from him. She was without clothing and the afternoon sunshine, the color of peaches, poured over her skin, engilding her, its apricity like delectable torture. It was so beautiful Camel sat on the edge of the bed and let tears slide from his eyes. Clam Tennen did not move.

"Clam," Camel choked out. "Beautiful Clam Tennen. If you only knew."

Without turning her face to him, she said, "I do know, Camel. I know that you are sad and I know why. I couldn't think of another way to comfort you. In my clumsy way I wanted to show you that you are loved."

"Clam," Camel said again. And then he was still.

Some golden minutes went by. Camel looked at the aureate skin next to him. He had but to reach out his hand to touch it. It would be chrysotherapy: gold-therapy. A gold rush. But he knew if he did it would kill him. It would stop his old heart. Clam's thighs were lit with tiny blond hairs, wee white flames. Her ass was as round as a Super Moon, and as close. Her back was like a billowing, blonde ocean.

Clam did not know what to do next. She was about to speak when she felt Camel's weight shift ever so slightly.

Camel placed one warm palm on one of Clam's perfectly mounded cheeks. He lay it there as if it were a handkerchief to cover her inappropriate nakedness.

Clam sighed. "I've thought of this so often," she said.

Camel put his other hand on her other cheek. He kneaded them gently.

"Oh," Clam said. "Oh."

Now one hand traveled up her shapely back and one hand traveled downward, gently squeezing a thigh. It was as if Camel's indecision was taking him in two directions.

"Camel, keep touching me, please."

Camel let his hands drift over her back and ass, like a wind. It rustled her hairs. It lit the inferno between her young legs. So young, so healthy. So ready to canoodle.

Now Camel bent forward and put his mouth to one round cheek. It was cool to his lips and it offered him a moment of divine peace and beauty. He held his mouth there.

Clam Tennen spread her legs so that Camel could see how wet she had become.

"Would you like to fuck me, Camel, darling?" she asked, quietly.

Perhaps if she had not said 'darling' Camel would have lost his place in the world. He was not her darling. And, though he appreciated the gift she was offering and was sorely tempted, he removed his mouth from her fundament and rose, unfolding his body upward, and walked out of her apartment. He walked all the way back to his car in the university parking lot, under the upturned indigo bowl of the October sky.

The afternoon was never mentioned again and later that semester Clam Tennen pulled the highest grade in

Camel's class on The American Novel. She was never again a student of Camel's.

I just heard

Said Hondo Minimum from Berkeley.

Said Dianus Pocs.

Said her husband.

Said Rudder Amidships from San Francisco.

Said Stinging Nettles.

Said Harry Ford from Japan, where he was attending a book conference.

Said Ellie Masonry.

Said Three Hushpuppy Brown, weeping.

Said Remark Kramer.

Said his wife.

Said Gary Snyder from Sri Lanka.

Said Richard Brautigan from Japan.

Said Lahna Darling.

Said Leonard Cohen from Ottawa.

Said Ohem Jee from Arkansas.

Said Etheridge Knight from Indiana State Prison.

Said Pharaoh Moans.

Said Allen Ginsberg from Tangier.

Said everyone who called, everyone, everyone, everyone. Every fucking well-meaning goddamned loving beautiful worthless friend.

The adventure of Allen the brave

And so it came to pass that Allen, post-surgery, was put through the medical procedure which involves flooding one's system with poison in order to rid it of an alien force working on one's demise. Chemo and radiation. Chemotherapeutic agents. Ionizing radiation. CTX and RTX.

Camel sat next to her, holding her hand, while they both read books, and the drip did its murky, necromantic work. Camel was reading a galley of Richard Brautigan's newest novel, *Sombrero Fallout*, while Allen was working her way through the *Complete Poems of Emily Dickinson*. Sometimes they stopped to share a splendid boil of language, to share a kiss, a wink, a nod, a smile, a simile.

Allen's hair fell out. She wore her bald head as if it were a miter. No scarves, no floppy hats. When the stubble returned, grey-white like flecks of ash in plaster, Allen thought it was the prettiest her head had looked in ages.

Allen was reading Dickinson because she had asked Camel for a list of the essential books, the texts that she had to consume before she went to join the Great Poet in the sky.

Camel, with an odd admixture of pleasure and dread, made her a list. It took him two full evenings. Who to include, who to exclude? Read only the Masters and skip the joyful genre writers like Raymond Chandler and John Crowley? Read only the best books by the chosen authors and omit their second-tier creations, even if the second-tier creations often offered pleasures that the best books did not?

Allen could have gone the other way, Camel thought: "I want only to re-read my favorite books." Instead she wanted to absorb all the Great Books, preparing her mind—*for what?* Melding with the Mind Eternal? Camel did not ask. Did he even wonder? He wondered.

By the time it was done—midnight hours of agony—the list looked like a family tree. Every book had a qualifier and numerous alternatives, adjectives sprouting from each title like vegetatively propagating tuber eyes. It was five tightly typed pages, with colored arrows and charts and sidebars. It looked like a map of Camel's mind, for indeed it was a map of Camel's mind.

"Camel, darling," Allen said, from her couch where she was riding out some toxin-induced nausea, "The time you spent over this!"

"Let me explain it," Camel said, settling his large male frame next to her fetal feminine frame. "This at the bottom is the legend."

So, not only did Allen have this—*chart*—she had Camel's long-winded explanation, to which she was paying half of an attention.

"Thank you, sweet man," she said. "Are there any more saltines?"

The next day, when Allen awoke, she found, next to her iron skillet of scrambled eggs—Camel's remedy for nausea was lots of protein ("I learned it from midwives," he said) and some wicked weed of course (thanks to Jim Dickinson for sending over his best jingo boo)—a pile of books, the first ten on the list. A book cairn, a gift, a starting point, from her bibliotaph husband. At the top was the divine Ms. Dickinson.

The change in Allen

Finally, Allen finished her chemo and radiation. The results were inconclusive, according to Dr. Worm. "Miracles happen," he told her, offering only twilight's smile.

Rather than wait for divine intervention, Allen spoke to some friends knowledgeable in the world of the dark arts (aka alternative medicine): some wiccans, some accoucheuses, some diviners, some earth-women, some wizards, some conjurors, some magicmen, some curanderos, some shamans, some quacksalvers, some angakoks. Pimps, priests, popinjays, prophets, pedagogues. Psychiatrists, physicians, philosophers, psychopomps. Allen would not go gentle into that good night. She sought monkey hands, gris-gris and John the Conqueroo, apotropaic medicaments. She learned things and they fed her soul, already as strong as Ajax's red right hand.

She sought acupuncture to get rid of the 'roping' of her surgical scar and balance her chi; reiki and meditation (and crystals on the nightstand) to increase her healing energy, and a psychic medium to understand why she was visited by this disease when she didn't fit the profile. The psychic convinced Allen she could also, while questioning the divine unbalance, cleanse any psychic wounds from her past.

Camel stood by in admiration and hopeful vacancy. He lived in hope. He dined on the food that gods had divined could make man believe in an immortality that was just beyond his grasp, just around the corner, just the other side of the ethereal wall that separated *this* from *the other*.

When Allen was not studying how to stay in the world she was making love, reading, sculpting or watching movies. She had contacted Edwin Howard, the movie reviewer at *The Press-Scimitar*, Memphis' afternoon newspaper, and he had provided her with a list of the best 100 films of all time, a list tidier than Camel's, but with less flamboyance. It was apparent that Allen intended to fill every *living* moment with art. She was wringing the sponge of life for its honey.

The only thing she would watch besides movies (*films*, she kept insisting—isn't Bergman *delicious?* she asked doting Camel) was *Jeopardy* and, during the commercials in *Jeopardy*, she worked crossword puzzles, and not just any crossword puzzles, but the New York Times Sunday puzzles. Aradia and Dianus sent over collections of crosswords by the boxful.

"Allen, baby, you can have some down time, you know," Camel said, gently.

"No time for down time, Lover," she would answer.

"There will always be time for us, Allen. Our love is like an aeonian Get Out of Jail card."

"I know, Husband," Allen said, setting down, with reverence, her copy of Iris Murdoch's *The Philosopher's Pupil.* "Fuck me now, please."

And Camel did. During sex Allen released her coiled spring. She relaxed her regimen and disappeared into the physical bond, which, for the Eroses, was like some kind of wholesome philter. They fucked until sweat ran down their bodies, until all fluids flowed like the 165 major rivers.

One afternoon, Camel came back from class, downcast and without faith. He was sinking.

As he unlocked the front door he could hear his wife singing. The notes were coming from her studio. Allen often sang as she sculpted. Her favorites were early Beatles and

Herman's Hermits. Sometimes Janis, though Janis could make her sad. Sometimes The Monkees.

Today it was this: "I'm not scared of dying and I don't really care. If it's peace you find in dying…"

Camel was overcome. He stood dead in his tracks. His heart opened like a sore. He returned to the car, got in, rolled up all the windows and wept. His sobs shook the car. His fishwife neighbor, Melba Tornado, stood in her yard, arms crossed over her chest, and openly stared. Her visage said, "Goddamn hippie crazies." Camel met her Baba Yaga gaze. He slowly raised his hand, wiped a tear from his cheek, smiled and gave her the dirty bird salute.

A party

At the end of the semester there was a party thrown. Who threw it? Hard to say but caught up in it were the usual suspects: Ricky Koeppel and Gordon Osing, from the department; Etheridge Knight, paroled; Pharaoh Moans, Stinging Nettles, Lahna Darling, Buddy Gardner, musicians; Percy Fledge and Clam Tennen and Ellie Masonry, students; Sarah and Vera Money, twins; Axel and Maya Eros, parents; Three Hushpuppy Brown, stoned as an owl; Peter Coyote, in town to star in the Memphis-made movie version of Mezz Mezzrow's *Really the Blues*, also starring Jane Fonda, Mick

Jagger, Lee Remick and a young homeboy named Chris Ellis; Aradia and Dianus Pocs, booksellers; Aba Herdsettler, nautch *moderne* and ecdysiast, various scene-makers and scene-crashers, selenographers, mycophagists, celebrants, magi, presbyters, bonzes, gyrovagues, three dogs, a ferret, a clown, and more poets, physicians, farmers and magicians. And lastly a hogshead of real fire.

The party was held in an area of Shelby Forest, to the north of Memphis, which seemed ancient and hag-ridden, dark and dreamy, deep (in myriad ways) and Lucullan. Some denizens of the area, some who gathered at the General Store for soda pop and fried bologna sandwiches, called the area The Holy Hollow, and they meant, *Stay Away*. Ancient spirits mixed with mixed spirits: rum, crockpot Kahlua, cracked-pepper Stoli, ptisans, mead, sake, various ciders, baijiu, Boone's Farm, Tusker and Harp, digestifs and aperitifs, stump water and hellbroth.

There was grass from sixteen different countries, not to mention Mississippi, pills and acid, uppers, downers and stabilizers, mushrooms magical and secular, homemade chemicals and store-bought medicaments.

There was food delivered by 16 vans: Mexican, Moroccan, Indian, Native American, Italian, Norwegian, German, Canadian (muktuk, and peameal bacon, food of the effing gods), French, Ethiopian, Irish, Louisianaian. Pizza pies, huckleberry pies, pies squared and pies triangulated. Edible nuts and berries, hen-of-the-woods.

Camel and Allen stood off to one side, with Camel's parents. The Eroses were sipping white wine and observing, as if the party had coagulated so they would have a tableau for their private viewing and musing. Camel kept a hand gently on his wife's empyrean hip, a hand not of ownership but of equilibrium. Allen was smiling her kitty-cat smile while in her head industriously naming the capitals of all 50 states, the names of all the popes, Shakespeare's plays in order, The Books of the Christian Bible backwards, all seven dwarfs, all seven continents, all seven Chicago defendants, all Seven Wonders of the World, and the ingredients for apple pan dowdy.

The makeshift band (some wag dubbed them Buddy and the Holy Hollow Hollys) was cooking some special Memphis homebrew. They sounded like Stax on acid. They sounded like the Dead but more alive and more grateful. They sounded like thunder and lightning and rain, which when it starts it's all the same, through a hash-filled drainpipe. And, when the Eros Elders joined, they sounded like Mingus Mellow Fantastic. For the final 18-musician, 55-minute version of "Astral Weeks/Your Auntie Grizelda," Clark Terry sat in on flugelhorn.

Buddy, who lately had fallen under the sway of singer/songwriter California, looked young again, re-energized by playing the music that birthed him. (A week later he would be dead of the rock and roll disease: suicide by booze and pills.)

"It's beautiful out here," Allen said. "The woods seem full of spectral figures."

"Will-o-the-wisps," Camel said, dreamily. He instinctually pulled Allen closer to him and further from the haunted woodland.

"Camel, baby, I've been thinking. Might we adopt a child?"

Camel smiled down at his bride. "Is that what you would like, my Allen?"

"I think so. I think we'd make dynamite parents, for one thing."

"You would."

"No, Camel, both of us. We're good together. We'd be good for a kid. He or she would feel it in their very marrow, our vibe, our limitless love."

"You're a wise woman, Wife. Let's pursue that. I don't know where to begin."

"I'll look into it. I bet Sarah knows."

"Or Vera knows," Camel iterated.

"This one's for Camel," Buddy roared from the makeshift stage set up for the makeshift band. And they launched into David Bowie's "Kooks." Camel's mother took the vocals and the song drifted upward, through the crepuscule, through the sky-hung branches, through the Earthbound clouds, through the Magellanic Clouds, through the dust of things dead and living, and into the asterisms like a bolide, like some longing galactic sibling looking for love, for love, for love.

Miracles and the elasticity of time

My time has been passed viciously and agreeably; at thirty-one so few years months days hours or minutes remain that Carpe Diem is not enough. I have been obliged to crop even the seconds — for who can trust to tomorrow?"
—*Lord Byron*

Time passed. Incomplete at first but eventually yardage was gained.

Dr. Worm and the entire cancer ward at St. Dymphna Hospital declared Allen a miracle. During her latest scan no cancer was detected. She had beaten the beast.

Dr. Worm, while joyous, warned Allen about cancer's surprise returns. "Like zombies the little bastards don't take death seriously. But, hope, Hope, Allen!"

"Like surprise lilies," Allen told Camel. "Sproing! One morning I wake up with cancer again when yesterday it was only death waiting inside the darkest soil."

"No surprise lily cancer in my house," Camel said. He kissed his wife's bristly head.

"There is such a thing as relief," Allen said, smiling under the kiss.

"Like the relief after you've sat through Ravi Shankar and George Harrison is about to play."

Time returned, its vagueness, its elasticity, its erratic speeds. Their lives resumed. Camel woke at 5 every morning so he could write. His classes were as onerous as ever but he was happy to not have to deal with beautiful, young, blond co-eds in short skirts. Not that he didn't have any in his classes but, this time around, there were no breaches of the student/teacher relationship. And, in his writing class, there was a student—Sylver Tuck—who he thought might be the best writer to come out of Memphis since Steve Stern. (Or Camel Eros.) Sylver Tuck was the real deal, influenced by the beats, like they all were, but already heading off on his own astonishing tangents.

"He writes a lot like Corso, if Corse were a young, black Memphian. Or a prose writer. He's really something. Here, lemme read this to you," Camel said.

He read the piece to Allen.

"It's grand," she said. "You're a generous soul, my husband."

"I'm not being generous."

"I mean, you find the diamonds, you acc—en—tu—ate the positive."

"Well, shore," Camel drawled like a Brautigan cowboy. "It's what I do, ma'am. I'm larruping good at it."

Also, in Camel's class was a young writer named Neill Rhymer, so shy he was almost invisible, but gifted, perhaps, in an imitative way, which can, Camel knew, lead, eventually, to an honest, personal voice.

Allen was still trying to fill every moment with bliss. It seemed less desperate, perhaps only to Camel, who began to settle down himself, to relax, to forget death's recent invitation to His Ugly Ball, the Last of the Season.

One morning Camel found Allen in the kitchen cutting up sweet potatoes for pancakes. He entered the room, his robe dragging at his feet like a slug's trail, his sleepy head full of hum. He heard Allen say, "Sorry, little buddy."

"Oh good morning, beautiful husband," Allen greeted him.

"Who you talking to?" Camel said as if his mouth were full of tawies.

"I only have one husband, last time I checked," Allen said, pursing her pretty lips for a good morning kiss, bad bed-breath and all.

Camel kissed her a good one.

"You said, 'sorry, little buddy'," Camel said, fetching himself a mug for coffee.

"Oh, haha," Allen said. She continued to cut the sweet potatoes.

"Allen."

"It was a little spider. He walked across the cutting board and I almost took one of his legs off." She looked up and her cat's smile bunched her flecked cheeks in a way that always broke Camel's heart. She was so pretty, his Allen.

"I see," Camel said.

He had noticed this lately, this reverence for everything living, even the creepy crawlies, the bugs, the lowest life. She had thrown out all traps, mouse, rat, roach. Another time she spent ten minutes trying to get a moth to land on her hand so she could usher it outside. This new saintly Allen made him smile.

How love lives forever: all the fluctuations are new adventures.

She also had this thing

She also had this thing about running out of stuff. Toilet paper, cashews, dark chocolate, wine, grass, coffee filters, ice tea, breath. If the ice tea pitcher got low she would start boiling water to make another pitcherful.

"We need a second pitcher," she told Camel, seriously. "If this one gets down to the bottom, especially the bottom with *dregs*, we won't have more ready."

And she bought toilet paper, paper towels, typewriter paper, by the reams. They always had a 24-pack of, what the Brits call bumf, stowed in the coat closet. Camel stumbled upon it and smiled.

"It's the finitude of things that eats at her," Camel told Peter Coyote when Peter called once from France where he was filming the life of Jerry Lewis.

"Of course," Peter said. "The finitude of *us*. Of humans."

"Yes," Camel said and his head went sideways into a reverie.

"You there, Buddy?"

"Yes, Pete, sorry. Yes. Jerry Lewis."

"Right. This film is going to suck. Just so you know."

'You're not playing—"

"Thank God, no," Peter said. "I'm Dean Martin."

Allen in the studio

Her new work was indescribable. It was unlike anything else she'd ever done. Possibly because coming close to death, at least that's how she felt, deepened her. Possibly because she felt free now to do anything she wanted. There were no strictures, no expectations. She could add colors, surfaces, angles, *life*, that, previously she had dismissed for a variety of reasons, weak or strong. She adjoined pepper, coffee grounds, apricot preserves, Dr. Bronner's soap, Dr. Bronner's soap bottles, hairpins and safety pins, jumping beans and garbanzo beans, ears of corn and ears of dolls. Little plastic army men. Scraps of paper with mere phrases of Camel's poems. It was all grist for her bright angelic mills.

"What is this new piece?" Camel asked. It was a thing with wires and masking tape forming what appeared to be alien legs, with a base made of ceramic painted with a Superman S. A tiny plastic arm reached out toward the light, as if, inside, a wee soul longed to be free.

"Mm," Allen said, looking over. "Not finished yet."

"Uh huh."

"The spider gave me this one."

Camel smiled at his wife. His heart filled.

"The spider told me the secret that brought that into being."

"I understand."

"Mm, I know you do, husband. Are you late for class?"

"Shit," Camel said. "I thought it was Saturday. I already put on my Saturday stain shirt. Shit."

And out he went, shirttails flying, to read Auden to restless adolescents who wanted to talk about comic books and television shows.

Allen turned back to her work. She picked up the spider. On the end of each tentacular leg she added one tiny drop of blood, like a little glimmer of sperm on the head of a cock. She smiled the secret smile that is vouchsafed artists when they believe something is just right.

"Just so," she said to her secret friend. "So, just."

Then she went to the kitchen and made a toasted cheese sandwich. While there she saw her calendar lying open. She had an appointment with Dr. Worm for the following day. She smiled again. "Tomorrow is such a long time," she told her friend. "If today were not a crooked highway."

Dr. Worm, the Conqueror Worm

"How?" Allen asked.

"Allen, it's not quite clear how. It's rarely clear. Do you need a how?"

"No, I guess not," Allen said.

"We can talk about what to do next. This does not have to be devastating news. Would you want to travel to a clinic in another city? There are hopeful new procedures when the cancer has reached this stage."

"How hopeful. How many years would they add? How many *days*?"

"You want statistics?"

"I want to live."

Dr. Worm was silent. He held Allen's hand and was absentmindedly turning her wedding ring.

"What happened to Tricky Dick's war on cancer. Not enough troops?" Allen asked, with a deadly smirk.

Dr. Worm wormed around in his seat. His smile was sweating.

"How many days?"

"I can check and get back to you."

"Ok. Any idea?"

"Honestly, not many yet. This is new science. We are hopeful."

"Uh huh."

"Do you want me to check?"

"On the amount of time? No. On the clinic? No."

"Ok." He let go of her hand and it stayed in the air between them as if it were floating of its own accord.

Camel and Allen dig in

It was a return to bunker mentality. Camel canceled his classes. Allen stopped sculpting. She stopped saving bugs. She stopped reading and watching movies. They took a short trip to the Mississippi Delta to visit the graves of bluesmen, to stand at the crossroads and ask the devil if his bargains were any more hopeful than cancer doctors' prescriptions.

Old Scratch did not show. He didn't dare.

"Jazz and blues and folk, poetry and jazz; Voice and music, music and no music;
Silence and then voice," Camel scat-sang as they drove.

"More please," Allen said beside him, her hair floating up around her Botticelli face and trying to fly out the passenger-side window.

They stayed in a bed-and-breakfast outside Yazoo City, which was also a peafowl-infested lily farm, or a lily-infested peafowl farm.

They made love, quietly, in their four-poster bed with the white, lacy curtains, so as not to shock the elderly couple who ran the place.

"Does this hurt?" Camel asked as he entered Allen from behind, lying side by side on the coverlet.

"No, my love," Allen said. "Touch my clit."

Camel did and was rewarded with a low moaning orgasm, Allen's song sweet though muted. Camel held himself snug up against her.

After a moment she said, "Nothing hurts right now. You don't have to be so gentle. The no-pain thing is part of the frustration. I feel fine." She said all this quietly, in a whispery dreamstate.

"My Allen," Camel said.

"Come, darling. Let's make you come. I want to feel it inside me."

Camel began to move slowly.

"Camel, do it. Come on. Hit me harder."

So he did. He gave her a slam-bang orgasm of his own. The old bed seemed about to crack like the ship after the albatross showed up. But it held and soon they were asleep.

Before breakfast they opened the front door, planning a short walk. They were greeted by a solid white peacock who opened his shimmering tail seemingly just for their pleasure. It was a benediction when they needed a prayer. It was a burst of the world's tired old beauty, as white as the yarn from the angels' spinning jenny, as white as blindness, as white as a single moment, frozen.

More quiet conversation

After a morning of plying young minds with the mind-altering substance known as Twentieth Century Poetry, Camel returned to his casa and it was as still as....a tomb. Camel's mind went *there*. His heart beat fast.

"ALLEN!" he cried, somewhat louder than he meant to. There was no echo and no returning salutation.

Camel began to jog through his house.

"Allen, Allen, Allen," he ululated.

Into the studio he ran, did a 180 and was exiting when he caught a glimpse of his wife in the far corner of the room, half-hidden by her drafting table, which, as per usual, was a wild disarray of drawings, pictures cut from periodicals, writing, drawing and carving implements. She looked like a skylarking child in her 'fort.' She was half-turned away, facing a corner of the room. She was dressed in white and, against the white wall, underneath a white drop cloth, his bride looked like an illustration by Yoko Ono. She looked see-through.

And she was whispering.

Camel approached slowly. His sneakered feet made no noise until he kicked a bucket of plaster of paris.

"Cripes!" he said.

Allen turned leisurely toward him.

"Husband," she said. "I didn't hear you come in. Did you hurt yourself?"

"What are you doing?" Camel said, hopping on one foot till he collapsed on a beanbag chair. "Apologizing to bugs again?"

"No, sweet husband. I'm talking to Challa."

"Challa," Camel said. He did not immediately grok.

"Here," Allen said, tilting her head toward the empty corner.

"Challa," Camel said again and it came back to him. Challa, the ghost.

"She's all in white, just like me," Allen said, dreamily. "We'll be through in a flash."

Camel smiled and nodded. He gave them their privacy.

In the living room Camel stretched out on the couch and was looking at the newest issue of *Poetry* magazine, in which he and his pal Ginsberg both had poems. Ten minutes later Allen emerged.

"Hello, Camel. Good day at school?"

"About the same," Camel said. "I'm thinking of springing Allen on them."

"Me?"

"Baby."

"Oh, Ginsberg. You mean reading him or actually bringing him?"

"Bringing him. He'd come, I'm sure. I asked and they want Robert Bly instead."

"Bly is lovely."

"Yes. He is, a lovely man."

"What do you want to do for dinner? Know what I really want?"

"Sweet potato pancakes."

"Camel, one of the reasons I love you is your clairvoyance."

"Do you wanna talk about Challa?"

"Sure. She's so sweet. She told me I looked like virgin snow."

"What does that mean?"

"You should know, husband. You're the poet. She's speaking figuratively, I imagine."

"Ok. Do you talk to her often?"

"Oh. No. Lately though, it seems like every time I turn around she's there. She loves my studio."

"You gonna sculpt her?"

"She asked me not to."

"Shy, I guess."

"Perhaps."

"Ok, Allen. Ok, Grimalkin."

"So how about it?"

"What?"

"Sweet potato pancakes."

"Anything you want, Love."

The final exam

"Allen, you look beautiful," Dr. Worm said, entering with a folder in his hand.

"Bullshit artist," Allen said. "I look like death. Literally."

"We don't know what death looks like," the doctor said, tenderly.

"Right. So, this is, as they say, it, right? My final exam? I flunked out."

The good doctor frowned and looked at his shoes. He sat and scooted his chair around to sit next to Allen.

"Is Camel here?"

"I made him stay home."

"I see."

"No change is good change?"

"In this case change is bad. I'm afraid it's much more aggressive than we thought."

"Oh." It was a wee oh, small as the tail-end of naught.

"Allen, we can make you as comfortable as can be. Good painkillers. No reason you can't see this through at home with your beautiful Camel by your side."

"Uh huh. Ok. That's it then."

"I wish I had a better plan."

"You're lovely, Doc. You've been extremely kind to me. Everyone here is. Last station, right? Everyone is nice at the last station because we're all going home."

"Yes."

Allen kissed Dr. Worm softly on the mouth.

"Thank you," she said.

Dr. Worm began to snivel.

"He said, I'd get good drugs," Allen told Camel that afternoon.

Camel spoke through a veil of tears.

"And we can supplement those. I'll get some kickass windowpane. You can go out on a cloud of pudding with Blake and Whitman pulling the tumbril. And Jimi and Janis singing "Busted flat in Baton Rouge….""

"I love that song!" Allen said and she burst into tears, also, and for the first time that day.

Allen leaving

Most days Allen was granted a few pain-free hours to work in her studio. Her late work is fiery and confounding and arresting and full of pain and sunshine, a potent poteen. Some days she spent on the couch rather than in the marriage bed. The couch was long and plush and had pillows that Allen had made herself out of old t-shirts stuffed with Delta cotton. Her favorite was a tie-dye with its words still visible: "Beauty will be convulsive, or it will not be."

(Andre Breton)

Camel reluctantly kept teaching. He asked Camel for a note that dismissed him from school—"Pin it on my sweater and sign it, with love, Camel's Allen"—but Allen wouldn't hear of it.

"I know your fear is that one day you will come home and I will be gone and we will miss the final parting but I will wait for you, Love, the way you have waited for me, the way we have waited for each other lo these many years."

So Camel taught.

Some say his lessons grew a dark tail and that, often, students were left with cryptic pronouncements when they asked for clarification. This may be rumor, written after the fact. Or it might be true. Our Camel had a shadow side, of course, and sometimes his old black dog, depression, which he had inherited from his mother, kept close company. Some nights, as Allen lay sleeping beside him—for she still slept mostly in the big bed—Camel would stay awake and watch. He thought, perhaps, that when The Angel of Death came, he could wrestle with it like in his friend Steve Stern's story, or like with Ole Dan Webster. In the white hours of two and three a.m., he was convinced he would win that fight, armed, as he was, with determination and whimsy. Whimsy is a powerful armament, Brautigan taught him. Thus, many days, he taught, bleary from lack of sleep, jacked up on coffee and bennies.

Sometimes his readings went something like this: "Peoplegettingdivorced/ridingaroundwiththeirclothesinthecar andwonderingwhathappenedtoeveryoneandeverythingincludi ngtheirotherpairofshoes…."

One night, after too many nights of scant sleep, Camel believed that Barghest, the goblin dog who brings Death, had entered his sleeping chambers, growling and slobbering, its ugly maw opened to reveal jagged teeth and small, burning demons, who danced on its terrible tongue. Allen was awakened by Camel pirouetting about the room with a hoe in his hand, swinging it wildly.

"Camel, Camel," she implored. "What are you doing?"

"I've got the bitch on the run," he said, eyes wild as Ian Anderson's.

"Camel, why do you have a hoe?"

Camel looked at the implement in question. "I won't have a gun in our home," he said, seriously.

"Put the hoe down," Allen said.

There was a tense moment.

Then they both collapsed with childish laughter. "Hoedown!" Camel kept saying. "Having a hoedown with demons!"

After a while he calmed and eventually fell asleep in his wife's arms, as if he were the ill one, as if he were failing.

And right before he fell asleep, he murmured, "I did get rid of the bitch."

Defeated by simpler and simpler tasks

This is what it came down to.

When it became difficult to stand in the studio for a long time she tried working from a rolling chair. When it became difficult to stand in the kitchen and slice vegetables she would leave them on the counter and take to the couch, pile a dozen quilts upon her gravely thin body because their rackety-packety house was poorly insulated and winter was a cumin in, dose herself with some Owsley and dream. Camel would come home to the aroma of liquefying vegetables and he would make room for himself on the couch, tunnel under the heavily-quilted Hogan, and hold his wife cheek-to-cheek.

Camel tried to create a salubrious air in their living space, real and cosmic. He brought in rose petal preserves, red clover, dandelion tea, fresh rosemary leaves, anise, ashwagandha and burdock root. He bought a Himalayan salt lamp. He played Erik Satie and Philip Glass and Brian Eno and Gimmer Nicholson. And *The White Album*. He dressed nicely. He painted suns on the walls. He wanted to surround Allen with beauty, healing beauty. He read his own poems over and over, like the best prayers.

Yet Allen's lovely, lithe, small-breasted, wide hipped, callipygian body began to fold forward, her spine, where the poison had seeped, seemingly as malleable as her sacred clay. "I am becoming a question mark," she said. "Fitting, what? Since I am the final question."

Camel laughed despite his grief. "Or the final answer," he chided. His wife would be funny in the shadow world. Good luck to all in the afterlife theater: Allen Eros was coming, armed with jokes and an all-seeing gaze and a flaming heart, never extinguished, never to be extinguished.

One afternoon Camel found her still in bed, books scattered around the counterpane like distaff clothing.

"Listen to this, my Camel. She reads: "I like the prince who was reading a book when the executioner touched him on the shoulder telling him that it was time, and he, arising, laid a paper-cutter between the pages to keep his place and closed the book."

"What is that, Allendear?"

"Djuna Barnes."

"Djuna," Camel said.

The adventure of dying

"Camel," Allen said into the phone. "I'm no longer busy being born."

"Wha—" Camel got out, then dropped the phone in his office in Patterson Hall and was in the car and on the way home before Allen could say more.

He hit the curb, bounced up into Melba Tornado's lawn and across her flower beds, and abandoned the car, still running. His key hit the lock fourteen times before it found its center and opened the door.

"Hello, Love," Allen said, from her couch. She was surrounded by Camel's collection of *Mad Magazines*. "You know I've never read these before. They're really funny. Look at this. 'Hack, Hack, Sweet Hasbeen.' Isn't that hilarious?"

"Allen, Allen, what is it? What's happened?"

"Oh, it's time is all," Allen said. Her skinny kitty face, freckled with teenish pimples (Camel loved every little ruby head) was still beautiful though pain had carved there with its dreadful scalpel. She *knew*, as if death were the child they had been seeking, and her earthly waters had just broken. The child would be Death, without siblings.

"How—how?" Camel got out. "Are you tripping now, my love?"

"No I stopped doing that. It made understanding difficult."

"Understanding," Camel echoed like an echo.

"Oh and Camel?"

"Yes, my love."

"I've never told you this, damn me. I love it when you pull your mustache."

A knot formed in Camel's throat. He smiled Merlin's smile and gave his mustache a tug.

"Camel, will you marry again? I can't believe I waited till now to ask you. There will be many suitors. How about Sarah? She adores you, you know? Just, well, don't marry that student, that Clam woman. She's, I don't know. She's not worthy I think."

"Clam," Camel echoed like an echo.

"Oh, you know, sweetheart. You marry who you want. Your heart is a great compass, my love."

"Allen, Allen, I don't want anyone. I don't want anyone but you. For all time."

"Someday, Baby. Someday, there will come a new love into your life. She may surprise you. She may not be what you had anticipated at all. She may be the anti-Allen, my opposite. She may be small and round and as young as ripe corn."

"Ok, Allen," Camel said, holding his wife's slim hand, its flesh stretched over naked bone, and letting the tears tumble down.

"Don't cry, my love," Allen said. Her voice, which had grown husky over the past few weeks, was now clear as the last bell. "There are pastures of plenty."

"Yes, my love."

"There are streams of milk and honey."

"Yes, my love."

"You know, that might not be true. I meant to ask Challa. She was here today, briefly. She told me to kiss you on the forehead and that that kiss would stay there forever. She's a very wise child, Camel."

"Yes, my love." Camel was looking into Allen's lime eyes, wide as dawn.

"Come here, bend close."

Camel bent over and Allen placed her mouth against Camel's forehead. She held her lips there for hours, days, years, millennium. And when they unpuckered she was gone.

It was December 8, 1980

"Oh chosen love, oh frozen love
Oh tangle of matter and ghost
Oh darling of angels, demons and saints
And the whole broken-hearted host,
gentle this soul, gentle this soul."
— Leonard Cohen

With the help of Sarah Money, Camel took care of the necessary things. There was to be a scattering of the ashes. There was to be a wake. Sarah offered her home but Camel wanted it in theirs, in the spaces Allen was familiar with in case she wanted to attend.

"Of course," Sarah said.

Also feeding Camel's black dog, at this time in the history of the world, was the news that the Republican Party had run his old nemesis Ronald Reagan for the Presidency of the United States and the chucklehead had won. Camel said, sadly, "He's a Muppet. And, instead of kind-hearted Jim Henson making him appear a viable living thing, it's the military-industrial complex pulling the strings." He found the world off-axis, an agley place of no hope, no light, no depth, and of no Allen.

Though the dispiriting presidential news had leaked through, Camel himself was not in the world as such. He did nothing. He neither read nor wrote nor watched TV nor read the paper. So it was in total bleary ignorance that he received a phone call from Yoko Ono.

"Hello, Camel, it's Yoko," she said. And then, "Ono." And then, "Lennon." In case Camel knew another Yoko.

"Hello, Yoko," Camel said. His voice was uninflected. "You're kind to call." A phrase he had said too many times so that now it was as threadbare as his favorite jokes.

"There are no coincidences," Yoko said.

Camel thought this over.

"We are all water," she added.

Camel thought this over, also.

"Camel, they're gone but they're not. You know what John would say?"

"What would John say, Yoko?"

"*Yes.*"

Camel waited. Then he realized that that was what John would say.

"Yes," Camel said.

"That's right, Camel. That's right. Shine on."

And she hung up.

When he recounted this call to Richard Brautigan at the wake, Richard said, "Odd that. Them dying on the same day. It was like being hit by Ali and then by Frazier."

"Right," Camel said. Then, "Wait. What?"

"John and Allen died on the same day."

"John's dead?" Camel asked. "Oh no," he said. And he dropped from a standing position to a sitting position, his ass hitting the floor with a dull reverb.

Richard, startled by the fall, let out a small shriek, and then lifted Camel under his arms.

"Hang in there, Buddy. They're on the next bardo."

"Yes," Camel said, shaking his shaggy head. "That's what I want to say. Yes."

The adventure of the wake

"Death is just where your suit falls off and now you're in your other suit. It's all right. Don't worry."
—*George Harrison*

Camel awakened for the wake.

That is, he came back into himself, his Camelness prevailed.

He sent out invitations. He called the wake The Magical Mystery Tour because he said the Tour had taken Allen away. The invitations went far and wide. Then they went near and narrow. They went hither for a while and then, briefly, before changing colors and fonts, they went yon. Scroll up through this story, now nearing its denouement, and find all the names (usually Proper Nouns, capitalized, to signify a living, or in-between, or deceased, Human Being) All the characters in this passion play were invited and they all came. No one begged off. Love for Camel and Allen was the main reason they came. But, let's be honest, some came to gawk at Camel's famous friends. Camel had famous friends. Some people like to stand next to a movie star, with a highball in their citizen hands, and bask in the radiance of a big screen tan.

No, Yoko did not come. But she sent a white box and inside the white box was an acorn (to plant in the yard with a pinch of Allen), a grapefruit, and a hand-done drawing of John's of a cloud and an angel with a kite for a head and on the kite was penned: "It's getting hard to be someone but it all works out."

Leonard Cohen came, dressed like a hipster banker, handsome as Dustin Hoffman. "I found Memphis," he said delicately to Camel. "My condolences to your loss in the war. You have my heart which I will hope you can use to heal the parts still healable." His mansuetude, gentlemanly voice stirred Camel's interior soup.

At Camel's house, during that festive, slipknot time between Thanksgiving and Christmas, there was delivered and donated foods from many lands. Jim Dickinson sent over a freezer he had down at the ranch to hold all the excess victuals which arrived seemingly like manna. There were turkeys, doves, ducks. There was beef, pork, venison, buffalo. Yams, turnips, carrots. Pickles dill, sweet and troubling. Strawberries, huckleberries, gooseberries, blue, black and red berries. Cardoons with marrow. Allspice seared moulard breast. Tennessee foie gras. Pot brownies and Rice-Krispie squares. Pot s'mores. Raviolo, Brussel sprouts and lamb belly. Boudin, falafel, lobster knuckle sandwiches. Salmon croquet, neckbones, okra boiled fried or pickles. Pickled beets, smothered cabbage. Ham hocks, hog maw, chicken fried steak, steak fried chicken, cold cuts, hot cuts, tepid cuts.

"Only God can make a cucumber, but only man can make a good pickle," Camel said.

And then came the ethanol-delivery fluids: Beer, ale, mead, wine (Richard brought rice wine which he declared the potable of the eastern gods), perry cider, gin, whisky, rum, tepache, soju, tequila, vodka, kvass, corn beer, brandy, applejack, slivovitz and moonshine.

It was a feast, a luau, a potlach.

Places to stay were scarce by the time the West Coast contingent began to arrive. There were even a couple couples bunking down at The Bookstore in the Pines. Aradia and Dianus had offered their space, as a bookish bivouac. Appropriately, Remark and Eedy slept there, along with Hondo Minimum and his new mate, Polly Cosinol, who, it was said, was Grace Slick's cousin and an even better singer than Grace, except that she had crippling stage fright. She arrived robed in a dress made of saran wrap and there was an appreciative crowd near her at all times. (On their way home from this wake, it was learned the next morning, Hondo and Polly were killed by a hopped-up ape wearing an NRA t-shirt. "Fucking hippies," he said. "I thought they were gonna scalp me." His death, you may recall, had been foretold.)

Camel was introduced to a man named Mr. Hughes by Ginsberg. Camel swore it was Dylan but, even later, Ginsberg denied it.

Ricky Koeppel and his wife came. Ricky gave Camel a small Mosher Press volume by Shelley, called *A Defence of Poetry*. Ricky nodded at Camel's moistened eyes and his grateful smile. His wife was dressed like a forest sprite and was as pretty as Audrey Hepburn in *Green Mansions*.

Billy Ass, the filmmaker originally from Indianola, Mississippi, you may remember, brought a small film crew. He had an idea for a documentary about the soul's journey from this plane to the next. He wanted to call it *Allen, Plane and Symbol*.

Early on Camel sat in a bentwood rocker in the living room and let the festivities churn around him. His life seemed arrayed like an enveloping aura, a throng that helped define him. He would live on after Allen but would he ever be that happy again?

Richard Brautigan sat to one side of Camel, both men pulling on their mustaches, both mothing out. Peter Coyote came in and dragged a wingback chair up next to Camel's, placed a consoling hand on his forearm, and, with those eyes that shine like chrysotile and that plummy voice which made women drop their linen without even seeking his words' meaning, he asked Camel how he was.

"Ok, Pete. Really. I'll be fine. It's just—well, you know, *sad.*"

"Sure, sure," Pete said. He joined Richard and Camel in silent contemplation. Then he spoke again. "You take this," he said. And from his hand he released a check for a considerable amount of money.

Camel looked at it and then into Pete's eyes. "I can't take this."

"Nonsense," Pete said. "I just wrapped a Walter Hill movie and I'm particularly flush."

"What for though?"

"What for? Anything, Camel. Anything. Funeral, wake, a little trip away from things after this is all over."

Camel decided to take the money. It meant a lot to his generous friend. Camel kissed him on the mouth.

Grace Slick came in on a cloud. She knelt before Camel and whispered, "When it's time I will bed you. When it's time."

Similar gifts and provocations came from many women and some men, including Cindy Ingaq, Stinging Nettles, Eileen Goff, Myriad Bling, Lahna Darling, Phyl O'Kalia, from the library, both the Pocs, Ginsberg, Corso and the ghost of Janis Joplin, who mostly sat in the corner next to Challa, trying to teach the young spirit the vocal calisthenics of "Mercedes Benz."

Bandy Lob from way back, from Trezevant HIGH, came. Camel hadn't seen him since the day, and Bandy had to re-introduce himself. He had shaved his head and was wearing a long saffron robe. He had given up music and his later job at Bombay Bicycle Club, to become a Hare Krishna. He handed Camel some Tulsi Japa Chanting Beads and said, faintly, "Carry om."

The band consisted of 86 musicians of varying skills and souls, old and young, rock and jazz, sousaphones and saxes and triangles and at least one washboard (thank you, Jimmy, who also named the musical conglom, Faux Bias). They played "All Along the Watchtower," and "You Can't Always Get What you Want" and "I Fought the Law and the

Law Won," and "Buttermilk Skies," and "Wooly Bully." They sang, "Memphis," "Julia," and "It Came out of the Sky," which segued into "Flying Saucer Rock and Roll." Melanie sang Allen's favorite song, "Beautiful People," and Camel felt a soft itch in the area of his third eye, where Allen's lips had left their deathless idolum. They ended the night with a 93 minute epicedium they called, "Allen and John, Their Sin-Eaters Looking for their Mittens in the Snow." Though the lyrics were adlibbed everyone seemed to know them ahead of time. The lead singers on this last epic rotated: Grace took a verse, Leonard, Bob Weir, Camel's mom Maya, Arthur Lee, Eric Burdon, Pete, Carla Thomas, Alex Chilton, Neil Innes, Pharaoh Moans, Lee Michaels and, in closing, a call-and-response duet by Neil Young and Joni Mitchell, that brought the stars down for a listen. The mysterious Mr. Hughes took a verse, too. He sounded like you-know-who.

Camel's eyes were red-rimmed but his smile was beatific.

The wake lasted 4 days. Some slept. Some stayed a-wake. Many previous strangers made love, especially at both sunrise and sunset. Many friendships were formed which have lasted until this day, children. At least one couple has gotten married: Percy Fledge and Clam Tennen re-met at the party and were married a week later by Ohem Jee at The Church on the River. A young Memphis singer-songwriter,

Rob Jungklas, wrote a song for them called "To Be in Love is to Be in Heaven." Camel, who gave away the bride, cried as Rob sang.

The wake lasted 4 days. Some stayed a-wake and everyone, eventually, drifted away. Some back to their Memphis beds, some back to their coasts, some back to the next bardo. Camel saw Challa just once (at least he thought it must be Challa) coming out of the fireplace in the back room which was still Allen's studio. The child stopped when she saw Camel and a smile spread across her little waning-moon cheeks, and she nodded once, a benediction, the final word, a jester's gesture, in the last act of The Magical Mystery Tour.

Camel writes again

A clown is a poet who is also an orangutan
—Wavy Gravy

Fourteen weeks later Camel began his first poem since the death of his bride, Allen Fermor Eros.

The first poem he wrote was entitled, "Everyone Who Was Lost is Found Again." It appeared in *The Kenyon Review.* The second poem he wrote was entitled, "At the End of the Tour the Priests Told New Stories." It appeared in *raccoon.* Altogether, in a red-hot blast of writing, which lasted 4 weeks and a day, Camel wrote 54 poems. They represented a whole. They were his next book, the one his fans had waited five years for.

It was published by Atheneum in August of 1981 and it was called. *After Sleeping in Nowhere*. It went into 3 printings in hardback alone, was a bestseller in paperback; it won the National Book Award and was a finalist for the Pulitzer. And he was given a Macarthur Genius Grant. He never had to teach again. He traveled some ("I gotta light out for the territory," he told his elderly parents), always alone (except for a brief trip to Japan with Richard), and he wrote more poetry in the next five years than he had in the previous twenty.

Camel was a poetry celebrity. They are rare.

Though a sadness sat down on his heart he developed a Panglossian outlook. He expanded as the world expanded around him. He saw ahead light, shadow, and sound. The sound occasionally seemed to be Allen's voice, the soft one she used to sing her personal songs, the soft one she used when she talked to insects or ghosts.

And, though he dated some, he remained alone, true to Allen in his heart and loins, and almost as sexless as the monks Leonard Cohen introduced him to. Camel was a solitary man but he never forgot Allen's premonition that he would, at some point, be surprised again by love. He imagined it could happen. He left his heart slightly ajar so the light could get in. It could very well happen, because life is long and because, as Len said, "God is alive and magic is afoot."

The final chapter: the adventures further on down the road

At the end of *Modern Times* Charlie Chaplin and Pauline Godard walk away from the camera, heading down a dirt road, toward a horizon that promises nothing except *more*. The music to Charlie's song, "Smile," plays.

Smile though your heart is aching
Smile even though it's breaking
When there are clouds
In the sky you'll get by

Camel's road stretched out before him without his heroine.

Also: On the final page of one of Carlos Castaneda's memoirs he steps off a cliff into empty air. The reader is left to imagine that he either plummeted, lemming-style onto the unforgiving rocks below, or that he stepped out into the air, as weightless as ole Wile E. Coyote before thinking destroys his momentary magic faith.

It can be forgiven if we imagine Camel also stepping off into the air because he did. He sailed above Memphis like a magic Cotton Carnival float. And he saw his be-treed city with new eyes and he saw that it was all good and, that, no matter where he roamed, he knew that Memphis was ground zero, home, Valhalla.

Afternoons, ruminating Camel liked to sit in an old sprung easy chair in his backyard. The chair had been rained on, pooped on by creatures great and small, and it smelled like a locker room for trolls. But Camel loved the way the chair seemed to hold him, the contours of his aging body caressed and held by the yielding ancient seat. It was Camel's Cathedra.

And, he would sit, as the sun fell into Big Muddy off to the west, and he would sip his bourbon, and toke his jay, and he would gather wool and he would daydream. He never saw Allen as a ghost and he never saw Challa again, but he knew that they were around. And, once, as the gloaming leeched the color out of his surroundings, until he felt as if he were the hero of an old Warner Brothers noir, he saw a figure that looked like Jesus, directly in front of him, sitting in a chair in the same attitude as Camel himself. A mirror Camel in a white suit and seated upon a white chair.

Camel did not startle or speak. He sat very still.

The Jesus apparition sat very still also. And then the apparition began to smile.

"You're not Jesus, are you?" Camel said. His voice was like water in a still pond.

"I'm not," the apparition said. "God knows." And the ghost laughed a ghostly laugh that sounded very somatous and very human, the kind of laugh a man laughs, when he's seen it all and he's kept his legerity sharp.

"I'm happy to see you," Camel said.

"I'm happy as well," the ghost said, in a scouse lilt. Around him a friar's lantern halo glowed, soft as pity.

"I don't need a message, really," Camel said. "I'm doing alright."

"I'm not a messenger," came the reply.

"Good then."

"Just one thing, Camel. You got a smoke?"

Camel fished around in the pockets of his vest, a beloved garment which was a gift from Gordon Osing because he could not make the wake.

"I don't seem," Camel said.

"I was only ribbing you, man."

"Ah. Well, then."

"Camel," the ghost said, and he began to flicker like a light bulb whose filament is crumbling.

"Yes?" Camel said. He opened his eyes wide, all three of them.

And the ghost began to sing. As the vision faded so did the sound.

Through the mirror go round, round.

I thought I could feel.

Music touching my soul.

Something warm, sudden cold.

The spirit dance was unfolding...

Camel blinked, all three eyes.

And Camel looked upward because it seemed right. The sky was the river (and the river was the sky) and, upon its coffee-hued, rippling surface, in the offing far from shore, sailed little folded paper poetry boats, moving toward Africa and beyond.

Epilogue:

Don't let it end like this. Tell them I said something.
[The last words of Pancho Villa]

THE END

ABOUT THE AUTHOR

Corey Mesler has been published in numerous anthologies and journals including *Poetry, Gargoyle, Five Points, Good Poems American Places,* and *New Stories from the South*. He has published 9 novels, 4 short story collections, and 5 full-length poetry collections, and a dozen chapbooks. His novel, *Memphis Movie*, attracted kind words from Ann Beattie, Peter Coyote, and William Hjorstberg, among others. He's been nominated for the Pushcart many times, and 3 of his poems were chosen for Garrison Keillor's Writer's Almanac. He also wrote the screenplay for *We Go On*, which won The Memphis Film Prize in 2017. With his wife he runs a 145 year-old bookstore in Memphis. He can be found at https://coreymesler.wordpress.com.